DOCTOR PERRY

KIRSTEN MCKENZIE

SSP

ISBN 978-0473419912

Published by Squabbling Sparrows Press
PO Box 26,126, Epsom, Auckland 1344
New Zealand

ALSO BY KIRSTEN MCKENZIE

The Old Curiosity Shop Series
FIFTEEN POSTCARDS
THE LAST LETTER
TELEGRAM HOME

Standalone Novels
PAINTED
DOCTOR PERRY
THE FORGER AND THE THIEF

Anthologies
LANDMARKS
NOIR FROM THE BAR

This book used to be dedicated to someone else, but now it's dedicated to Chocka - my daughter's imaginary friend.
Like Chocka, this book is a work of fiction, plucked from my imagination, and is in no way, shape or form, real.
Sadly Chocka is long gone, so there's no one to blame when things go wrong. So if you do find anything wrong with this book, it's probably my fault.

Elijah Cone's fingers looked more like sausages than these sorry looking excuses for frankfurters did. His appetite fled after prodding them with his fork. The thud of cutlery in the dining room representative of how the rest of the folk felt about the evening meal. Insipid chatter between people who thought the Watergate saga was current news was the only accompaniment to the metallic clang of forks and knives on industrial crockery.

"You not eating, Elijah?" asked Benson Flag, an orderly.

Elijah looked up and shook his head. "Not today Benson, hurts too much to hold the knife. A shame when it looks so fine."

"You want me to cut it up for you?"

Anger flared in Cone's eyes. The orderly meant no harm, but no one likes being babied. It hadn't been a lie, what he'd told the other man, cutting the sausages had sent a flame of pain so sharp through his knuckles that he thought he'd sawn off his own fingers.

Abandoning his meal, Elijah shuffled back to his room. He didn't belong in this place, he belonged on the field with a whistle clamped between his teeth and a team of lads hanging off his every word. The great coach, Elijah Cone, who couldn't even cut his own sausages.

Shutting his bedroom door, he lowered himself into the armchair he'd brought with him; a *luxury item* they'd called it. He could've brought a television too if he'd wanted but there was no chance of that — he didn't care to watch any more. Didn't want to chance seeing any footage of the game he'd once loved. You couldn't trust television programming these days; you never knew when the networks might slip in game highlights or breaking news about the players. Reading was his only pleasure now.

Picking up his book, an old autobiography of a long dead actress — where the likelihood of her mentioning sports was as slim as the level of joy in the Rose Haven Retirement Resort, he settled down to fill in the hours before lights out, like an eight-year-old waiting for his mom to kiss him goodnight. The minutiae of the actress's lack-lustre life sent Elijah to sleep — a pain-wracked sleep. A sleep fractured by the half heard screams of someone else, someone from his dreams, someone from a lifetime ago. Or perhaps from someone down the hall.

BENSON KNOCKED on Elijah's door, waiting for a response before letting himself in. Prising the book from the sleeping man's talon-like hands, he covered Elijah's legs with a crocheted throw from the bed. Poor guy needed better pain relief for his hands. It was damn hard for the residents when their insurance covered none of the effective arthritis meds.

Making a notation on his clipboard, Benson slipped out, locking the door behind him. Doctor Perry could prescribe something for old Cone, something stronger. Doctor Perry really looked after the patients well. That was the one good thing about this place.

BENSON WASN'T the only orderly doing the rounds. Ricky Donovan snaked his way past an overstuffed armchair and matching footstool, a rainbow-coloured crocheted rug and a magazine rack heaving with umpteen copies of every woman's gossip magazine ever produced, before reaching the old oak bureau on the opposite wall.

"Shit," he muttered, stubbing his toe on another pile of magazines at the end of the bed. This old hag hadn't followed the bloody rules, only one piece of personal furniture. The fucking rules were there for a reason.

Eyes acclimatising to the dark room, he smiled as he spied what he'd come for. Pocketing the ornate silver frame from the top of the writing desk, he turned carefully on the spot. He wasn't stupid enough to stub his toe a second time. The old bat probably wouldn't even notice it was gone. This room wasn't on his duty list so he knew he wouldn't get the blame if she did notice. The woman groaned in the bed and Ricky froze, or froze as much as he was able to, given the incessant itching under his skin. It felt like tiny bugs were running relays through his arteries. Absently he scratched at his arm, reopening an older scab. Focused on the woman in the bed in front of him, he was oblivious to the blood seeping out from underneath the scab.

Satisfied she was still asleep, Ricky fancied he tiptoed silently out of the room, closing the door softly behind him. Disturbed, the woman in the bed pulled the covers further up to her chin, her old nose wrinkling at the sour odour left behind by Ricky's departure. Someone had been in here.

2

Doctor Perry tugged at his sleeves. No matter how carefully he hung his jacket, the fabric always looked as if he'd slept in it. He could invest in a better quality suit but that would waste money. His clients didn't care how he dressed... most of the time they didn't even dress themselves.

He checked his schedule. Neat appointments lined the page, allocating each patient twelve minutes, leaving him three minutes to write his notes and prepare for the next one. Would it be possible to shave another minute off each appointment? That way he could fit in more patients. He must remember to ask his receptionist to look into it. The extra funds would be welcome.

His smile widened as he considered Molly. A talented receptionist and an efficient patient wrangler. Better than the last one — less curious. He'd found that an essential trait in an employee. Curious staff were a liability.

Noting the regular booking at the Rose Haven Retirement Resort in his schedule, he smiled. Elderly patients without family made for profitable patients. He didn't want long-term relationships with his patients. Relationships invariably involved grown-up children further down the track. Having a whole old folks home on his books had been a boon to his bottom line, especially the Rose Haven Retirement Resort. He chuckled over the word *Resort* — the Rose Haven was as far removed from a resort as possible. Reeking of cabbage and urine, it housed pensioners too poor and unloved to go anywhere else. The dregs of a throwaway society. No one wanted them, no one except Doctor Perry.

"MOLLY, please send through the first patient," Doctor Perry instructed through the intercom.

His schedule listed the first client as Clarita Swann, a new patient. He loved new patients. Before they walked through the door, there was always that delicious moment of not knowing whether they might be ideal for the little sideline he had running. There was always a chance today would be the day.

3

Elijah stared out the window. He wasn't antisocial but there was a television in the communal lounge and even from here he could hear the sports channel. People might ask his opinion of the game, the players, or for deep insights into what was happening on the field. He couldn't bear it so he'd just sit here till lunchtime. It was a Wednesday, meaning meatloaf was on the menu. He'd be able to manage that, along with the limp lettuce masquerading as salad which usually accompanied the meatloaf, followed by a tub of jelly for dessert. What was the reasoning behind serving jelly to the residents of a retirement home? Understandable at a kindergarten, which was a far more appropriate place for jelly. Mind you, he had his own teeth while half the other residents gummed their food to death. It was depressing to think he had a couple of decades of jelly on Wednesdays ahead of him.

Gazing outside, he appreciated one of his few blessings — that his room looked out over the main road, where cars, bicycles, and dog walkers kept him amused. He'd created lives for the regulars who passed by. There was the Rat Lady - an elderly woman walking a rodent-sized dog on a lead. Elijah had no time for anything smaller than a Labrador, so had no idea what breed of dog came that small. The Rat Lady always wore a beige jacket regardless of the weather and he imagined her stark naked underneath. He'd never seen her face as she always averted her eyes from the Rose Haven every time she passed, as if by merely looking at the dilapidated building she'd be sucked in. Today she teetered by in an ancient pair of cork platforms, giving her a bizarre hunched shape and in her ill-fitting beige jacket she looked almost spy-like.

He checked his wristwatch. Unlike his own ticker, it still kept time, never missing a beat. Any moment now the School Mum would hurry by wielding an enormous pram like a Normandy landing craft. Dawdling behind her would be her twins — two boys of such an incredible likeness he considered it wicked of the mother to dress them the same. For weeks he'd examined them as they walked by, looking for differences — did one dawdle more than the other? Was there an affectation to a smile or a gesture? He continued his quest today, watching the children in their matching shorts struggle under identical backpacks.

A commotion in the corridor turned his attention away from the street — someone was playing up. He hoped it wouldn't impact on morning tea although if it did he wouldn't be missing much — lukewarm tea and cheap arse cookies days away from their best before date. He mourned the days of sugar-laden muffins slathered with butter, washed down by a mug of strong coffee. Coffee wasn't on offer at the Rose Haven Retirement Resort although its scent filled the halls, so he knew it was available — just not for the residents. It also lingered on the breath of the staff who revelled in making the resident's lives as uncomfortable as possible, pushing them into an early grave. Retirement homes were all about the churn, turning the residents over as quickly as possible without resorting to holding a pillow over their heads. Every time one of them died, the next person who moved in had to pay more for the privilege of living there.

Elijah jumped at a thud against his door. The commotion outside might be worthwhile getting out of his chair for. He leveraged himself out of his chair trying not to use his hands more than necessary. His curiosity grew — yelling had joined the ruckus in the corridor.

Gritting his teeth, he grasped the door handle. You'd think an old folks home would have handles easy for the residents to use, but no. Opening his door was an almost insurmountable obstacle every day — just turning the doorknob made it feel like there were thousands of shards of glass embedded in his hands. He swallowed the pain to avoid drawing the attention of the nurses who were already in a lather over the performance in the hall. Any deviation from the prescribed daily programme wasn't tolerated at the Rose Haven, and retribution was always swift.

With the door open enough for him to look out, Elijah saw two orderlies sitting on Johnny Paulson, with a nurse yelling into her radio. Management had recently issued the staff with handheld radios and the flustered nurse was using hers to summon help from the bowels of hell, or she would if she could use the thing.

This was the most entertained he'd been since coming here. He'd offer to help, he had plenty of experience with handheld radios from his years on the sidelines, but knowing how vindictive the staff were here, he held his tongue.

Frightened faces appeared at the edges of the corridor and from behind doors the same as his. It was worth missing out on morning tea to watch this play out. He momentarily forgot his own pain.

4

She'd presented with a minor skin complaint — one a hydrocortisone creme would sort out. And with another seven minutes left of her appointment he had time to check her blood pressure, temperature, weight — normal procedures for any new patient. He had a few additional questions he liked to ask new patients, questions peculiar to his medical practice. Ones which gave a more rounded overview of a patient and their background. Questions about family support, friendships, relationships. Most patients never thought to question why he needed to know.

Doctor Perry recorded the results in a peculiar shorthand, illegible to anyone else. Hand written notes stored in patient folders filed alphabetically in floor-to-ceiling bookshelves in his office, some files fatter than others, and some as slender as a fingernail — holding only one or two sheets of paper. He didn't trust computers, too easy to access remotely, and since maintaining patient confidentiality was of the utmost importance, he maintained this anachronism — an old-school paper-based filing system.

"So, Miss Swann-"

"Clarita is fine," she replied.

"Your results are nothing concerning but I want to monitor your blood pressure. Are you under much stress? For your age, it's too high for my liking," he said, steepling his fingers.

Clarita Swann squirmed in her seat and Doctor Perry smiled — he liked it when patients replied nonverbally. She was holding something back, he could tell.

"You don't have to tell me but come back in a fortnight and we can run more tests and try to manage this before it gets out of hand. In fact, I'll write you a prescription for the lotion for your hands and I'll add some pills which may help with your anxiety. Moving to a new town can be stressful."

Clarita protested but Doctor Perry was having none of it.

"These pills are all natural, I try not to prescribe my patients drugs when they don't need them. It's a natural remedy which I've found works well for people suffering from the beginnings of stress, they help ease things. Two weeks and I'll see you again, and I'm sure there won't be anything to worry about then and if there is, we can talk through some treatment options, hmm?"

After escorting Clarita to the door, Doctor Perry returned to his desk. And in the upper right-hand corner of the file, he added a small red circle with his special red pen. A circle no bigger than a newborn's tiny fingerprint.

———

CLARITA SWANN LEFT the doctor's surgery after making another appointment with the receptionist. She'd felt fine coming in, apart from the ugly rash on her hands, but since the nice doctor had mentioned her stress levels, she remembered noticing fine lines round her eyes and a sprinkling of white hairs at her temples this morning, and other mornings if she was being honest. They'd terrified her, but having just moved into town, finding a hairdresser and a beautician were the least of her concerns.

If it was stress causing the rash on her hands, it was a relief the doctor had prescribed something natural to help. She hated quacks who wrote out scripts for antidepressants at the drop of a hat. She had a good feeling about this one.

DOCTOR PERRY HANDED Molly the Swann folder to file. The appointment had again showed he could shave a minute off each appointment. He'd track it for another week, keeping a record of the potential time savings, then he'd instruct Molly to amend the appointment scheduler. Evidence. Medicine was all about evidence.

He checked his watch — one minute before his next appointment, enough time to go to the toilet and wash his hands. Washing hands was such an important part of good health and it was a shame more people didn't subscribe to that belief. But then if they did, half of them wouldn't be sitting in his waiting room.

Ready for his next patient, he plastered a professional smile on his face and began his usual interrogation. Doctor Perry liked asking the questions first and never invited the patient to say what their complaint was until he'd run through his own set of questions — questions vital to tracking the health of his clients. After all, he was the doctor, and knew best.

And so the day progressed, patient after patient. A scheduled lunch break of twenty minutes, enough time for a chicken salad, two cups of peppermint tea, and a slice of cake.

5

The orderlies had dragged Johnny Paulson down the hall and out of sight, leaving behind a foul puddle of urine on the old carpet, a carpet which crackled underfoot with age. The nurse called for another orderly to clean it up but until then, the wet patch mocked the residents' as they filed past to morning tea.

A subdued atmosphere lay heavily on the residents as word of Paulson's episode made it around the Rose Haven faster than a bout of dysentery. By the time the rumour reached Elijah's table, Paulson had been fighting three nurses and was brought down with a tranquilliser gun. Elijah had seen what had subdued Paulson — the embarrassment of wetting himself in public. So much for a healthcare system designed to protect the elderly. Instead it subjected them to a fate worse than dying in a pensioner flat, bodies gnawed on by a menagerie of cats drowning in their own faeces.

Elijah drank his tea and ate his biscuits quietly as he remembered hearing Johnny begging to get up, swearing he was only looking for the toilet, that he'd got confused and had gone into the wrong room. Elijah knew it was easily done, the corridors all looked the same — insipid beige avenues where even the pot plants in the halls were identical — plastic ferns covered in decades of dust. There was a sense of unease in the dining room over what had happened and even though he didn't want to get involved, Elijah wouldn't forget the anguish on Paulson's face nor the venom in the voice of the nurse as she'd instructed the orderlies to take him, no, to drag him, to the sick bay.

As always, Elijah rebuked all efforts at conversation, refusing to be drawn into any discussion about Johnny. He wasn't here to make friends. He was here to die.

Elijah finished his tea and hurried from the room as best he could on arthritic knees. He should have had knee surgery when he'd had the money but it was too late now. He could have had top of the range titanium knees, but he'd been too scared to go under, he'd seen so many surgeries go wrong. Now there were knives under his kneecaps, in his fingers, his shoulders, his hips. He was a living Freddy Kruger instead of the Bionic Man.

Back in his room, he twitched at the curtains. He wanted nothing to do with any living creature, but once a day there was a tiny moment of joy. Every day, regardless of the weather, a woman would jog by, a creature of habit like him. He had his habits, even in this early grave he was living — wake up, breakfast, shower — if it was a day he was allowed his allocated time under the lukewarm water. Federal prisoners were treated better than pensioners although he didn't deserve the luxury of prison. This life was punishment enough for being alive.

Hands on the fabric arms of the chair, he breathed through the minutes, isolating the pain in his hands and putting it away. He'd allow himself to feel it later but for now he'd savour the simple pleasure of watching a woman jogging by, lycra-clad legs sculpted from shiny black marble.

And there she was, legs moving rhythmically along the footpath, her top a kaleidoscope of geometric colours, a long ponytail swinging behind her. His youthful self imagined it loose across his pillow, although not across the pillows at the Rose Haven Retirement Resort, where the industrial cotton pillowcases were rendered as dry as the Sahara by the harshest of washing detergents. Elijah laughed at the absurdity of his thoughts — the thoughts of a decrepit old man imprisoned behind glass.

From the corner of his eye he noticed the Rose Haven Retirement Resort van backing out from its position in front of reception. He'd never had the privilege of travelling in the van, a sign-written vehicle the Rose Haven's advertising literature said was used for taking happy residents to the theatre, the casino and on vineyard tours out of state. As far as he knew, the only people who used the van were staff on emergency runs for cigarettes and candy — luxuries forbidden to the residents. Today, Johnny Paulson was in the back of the van and their eyes met.

Elijah turned his attention back towards the jogger, earphones snaking into her ears, her head down as she fiddled with her phone. Changing the music? Checking a message? Whatever, it meant she wasn't looking. He turned back to see Johnny hammering on the windows of the van, screaming, distracting the driver.

The driver was the orderly known as Smokey, Bart Stubbs - a man who spent more time smoking in the courtyard then he did carrying out his duties, rain or shine, night or day. Today he was driving and smoking and yelling at Johnny, and the jogger never stood a chance.

The sign-written Rose Haven Retirement Resort van

backed right onto the woman, jackknifing her in the middle, her black legs swallowed by the white van.

As if in slow motion, Elijah lunged at the window, pressing his hands against the glass, trying to push the woman out of the way, through the transparent barrier.

The jogger lay motionless on the sidewalk.

Doors opened and slammed and voices tainted with fear filtered in through the window. No double glazing and the cheapest seals on the market allowing the noise to leak into his room. Elijah wanted to go out but had nothing to add, no skills to assist. What use was he anyway? He was a useless old man. A burden. Better not to get involved.

A wail of sirens joined the voices on the sidewalk. Nurses and admin staff circled the van, like sharks around a lone surfer. Someone finally turned the van's engine off, which was worse as the engine had been drowning out Paulson's manic screams.

The ambulance arrived with medical staff on board who showed more professionalism than all the Rose Haven's nurses and orderlies put together. The paramedics had the woman on a stretcher and into the back of the ambulance faster than he'd thought possible. Before the doors closed, Elijah saw a flutter of the jogger's hand — the smallest of movements but enough to lift his heart. She was alive.

Elijah pushed off from the window as the ambulance sped away, its lights flashing in concert with the waves of pain coursing through every one of his arthritic fingers. She was alive but he doubted she'd be running anytime soon, which turned Elijah's world a little greyer. The disappointment nudging death a little bit closer.

6

Doctor Perry ran his eyes down the patient list with a widening smile as he reached the final name — booked in for a double appointment. His special patients needed a longer time so he always scheduled those for last thing in the day. On those nights he'd send the receptionist home early, promising faithfully to tidy and lock up the place behind him.

In neat cursive he made a small notation in the margin, his smile playing on his moist lips until the ink spat out from the nib of his fountain pen leaving a small blot of red ink on the pristine appointment schedule. No matter, a few more of these appointments and he wouldn't need this schedule for much longer, it was almost time to move on. He'd tell his patients he was retiring, that the clinic was closing down as he didn't want the bother of selling it. It was prudent to quit when things were going well. There were still a few more late night appointments ahead of him, patients whose treatment regimes he wanted to complete. Slow and steady won the race, but experience had shown it was important to quit when you were ahead. Not long now.

Recapping his fountain pen, he slipped it into his breast pocket. It was time for the first patient of the day.

Molly showed the patient in, blushing at the banter from the man — his dark hair lightly salted and the beginning of fine lines giving him a touch of George Clooney-type magic. Doctor Perry's receptionist cast an appreciative glance at the patient before closing the consulting room door. Yes, Molly would have to be dealt with soon. It didn't pay to let the staff get too close to the patients.

"Don, I'm surprised to see you again so soon. Joint pain again?" Doctor Perry appeared to consult Don Jury's patient file but knew off by heart what his shorthand cursive notes said and that this appointment was hardly a surprise. They always came back. Especially those with a tiny red circle in the upper righthand corner.

"It did work Doctor Perry, which is why I'm here. The pain in my knees has completely disappeared. They feel like they did when I was twenty, as if I could take up competitive football again. Now I'm here about my shoulder. Years ago I had some issues with my bursa joint and, well, it's flared up again."

"Oh?"

"Probably something to do with all the swimming I did on a cruise round Hawaii - best swimming pool ever, even had a tank full of dolphins. I swam every day which seems to have really damaged my shoulder."

"And you thought of my joint tonic?"

Don Jury nodded. For a man his age, he carried no extra weight, and his previous blood tests hadn't shown any drug use, illicit or otherwise. Apart from over exercising in his youth, Don Jury was as healthy as a man of sixty could hope to be.

Doctor Perry took a serious tone, "I'll need to run my usual tests, check your cholesterol and iron levels but, yes, I think the joint tonic will definitely help relieve the bursitis symptoms. Come through to the examination room and I'll check that shoulder."

Doctor Perry made a show of rotating the man's shoulder, unmarred by any childhood scarring bar the standard circular tuberculosis mark on his upper arm.

"We should be able to fix this up in no time, I can't feel any serious damage. I'll administer a dose of muscle tonic today and you'll need to make an appointment with Molly to come back next week. Make it the last appointment of the day so I can do some manipulation of your shoulder. Then one more dose and you should be right after that."

Doctor Perry measured out a milky dose from a brown glass bottle. The viscous liquid moved as if it had a life of its own, like a tide pulled by the moon. He tipped a drop back into the bottle, it wouldn't do to overdose a patient. He had to be careful. There'd been errors in the past, which still made him shudder. He hadn't had any accidents for a long time now and it had to stay that way while he tidied up his affairs, before he moved on.

Don knocked back the liquid in one gulp, his pink tongue snaking around the rim and only handing back the medicine cup when he'd licked it clean.

"Ten minutes in the waiting room, to be safe, then you can be on your way," Doctor Perry smiled. He could already see the tonic taking effect although he was sure his patient wouldn't notice anything yet, maybe by tonight. Next week's appointment would go well if he was reacting this quickly to the small dosage he'd administered.

Don Jury left the doctor's office and chatted

humorously with Molly. Doctor Perry's shoulders twitched. Their banter made him uncomfortable. There was no point worrying too much about it. It'd all be sorted soon enough but it left a sour taste in his mouth. Molly needed to concentrate on her work, not form relationships with the patients, with his patients.

DON JURY COULDN'T HIDE his excitement. He felt younger and fitter than he had in years and after the doctor's magic tonic today he was certain his performance problems down below would also be solved and that would change his life. It was as if every time he saw Doctor Perry, he felt younger and younger. A miracle he wasn't willing to share with anyone else. Retirement really was all that he'd been promised. Now he just needed someone to share it with, and Molly was looking like an attractive proposition.

THE DAY PROGRESSED AS NORMAL. The doctor stopped for lunch at midday — his chicken salad exactly the same as the chicken salad he'd eaten the day before and which he'd eat tomorrow, each mouthful as bland as its predecessor. Sipping his tea gave him a moment of peace he'd been missing since Don Jury's appointment. Doctor Perry didn't look at patient paperwork during his lunch break, his mind needed the rest. Half his patients didn't take a lunch break so it was no wonder his appointment book was full. If only they followed his advice, most of them would never need him. Some would wish they'd never come to him.

There was a buzz on his intercom.

"Sorry Doctor Perry, but there's an urgent phone call

from the Rose Haven, they want to know if you can schedule a visit now or if they can bring one of the residents in. I didn't know what to say because your schedule is full, and you've got Mrs Webb coming in this afternoon, and I've already rescheduled her twice?"

Doctor Perry wiped his mouth. Crumbs around the mouth was not a professional look. He swallowed down both the mouthful of sandwich and his irritation with the interruption to his lunch break. He tried to summon a smile but it barely made it past the sides of his mouth. "Transfer the call through Molly and I'll deal with it. We can't reschedule Mrs Webb again."

Doctor Perry answered his extension.

"Good afternoon…no problem at all, how can I help?…Yes, hmmm, you'll need to bring him in…I have no time today to…yes, hmmm, tomorrow first thing. Yes, that will be fine, put him in there. Yes, thank you. See you tomorrow."

The doctor made a notation on his desk pad. It bothered him immensely scribbling on the stark white paper but it was a momentary nuisance and he didn't want to forget the details; *Ryman Spittle, possible chest infection, new resident, widower*. He liked having widows and widowers on his books. Not in a scurrilous way, but more because it made treatment options easier, without a worried spouse interfering. A widower living in a retirement home was even better.

7

After such a promising start Molly was now proving to be troublesome, too many questions, just like Lily before her. Why couldn't they keep their painted mouths shut and their eyes on the patient schedule? He'd have to deal with her, but not today... today was for home visits, a lucrative part of the practice but he didn't like being away from the surgery, you never knew what the staff might find. Lily found out what happened if you didn't keep your nose out of other people's business and now Molly was heading that way.

Doctor Perry tapped his fingers against the steering wheel of his sensible mid-range sedan. He'd considered purchasing something European, but it was best not to advertise your wealth too much. Clients might take it the wrong way or it could attract the attention of the wrong people. Still the air conditioning worked and it was reliable. The radio off, he entertained himself with his own thoughts as he considered the first patient of the day - Mary Louise Jackson. Pulling into the driveway of a brick bungalow, he noticed the shaggy lawn, a post box heaving with junk mail, and the garden a symphony of weeds, indicating that Mary Louise Jackson hadn't received any recent visitors. It paid to be mindful of these things in his line of work.

Climbing out of his car with an old-fashioned leather doctor's bag in hand, he walked up the weedy path and knocked on the door. Inside, the chimes of London's Westminster bells echoed through the house.

The door swung open and Doctor Perry stepped through, closing the door behind him, hiding him away from any prying eyes. He needn't have worried - Mary Louise Jackson lived in a working class neighbourhood where everyone went to work. Everyone except Mary Louise. She couldn't work now and not for the foreseeable future. She knew it and Doctor Perry knew it.

"Thanks for coming," Mary Louise said, showing Doctor Perry through to the kitchen, the air moving like a somnolent fly flapping lazily through the room, in no hurry to get anywhere.

"I'm more than happy to shoulder the hospital's overflow, they're so understaffed these days it's a travesty," Doctor Perry smiled with eyes barren of any warmth.

Oblivious to the disconnect, Mary Louise lowered herself into a chair; a higher than usual chair with padded arms and a straight cushioned back, its feet clad in non-slip rubber stockings.

Her crutches clattered to the floor and the doctor bent to retrieve them, returning them to the edge of the table.

"You look uncomfortable, how is the pain level?"

Mary Louise turned her opiate addled eyes away from the crutches and back to the doctor.

"They gave me painkillers at the hospital but I don't think they're working. I can't sleep, and every time I roll over the pain wakes me. Is there something you can prescribe me?"

Now Doctor Perry smiled properly. "We can't have you in any discomfort. The staff at St. Albert's are excellent but their pain management techniques are ancient. They see opiates as a panacea for all ailments whereas I have a more holistic approach. Pain relief needs help to work, to speed things up," he said, rifling through his bag. "Based on the clinical notes I received, I came prepared."

Doctor Perry produced a brown pharmacy bottle filled with milky viscous fluid and he saw relief flash across Mary Louise's face. His patients wanted to be better and rarely questioned the means, especially when it was their doctor offering the cure. Everyone trusts their doctor.

"I don't need the pharmacy?"

"Oh no, I have everything you need right here but before I administer your first dose, let's check these injuries. My notes say a vehicle drove into you?"

Mary Louise recounted the painful details of her accident, itemising her injuries without once taking her eyes off the brown bottle.

Doctor Perry made sympathetic noises. "I'll examine your ribs first. Four broken ribs with one piercing the skin? I hope the driver is being held accountable?"

Pulling on a pair of disposable latex gloves, he lifted the woman's t-shirt revealing a swathe of white bandages. "That's good, no seepage. I'll check for any sign of infection under the dressings."

His patient didn't answer but nodded along to his ministrations. The combination of opiates, pain, and lack of sleep turned her as docile as a newborn lamb.

Doctor Perry removed her dressings, prodding at the ugly stitches holding her together. *A shame.* The scar would stay with her forever now, no matter what he did. He hated his patients scarred, preferring them perfect, as did his clients. Still, she'd be a profitable addition to his books regardless of the scar. And scars faded.

"It's healing but you'll need something to reduce the scarring."

Mary Louise sobbed, huge gulping sobs wracked her body and forced globules of snot from her nose. Doctor Perry turned away, his stomach roiling in disgust.

"And my face?" Mary Louise asked through her tears.

"Just grazes, they'll heal without interference and they won't scar. Trust me. They will heal faster once your pain is under control," Doctor Perry said, offering her a box of tissues, turning away from the mucus covered face of his patient. He loathed this side of doctoring.

Mary Louise blew her nose, filling the flimsy tissue, followed by the *shush shush* sound of more tissues being pulled from the box, and more moist blowing sounds.

Once he was sure she'd finished, Doctor Perry returned his attention to his patient, to her plaster cast covered limbs. Bones broken when a white van slammed into her, breaking four ribs, lacerating a kidney, breaking her arm and hyper-extending her left leg until her knee socket shattered.

Doctor Perry opened the medicine bottle and poured a measured dose of the opaque liquid into a small ceramic cup. "I apologise for the bitter taste, it's true when they say the worst tasting things are always best for us," he chuckled, watching Mary Louise as she tipped the liquid down her throat. Satisfied, he whisked the cup away, tucking it back into his bag.

"Whilst it's a long-acting formula, I must administer another dose next week-"

"How long till it works?" she interrupted.

"You should feel relief tonight. Keep taking the

medication the hospital prescribed, they'll work in tandem and I wouldn't be surprised if you felt like a new woman in the morning," he laughed. A dry, mirthless laugh which echoed around his chest and up through his throat but never made it to his eyes. Doctor Perry pulled off his gloves and packed away the brown bottle. "Have you got anyone to look after you?" he asked innocently.

"I have no family nearby, or friends yet. The nurse was coming twice a week, but that's finished now they've passed me onto you. I'm using a grocery delivery service but if I'm not back at work soon I won't be able to afford that for much longer, so no, not really."

"We'll concentrate on getting you back on your feet as soon as we can and you'll be rejoining the workforce before you know it. Take care and ring my office if there's no improvement in your pain management in the next couple of days."

As Doctor Perry climbed into his nondescript mid-range sedan, a smile finally made it to his eyes. He patted the bag on his passenger seat affectionately before backing out of Mary Louise Jackson's driveway. The driveway of his new favourite patient, one with no family or friends. The perfect patient.

8

The residents of the Rose Haven Retirement Resort didn't see Johnny Paulson at lunch or dinner. By the next day half the residents had forgotten him altogether, and not just those with dementia.

Elijah Cone hadn't though. He looked for Johnny Paulson at lunch and at dinner and by breakfast the next day he assumed they'd locked Johnny up. He didn't want to get involved. It was Johnny's tough luck and nothing to do with him but Johnny Paulson was the closest thing to a friend Elijah had. The only resident who didn't try talking sport with him, instead he'd been happy to compare books and discuss politics — local more than national, with an occasional foray into political events further afield. Now his life was empty, which as he deserved.

"You're not eating again, Mister Cone?" Benson asked, appearing at his elbow, bending to cut the dry chicken breast Elijah was struggling with.

"Leave it, I can do it," Elijah snapped. "Why are you here? It's not the weekend already is it?"

"I'm in covering for Smokey, he's on leave," Benson replied.

Ah, Smokey, the orderly who'd run over the jogger, the one who smoked more than a chimney at a crematorium.

"What happened to the jogger, Benson?"

"Don't go asking me, they don't want us chit chatting about what happened, best leave sleeping dogs lie," Benson said, checking over his shoulder.

Elijah didn't want the details, he didn't care, but he wanted to know about the jogger. "The jogger, is she okay?"

Benson straightened, his hands brushing at imaginary crumbs on the table.

"How are we today, Elijah?" said a voice like nails on a chalkboard - Tracey Chappell, the manager of the Rose Haven Retirement Resort, a gussied up sow in a silk purse. Blonde hair, blue eyes and a nasty streak. It was no wonder Benson stood as if he had a poker up his backside.

"Fine," Elijah muttered, keeping his eyes on her face despite the acres of bare flesh displayed below her neckline.

"I noticed Benson assisting you with your meal. We aren't able to cater to *residents* with high needs in the *Rose Haven*," Tracey Chappell enunciated, taking great care to protect the illusion she was running a pensioners' holiday resort and not a low cost rest home shoehorned into an old hotel complex altered on the cheap to meet planning consent requirements.

"I didn't ask him. He did it off his own back," Elijah said, regretting the words as soon as they were out.

Tracey turned to the orderly, "Benson, a word in my office after your shift has finished," she said before returning to Elijah. "Regardless, those fingers look like they are becoming a problem. We'll schedule you for a visit to the *Resort's* doctor. You haven't had a check up since you moved in with us, and we prefer that our *Residents* maintain their health so it's timely. Enjoy your meal." And she swanned off, surveying her domain, checking for the slightest infraction, leaving residents hunched into their meals hoping she wouldn't pounce on them. For many residents, the Rose Haven Retirement Resort was the only affordable assisted-living facility in a two-hundred-mile radius.

"Sorry, Benson," Elijah started.

"Not a worry Mister Cone, her bark is worse than her bite. I'll be okay. Now are you going to eat that chicken or am I going to feed you?" Benson chuckled, the tension broken.

THE MEAL OVER, Elijah walked the long corridors, passing room after room, doors ajar, the volume of their television sets creating an impossible cacophony of noise. He quickened his step least one was tuned to a sports channel. As he rounded the corner, he collided head first into an immovable object. *Oomph.* Elijah bounced off the object, reeling with the force.

"Hey there," boomed a voice.

Elijah looked up, he had to — the woman standing in front of him was at least six foot with a girth to match. The colour of charcoal, her skin glowed under the shuttered bulbs decorating the long corridors — leftovers from when it was a hotel, the current management would never have sprung for such expensive fittings.

Swathed in layers of a jewel-coloured fabric, gold dripping from her ears, her wrists and her ankles, she tinkled as she breathed. Rheumy, milky eyes the biggest nod to her age.

"Hello," Elijah replied.

"It's a fine way to meet new people, bumping into them. I find it's the best way to start a conversation," she chortled, the heavy earrings dancing in her lobes, dragging them down towards her shoulders.

Making small talk wasn't something Elijah enjoyed any more, but he still had manners, "When did you get here?" he asked.

"To this country or this place? Been in the US longer than I care to remember, but arrived here today. Sorry sort of welcome I got though, can't find my way to lunch, lost my room, and you're the first friendly face I've seen. Not that I can see it very well, I've as much eyesight as the President has brain cells, and that's saying something."

Elijah was desperate to get back to his room, but she hadn't moved, and he didn't think it polite to squeeze past her bulk when she was lost. "I can walk you to the dining room?" he offered, hoping she'd decline.

"Do I *want* to eat the food there, that's the question? Can't be fading away. Too many malnourished skeletons walking the world as it is. So yeah, sure thing, that'd be great."

Reluctantly he offered the woman his arm, wincing as she grabbed it a little too hard. She loosened her grip and rested her fingers on his arm as they walked down the hall to the empty dining room. No one lingered over their meals here, the staff made it clear that loitering was against the rules. Turn up on time, eat what's on your plate without complaining, go back to your rooms. Rinse and repeat.

Benson appeared at his side, "There's no seconds, Mister Cone."

"Not here for more, Benson, I'm escorting... sorry, I don't know your name?"

"Sulia Patel, just moved in. Nice to meet you but I'm starving and could murder a burger or a big plate of lasagne." She laughed at Benson's confused face, "I'm not all curries and korma. I've been living here longer than you've been alive and I enjoy the taste of a good burger as much as you do. Now lead me to my table."

Elijah made to leave, reluctant to hang around, but the woman called out, "I'm not eating alone, come sit here and tell me about the place." Her request brooked no argument and before Elijah knew it he was sitting by her side watching Sulia hoover up the rehydrated potato and chicken breast, her knife and fork working in harmony, ladling the food into her cavernous mouth, teeth chomping at the dry chicken flesh, smacking her lips as though savouring a gourmet meal.

"Not bad, not bad at all," Sulia said, wiping her mouth with a paper napkin. She rubbed her stomach before turning her cloudy eyes towards Elijah. "Nothing like a full stomach to settle the nerves. You wouldn't expect I'd be nervous moving into a place like this. But boy oh boy it reminds me of being the new kid at school. I was the only Indian there too. Am I the only Indian here?"

Elijah flicked through the faces of the other residents, and he couldn't think of a single resident who wasn't a subtle shade of beige, except for Bill Chen, who, despite his surname, didn't look Chinese. Elijah muttered a quiet *yes*.

Sulia snorted. "Thought as much."

Elijah flushed with shame. Not at the lack of diversity in the Rose Haven but that he hadn't even noticed. He'd been so introspective he hadn't realised the residents of the

Rose Haven Retirement Resort were a recruiting poster for the Ku Klux Klan.

"I can feel the heat of your blushing from here. Don't worry, I'm used to it. Doesn't bother me. They'll get used to me, they always do. Before long we'll be tucking into plates of chicken korma and more poppadoms than you can shake a stick at."

Elijah thought the idea of the Rose Haven altering their cost-effective meal plan was unlikely but wouldn't tell Sulia that. Let her work it out for herself. No need to open his mouth, or to get involved. Getting up from the table, he started to make his excuses, he wanted to be back in his room.

"Your voice... I recognise it now. Took me a while, but yeah, you're Elijah Cone, what on earth are you doing here?"

Elijah sank back into the chair, the plastic covered seat squeaking.

"It's no secret who I am," he replied.

"You disappeared a kind of a sudden though didn't you? Vanished from the face of the earth. I'd recognise that voice anywhere, heard it on my television for too many years not to. If my friends could see me now, sitting here with a celebrity," she laughed, her enormous girth undulating like jelly in an earthquake.

If Elijah wasn't in so much pain, he would have bolted but with his arthritis he needed five minutes just to stand up.

"Where you've been? What have you been doing? Must be five years since you were on my TV set. You been here all that time?"

Elijah stared at the table, this was the last thing he wanted to talk about.

"Why d'you disappear?"

Elijah almost answered but Benson reappeared at the table.

"Sorry guys, but we need to clean the dining room now, for the supper service."

"Right, yes," Elijah replied, his voice full of relief. He pulled himself up, avoiding Sulia's cloudy eyes, wincing as he shuffled out from the table and hobbled from the room.

"I'm almost blind but I don't need eyes to see he's hurting," Sulia said as the door closed behind Elijah.

"Arthritis is an indiscriminate affliction. Elijah masks it well though, won't let anyone help him. Do you want me to show you to your room or to the lounge with the other residents?"

"The lounge, thank you."

They made an odd couple walking the halls — the orderly's skin unmarred by life against Sulia Patel's wrinkled features which were a road map to life well lived. She carried luggage under her eyes like a hotel porter working a convention.

Benson left Sulia in the funereal lounge, oblivious to the depressing atmosphere — his mind already on his meeting with Tracey Chappell. Completing the lunchtime handover sheet, he noted down the increasing difficulties Elijah Cone had with his hands. He didn't want to give Tracey any excuse to fire him and recording concerns about the wellbeing of the residents was part of his job, and he needed this job. He never once considered that he'd just started the ball rolling on a destructive force which might crush them all.

9

Molly smudged pink gloss on her lips and admired the colour the hairdresser had run through her hair, subtle streaks of auburn which looked better outside than under the doctor's florescent lights but if it went well tonight, it wouldn't matter what her hair looked like under lights, or under the covers.

Snapping the mirror shut, she popped it away in the top drawer along with candy floss coloured lip gloss. Molly didn't think about being the latest in a long line of receptionists who'd kept their belongings in that drawer. She ignored the yellow comb and the half used compact of pressed powder and had thrown out the old bottle of Dior perfume, the scent so overpowering she'd sneezed every time she opened the drawer, but she never stopped to wonder why her predecessors had left those things behind, including address books and asthma inhalers, house keys and expensive tubes of hand moisturiser. But at her stage of life, she wasn't prone to worrying over such inconsequential things.

She'd filed all the patient reports for the day, except for

the one belonging to Doctor Perry's last patient, who hadn't yet arrived. With nothing left to fill in her time, she read his file. For someone so good looking it was odd that he wasn't wearing a wedding band. He didn't strike her as gay, especially as he'd definitely been flirting with her the last time he'd come in, and the time before that. Tonight she hoped he'd ask her out. She didn't have the luxury of time, her reproductive chances diminishing with every sweep of the clock, so if he didn't ask her this time, she'd decided that she'd ask him.

The surgery door opened and Don Jury entered. An ocean-wide smile split Molly's face as he approached the counter.

"Hello," she said.

"Hello, Molly," he replied.

Molly blushed. He'd remembered her name. She forgot that it was on the nameplate on the counter as she imagined their future wedding. Despite his age, he'd look perfect at the end of the altar.

"Is he running on time?" he asked.

Molly bobbed her head, her power of speech lost.

Don smiled, showing rows of perfect white teeth, like a shark. Oh, they'd have such handsome children Molly fantasised. She overlooked his sloping shoulder and the odd stray hair threatening to sprout from his ears if left unattended for too long.

"Shall I take a seat?"

Molly nodded again, a blush working its way up her chest, snaking across her throat and staining her cheeks.

Don walked towards the chair closest to Doctor Perry's consulting room before spinning on the spot. Molly's heart stopped, this was it, he was going to ask her out.

"Is there any chance I could grab a glass of water? I'm

parched and I don't want the doctor accusing me of being dehydrated."

Molly deflated like a balloon in the sun. Shoving her chair backward from the desk she disappeared into the kitchenette. There was a water cooler in the waiting room but she'd already removed the empty bottle ready for tomorrow's fresh water delivery.

Molly's face betrayed her feelings and Don looked surprised at her discomfort as he took the dripping glass, his fingers brushing hers.

"Thank you," Don said.

Molly sniffed as she walked back to her desk, the sunshine on her face replaced by stormy clouds.

"Molly?"

"Yes?"

"I wanted to give you this," Don said.

Molly turned to see Don holding out a cardboard rectangle — a laminated business card.

"This is my card. Call me in the weekend and we could grab a drink, to get to know each other better?"

And just like that, the sun came out again as Molly smiled, whipping the card from Don's hands, and slipping it into her pocket just as Doctor Perry opened his door. Timing was everything.

"COME THROUGH, DON," Doctor Perry said, his eyes taking in the glass of water and Don's proximity to Molly. His intuition failed him this time as he disregarded the scene as irrelevant. "Thank you, Molly, that's all for tonight. I'll see you tomorrow." Doctor Perry dismissed the girl. He might keep her on until he retired, her legs were still a delight, despite her being too social for his liking which he hadn't realised when he'd hired her. He preferred his receptionists to be more circumspect with their lives, and preferably without a social life.

"Good night, Doctor Perry," Molly said, gathering up her purse and fair dancing out the door, locking it behind her.

Satisfied she'd gone, Doctor Perry followed his last patient of the day into his surgery, closing the door and engaging the well-lubricated lock behind him.

"How are you?" Doctor Perry asked, steepling his fingers on his desk.

"It's been a rough week, wrenched my shoulder again," Don replied, favouring one side which gave him a lopsided Quasimodo gait.

"More swimming?"

Don shook his head and swallowed hard, tears forming in his eyes. "My dad died, and I was a pallbearer," he said. "I had the heavy end."

Doctor Perry closed his eyes. He'd been cultivating this client for weeks and this was the first time he'd mentioned any family. His enrolment notes hadn't shown a next of kin and even when he'd asked about partners, Don Jury had been quick to say that there wasn't anyone. Jury had just retired from his job, a job which saw him spending long stints travelling out of state. No one relied on him and with no dependants, he'd appeared to be the perfect patient.

"And your mother?" Doctor Perry asked, fully prepared to abandon his plans for this particular patient. Annoying, but prudent.

Don grabbed a tissue from the box on the desk and shook his head, explaining that his mother had died years earlier and that his father had been suffering from dementia for the past ten years, in full time care for nine of those. As an only child he had the responsibility for his father's care, with the funeral being his last act.

"It was a grim affair. Just me, some of the staff from his care facility and two of his old work colleagues. And I'm pretty sure they were only there for the free food. I don't think they really knew Dad at all. We had a cup of tea afterwards and that's it. It's an ignoble way to go, drooling into your cereal every day."

Doctor Perry straightened his shoulders. Excellent, Don Jury was still the perfect patient. Time to start, there was work to do.

Washing his hands, Doctor Perry considered his procedure for tonight. His tonic was ready on the side, and the restraints tucked out of sight. He'd need to dispose of Jury's clothing on his way home — he used the charity clothing bins for that, far away from the office. Disposing of Don's wallet and cellphone were more problematic but not insurmountable, given caution and timing. Satisfied with his preparations, Perry dried his hands before turning back to his patient.

"Up onto the bed please, just sitting and let's look at that shoulder."

Doctor Perry made a show of examining Don's shoulder, poking and prodding like any conventional doctor. He was pleased that Don kept himself fit. With no extraneous weight, the procedure would go faster, and he smiled to himself as he poured a precisely measured dose into a glass he'd prepared earlier.

Doctor Perry handed Don the glass filled with the milky liquid. "Drink this, it's a stronger dose than before. Give it a few minutes to kick in and then I'll start the manipulation. It will hurt, so I apologise but my tonic will take the edge off. And by bedtime, you'll be as good as new. Trust me." Moistening his lips, Doctor Perry watched as Don swallowed the lot in one gulp. Now the fun would really begin.

JURY SCULLED THE LIQUID, eager to get on with life without his father and the resulting drain on his own finances. The doctor's milky liquid slipped down his throat, reaching its icy fingers out towards his extremities, slinking along his arteries and inching along every tiny blood vessel. He fancied he could feel it seeping through his hair follicles and out his fingertips. An iciness filled his flaccid penis and Don lurched backwards, a sudden dizziness overtaking him. His skin prickling at the sudden coldness engulfing him. Closing his eyes relieved the nausea but also made it feel as if the hairs on his face were being sucked into his skin. He tried opening his eyes but he gave up fighting the tiredness and inertia took over. He let himself drift away from his worries, away from the dreariness of caring for a father who didn't recognise him, away from a career which did nothing for his soul, away from a life void of love. Somewhere he could hear the muffled sound of Doctor Perry talking and thought perhaps that the good doctor was reminding him about the pain. Don tried smiling, he was ready for it he wanted to say, but when the pain came he screamed. And he screamed, and he screamed, and he screamed.

AFTER YEARS OF PRACTICE, Doctor Perry had his timing perfect, and he'd strapped Don down as soon as his eyes had closed due to the effects of the tonic. Doctor Perry gave each of the straps another tug, reassuring himself there'd be no injuries during the changeover. Injuries had occurred a few times in the early days, and it was hard explaining away broken limbs when his patients had come in without them.

Doctor Perry stepped back as the tonic worked its magic on the man on the table. Perry didn't enjoy being too close, the screaming hurt his ears. He'd tried gagging them in the past but that had ended badly so he hadn't tried it again. Instead he tolerated the noise, knowing they were alone in the building and there was no one to hear the screaming.

And Don Jury carried on screaming as his bones shrank one by one, and his nails pulled away from the shrinking skin. Pools of blood bloomed on Don's fingers and toes but Doctor Perry wasn't concerned — it was part of the process. With nothing to do now except wait for the transition to finish, Doctor Perry settled at his desk to write up his notes. Every patient's reaction differed, and as a good doctor, he recorded those vagaries for analysis at a later date.

Through it all Don screamed until his throat was raw, and his memories vanished along with his facial hair and elongated toes. The gristle of his ears absorbed itself until only tiny newborn ears remained, which looked absurdly small on Don's adult sized head. No matter how often he'd tinkered with the formula, the head was always last. Doctor Perry shuddered as he considered some of his early patients and their unfortunate outcomes, their files still part of his research library. It was a shame he'd never be able to share his library given how fastidious he'd been at recording his trials over the years.

The pitch of Don's screams changed and Doctor Perry looked up from his notes. *Ah*, the cranium was shrinking. Perry watched as gleaming white adult teeth disappeared back into Don's jaw, the sucking noise setting his own teeth on edge. Finally, Don's eyeballs liquified and reassembled themselves into cloudy unseeing newborn eyes with infinitesimal baby eyelashes.

The room fell silent as the straps loosened around the mewling infant on the bed. The baby was in no danger of falling off for it would be weeks until it mastered the ability to roll on its own. Normally Doctor Perry didn't reverse his patients this far back, but intuition told him time was running out and he'd been around long enough to trust his gut.

Opening a bag he kept in his bathroom, he selected a blanket and swaddled the baby boy with a practised hand. He felt nothing for the child, he never did. Babies were just part of his stock, and stock control was key to his other business, a more profitable business.

10

Elijah arrived late to dinner, to ensure he sat as far away from the newest resident as possible. He could see Sulia in the corner by the window, her table companions slack-jawed at her vivacity so he slipped into a vacant chair at the nearest table, not noticing who else sat there, until a quiet voice murmured *good evening*.

He looked up to see Muriel Lincoln, bundled up in a canary-yellow cardigan and sweater. A pearl necklace lay loose around her wrinkled neck which matched the crumpled skin hanging from her tiny frame. Old age seemed to pull the skin from her body. A quiet woman, she received no visitors and made no outings. She was waiting to die. Just like the rest of them.

"This isn't your usual table," she said across the plastic-covered table.

The tablecloth crackled as he tried to get comfortable, turning his body away from the woman's inquisitive look, refusing to converse. He was here for dinner not for conversation. He usually ate alone, in the corner. In the corner the larger-than-life Sulia entertained her table companions — all people he'd never once sat with.

"It's fish tonight. I hope they've cooked it better than last week," Muriel tried again.

"It'll be fine," Elijah replied. He didn't want to discuss the quality of the food, the food was shit, like his life. He deserved nothing good. The best thing about tonight's serving of fish was that it would be easy to eat; always overcooked and served with peas and mash and rice pudding for dessert, a meal he could manage with the cutlery provided, so tonight he'd be going to bed with a full stomach.

Their meals arrived — fish, mashed potato, peas. No surprises there. Jugs of weak juice joined the plates of bland food and the clink of cutlery against crockery filled the room. Laughter pulsed from Sulia's table. *They'd stamp that out soon* Elijah thought. The Rose Haven Retirement Resort did not encourage happiness, despite what their advertising said.

The orderly, Preston Sergeant, was thumping plates onto the table next to them with all the finesse of a performing bear. Elijah watched as plate after plate of mediocre food landed on the surrounding tables. It wasn't a surprise when a crumbed fish fillet fell off one plate and onto the floor. Preston bent down, picked it up, and whacked it back onto the unfortunate diner's plate, and moved on.

"This was on the floor!" the resident complained, a diminutive man, one Elijah didn't recognise.

"And now it's on your plate for you to eat. Stop your complaining old man," Preston said.

"But it's been on the floor."

"And I can put it back on the floor if you like, now shut up and eat your food, you dumb shit."

The newcomer backed down, and poked at his meal, wiping the dust and hairs clinging to his crumbed fillet. And once again, Elijah pondered the choices which put him in this chair — poor judgement, alcohol, financial misfortune. A shopping list of bad decisions had forced him into this waiting room of death, a segment of society abandoned by their families. Retirees who considered living here preferable to being eaten by their decorative lap dogs on the bathroom floor of their decrepit homes.

Across from him, Muriel had pulled a pack of playing cards from her pocket and was laying them out on her side of the table, her fish abandoned on her plate. The flicking over of Muriel's cards was mesmerising, and Elijah found himself fantasising that he could predict which card would come up next. He was so focussed on Muriel's game that he didn't notice Sulia lumber over.

"Elijah," she boomed.

Elijah jumped up, knocking his chair backwards. Grabbing for the chair, his fingers brushed its steel frame sending daggers of pain through his deformed fingers. He jerked his hands back but with his forward momentum already in effect he fell heavily onto the chair and floor.

The dining room erupted and staff rushed towards the commotion. Their performance bonuses rested on keeping the peace, avoiding injuries to the residents, and mitigating risk everywhere.

"Clear the way, clear the way." A tiny Filipino woman pushed her way past the crowd clamouring around Elijah. Like a fog lifting, they made way for the one person they all respected, Tala - the head nurse.

"Elijah's fallen over, he didn't even put his hands out," offered one resident.

"Tripped right over," said another.

"Thank you yes, I can see that. Give him some space," Tala said.

With a hidden strength, Tala heaved Elijah onto the straightened chair, strong hands firm under his armpits. He didn't even notice — the pain in his fingers and joints so intense the world had faded to a pinprick of white.

"Can you walk?" Tala asked, her voice soft with the melodic merging of her native accent with that of her adopted homeland. She had to repeat herself a couple of times until she got through to him.

"Yes," Elijah whispered.

"Good, up you get then. I'll take you to your room," Tala said. There was no discussion about it.

TALA NEEDED him up and out of the dining room before any word reached management. They would place the blame for the fall on one of the staff, any excuse to deny a performance bonus or promotion. She put up with their erroneous judgments because she needed this job, and they kept her on because she often turned a blind eye to their more dubious practices. And she was a good nurse. She wanted to fly home for her mother's birthday soon so she was counting on her annual performance bonus. She needed it.

Tala tried hurrying Elijah down the hall. She'd taken him the long way back to his room to avoid the main office, but Elijah was shuffling along too slowly, Tracey could come by at any time, or one of her loyal lackeys.

"You need to pick up the pace for me now, come on," she chided.

Elijah limped faster, she was sure he knew why she needed him to. He kept to himself but she knew he wasn't

47

as addled as some other residents. She also knew what was in his patient file, the circumstances of how he ended up here. She wasn't one to judge, but she felt sorry for him. Lambasted through the media, in front of the entire nation. No wonder he kept to himself. She wasn't sure she could have withstood the media firestorm that he had.

"We'll get you to your room then I'll find something for the pain," she said, loosening her grip under his arm.

Elijah nodded, keeping up the pace she'd set. She was grateful he had few words, it reduced the risk of being overheard.

Once in Elijah's room, Tala lowered him into his chair. She winced as he cried out, shushing him frantically.

"Sorry, sorry. I'll be back soon but I'll close the door to keep away prying eyes. You understand?"

Tala ducked out, pulling the door behind her. Out in the hallway she closed her eyes and recovered her breath, she was strong but Elijah was a big man. Seconds later the smell of nicotine wafted over her. She didn't need to open her eyes to know who was there - Bart Stubbs, Rose Haven's laziest employee, one who seemed impervious to any form of disciplinary action. Every accusation of incompetence, impropriety, theft or abuse, bounced off him. He spent more time smoking in the covered courtyard than he did working.

"What're you doing outside Cone's room?" he asked.

Tala recoiled from his toxic breath. "What are you doing?" she countered.

Bart's lip curled over his yellowed teeth and his eyes narrowed. He coughed, a hacking precursor to emphysema.

"You should get that cough seen to, you don't want to be passing it on to any of the residents," she suggested. From her years of nursing experience, the only passing which would come from Bart's cough would be his passing into the afterlife.

Bart Stubbs seized upon her words as expected. "You think I need a doctor? You think one of the old tossers has given me this cough? Cause if they have then Rose Haven needs to be paying my doctor's bill. Can't afford it on my salary here…"

Tala sighed, inevitably Stubbs was as tight fisted as he was lazy. She'd have to factor his doctor's bill into her budget but it was worth it to protect herself and the other staff. She'd do what she had to, to protect the others.

"I'll make an appointment for you with Doctor Perry. You should be able to see him today if you go now," she suggested. Stubbs leaving now wouldn't make any difference to the workload of the others — they all operated as if he wasn't part of their team as it was.

Stubbs coughed again, and the sound of phlegm navigating its way from his nasal passages down his throat turned her stomach, but at least he'd agreed to go to the doctor. Maybe the doctor would persuade him to give up smoking.

11

Doctor Perry stretched out, the cotton sheets cool against his skin. It would be a shame to leave this behind him but it wouldn't take long to build it all up again — the anonymity of online shopping was so convenient. He was still tired from the procedure the night before. He always got a headache after one of those sessions. Not for the first time he considered building a properly soundproofed room, he hated listening to the screaming. Maybe when he moved.

A shape stirred underneath the covers next to him. His current wife. A masterful cook and a fastidious home keeper, she'd been a fine selection, at the time.

Her head appeared above the covers, tightly furled curls the colour of burnt honey and a hundred different shades of blonde. She looked to be on the cusp of thirty or so.

"Good morning," he said, before frowning. "I don't like the look of those lines this morning."

Myra Perry pulled away as he reached out to stroke her forehead, batting his hand away and swinging her legs out of bed onto the wooden floor.

"They're fine," she said, slipping her arms into her robe and padding off towards the kitchen.

Doctor Perry frowned at his wife's back. How long had it been since he'd last given her some tonic? It bothered him that he couldn't remember. Must be too long ago he decided. She'd need another dose before they moved, if indeed he took her with him. It was good to have someone to cater to his every need, but that someone didn't have to be Myra. He luxuriated in bed a moment longer imagining the possibilities, whilst giving Myra enough time to make his breakfast, as was her job, every day.

A GINGER TOM cat rolled in the dirt of the back yard, a long feather clutched between its paws. Gnawing at the brittle quill, engrossed in his endeavours, he was oblivious to the audience at the kitchen window.

Myra watched as the cat tired of the feather and tore into the dismembered corpse of what had once been a gull. Myra moved a fraction of an inch, spooking the cat, who looked up from his meal, his whiskers smeared red.

A wail from the nursery reached Myra's ears and those of the cat, who took off, abandoning his prey, torn ears flat against his head. He'd be back soon, he always came back, hungry for the love and attention she'd given him for the fifteen years she'd had him. Myra ignored the baby, she had to get her husband's breakfast ready first and the baby would be safe in his crib for a while longer, hungry but safe.

Multitasking, she measured the formula powder precisely while waiting for the eggs to fry. She knew the repercussions of not measuring correctly, her husband had drummed it into her over and over again; his lessons spectacularly driven home the one and only time she'd ever been to the Juvenile Detention Centre where they'd first met.

She'd dropped in with a box of her childhood books in her arms, rescued from her family home before developers crushed it to a pulp and replaced it with soulless concrete boxes. She'd buried her parents a month earlier and her time had been filled with sending their treasured belongings off to auction, delivering cartons of linen and crockery to the local charity shop, and now this — donating the final vestiges of her childhood to those who needed them more than her. Her barren womb wouldn't be producing any children to enjoy them.

There'd been no cheery-faced staff at the door, no chortles of delight at the books she'd brought with her. The halls were filled with children of every sort and every age, abandoned by a system lacking the skills, the money, or the patience to adequately deal with damaged goods. Stunned into silence, she'd carried her box of books, aimlessly looking for someone to leave her box with. Child after child had followed her with their eyes but made no move towards her or the box, over the rim of which peeped the hard plastic faces of play-worn Disney characters. The children an eerie cast of tiny mannequins living amongst the scent of urine and neglect. She'd turned to retrace her steps and was confronted by a young girl, with a somewhat familiar face.

"Help me, please," the girl had said, stepping forward, eyes darting back and forth between Myra and the empty corridor. "Can you get me out of here?"

"What? No!" She'd backed away from the child but the girl had grabbed her wrist.

"You have to get me out of here. I need to go home.

Look at them all, we're all prisoners here," her little-girl voice had been filled with panic.

They'd drawn a crowd of blank-eyed children, who'd shuffled closer in identical slippered feet, surrounding them. Myra remembered pushing through the slack-jawed children, the girl child clutching onto her. She'd tried to shake her off but it wasn't until she'd found her way back to the front door, where the underpaid immigrant worker had absently let her in, that she finally broke free. From the safety of her car she'd watched as an older man had ushered the girl back inside, the little girl wailing, beating at him with her small fists. Myra had slunk down behind her steering wheel, tears melting the makeup she'd slathered on that morning. It wasn't until a hand had rapped at her window that she'd looked up from her rage at the injustice of the world. It was then that she'd met her husband, the kind Doctor Perry, the same man who'd ushered the wailing child back inside. How long ago had that been now? It was so blurry. Her mind had a hard time focussing on anything other than the immediate tasks within her own house and the parade of foster children they cared for, least they end up in a place like that.

He'd given up working at the detention centre after they were married, apparently something to do with government cutbacks and integrating the less problematic children into mainstream schools, including the child she'd spoken with. She'd never forgotten what he'd said about how that little girl was suffering from irreparable brain damage after being given the wrong dosage of an over-the-counter adult pain relief. It was a lesson she never forgot, a lesson her husband never let her forget.

Myra dished her husband's eggs onto a slice of unbuttered wheatmeal bread, he couldn't abide butter. She straightened his cutlery and mentally checked off the breakfast list — toast, eggs, cutlery, napkin… juice, he needed a glass of juice, that's what was missing. Glass bottles clinked in the refrigerator door as she reached for the orange juice. Her hand paused above bottles of her husband's special tonic. After his comment today, he'd make her drink some before the end of the week. Myra had no idea what the tonic contained and although she'd come to appreciate how it made her look, she had a suspicion that the tonic was messing with her memory. She had flashes of memories of faces and people, memories of a life she didn't have any more, and had trouble grasping those wispy thoughts and twisting them into anything coherent. The online forums she frequented called that *mommy brain*, but she'd never been a real *mommy*, only ever a foster mom. No one in any of the online forums ever said anything about their husbands making them drink a concoction to make them look young and beautiful…

She grabbed the juice they had delivered with the rest of their groceries every week and slammed the fridge door shut. She never went to the store, an *unnecessary outing* her husband said and besides, she needed to be here for the children, for the babies. Myra poured the juice, careful to only fill the glass three quarters full. Doctor Perry was very particular about that sort of thing.

12

Elijah's arthritis made sleep impossible, the pain more excruciating at night than during the day. Sitting upright eased it somewhat, so he'd given up trying to shut the demon memories from his mind and had lumbered over to his armchair. Another long night in the chair hoping to die before the sun rose.

He'd dozed off when the sound of an engine jerked him awake and the flash of headlights poured into his retinas like lightning. Maybe someone had snuffed it during their sleep, the lucky bugger. The lights of reception flicked on following the slamming of the car door, illuminating the Amazonian figure of Tracey Chappell, her skirt too far away from her knees to be anything more than a belt, and her ropes of costume jewellery too gaudy to be fashionable in any decade.

The lights from reception showed the witching hour visitor to be the amiable Doctor Perry, his cliche leather doctor's bag clasped in one hand, his other outstretched to pump the manicured fingers of Rose Haven's manager.

They disappeared into the building, locking the door and extinguishing the lights behind them.

Elijah pondered which poor soul needed the ministrations of a doctor this time, the time of night when old tickers gave up the ghost and tired lovers walked away from trysts gone stale. Was it Johnny Paulson or someone else? He hoped whoever it was had a quick and painless exit from this purgatory. He deserved to be here, but prayed to whatever omnipotent being was overseeing them that his number would be up soon because then the nightmares would stop and the pain vanish. Elijah imagined an afterlife akin to sitting on the edge of a lake in late spring, fishing rod in hand, his wife by his side… or at least that's what his heaven would be if it existed, if he ever got there, but the odds weren't in his favour.

Tonight the building was silent. Most nights the cries of his neighbours; their moans and groans and the grinding of their teeth became the symphony to which he slept. But tonight was quieter than the dark lane which had robbed him of the life he had loved. Where even the owls observed an unnatural silence at the atrocity he had committed and only the hissing of a cooling engine, and a dripping from the bottle, could be heard.

He woke with his own cry, the crushing of memories as painful as the roof of the van pressing down upon him and his passengers had been that fateful night. The sound of a car door opening once again waking him from his uneasy slumber in the chair.

The good doctor was back outside, Tracey Chappell simpering at his side, a wrapped bundle in her arms. Elijah watched as Tracey handed the package over to Doctor Perry, who put the package into the car, the bulk of the sedan hiding any further view of what he was doing in the back seat.

The doctor straightened and shook hands with Tracey before handing her an envelope. The smile on Tracey's face was big enough to light up a ballpark. Just before the good doctor closed his car door Elijah swore he heard the mewling of a newborn baby, cut off by the gentle rumble of the engine as the car backed out of the driveway, leaving only the exhaust fumes to infiltrate Elijah's room, instead of the long-forgotten sounds of a baby crying.

The lights at reception went dark as Tracey Chappell disappeared inside. Elijah knew too well she couldn't abide wasting electricity. The electricity bill probably cut into her holiday fund, or her Botox fund, or any other fund which might divert profits away from her. She wasn't known by the residents as one who liked spending money on anything Rose Haven Retirement Resort related, least of all electricity.

13

Myra's husband popped his head into the nursery to say goodbye before leaving for the day. He rarely had anything to do with the children they fostered, other than picking them up from wherever they came from, then delivering them to their eventual families. Sometimes the new parents came to the house, but more often than not her husband strapped the babies into a carseat and delivered them himself, telling her it was Social Services policy. Myra tried not to think about the babies after they left, but saying goodbye got harder and harder. She didn't mind the tiredness which came hand-in-hand with caring for babies, but she did miss the luxury of having a day to herself; a day of pampering or lying in the sun, cocktail in one hand and a paperback in the other. Since becoming a doctor's wife and then a full-time foster mom, she never even got to go to the local library any more. Her husband had given her an eReader and a subscription to a book service, pointing out that she didn't need to go to the library any more because the breadth of choice online was superior to anything at the library and that the children needed her at home. That, coupled with their grocery delivery service, her husband's stringent rules around who could visit — they had to have had recent vaccinations and not be sick, etcetera etcetera, left her a virtual prisoner in the house, bound by baby wipes and nap times.

Feeding, burping, cleaning, changing, then settling the baby all took time, and in a couple of hours she'd have to do it all over again. For now, she had a small window for a shower and to gulp down some breakfast.

Tossing the empty baby bottle into the sink on her way past the kitchen Myra saw a familiar medicine cup sitting next to the kettle and froze mid stride. Her husband's throwaway comment about the lines on her forehead clearly wasn't so throwaway after all. Her fingers sought out the offending furrows on her brow, then feathered across the lines she knew were forming alongside her hazel-coloured eyes. Contemplating the precisely measured vial of liquid her husband the doctor expected to her drink with her breakfast, she picked up the medicine cup and carried it through to the bathroom, tipping the milky liquid down the sink. Leaving the medicine cup on the side of the sink, she stripped off and stepped into the shower cubicle, the hot water washing away her unease at defying her husband.

DEEP in the sewer under Doctor Perry's house, a family of rats sniffed at the odd coloured liquid dripping from the pipes. They ignored the tang of shampoo and the eggy sludge from the doctor's breakfast, instead licking the milky residue forming along the edge of the old pipe damaged by the big tree in the front yard; damage which had gone unnoticed by anyone, despite the increasing bogginess of the earth in that part of the garden.

Being creatures of habit and with their stomachs full, the rats scurried off to their next port of call. Although they didn't have the words to name it, they and all their brethren made their way towards the various laneways and roads frequented every Monday to Friday by the small humans — the ones who tossed unwanted sandwiches and the crumbs from their cakes on their way to school. Mana from heaven; it was an event not to be missed.

As they scurried from their dark corners and their stinky pipes, from behind dumpsters and underneath bridges, there was one family of rats who lagged behind, their minds suddenly foggy. Physically they were fine, their multitude of aches and ailments had vanished; a lifetime of bad food snuffed out in an instant. Their arteries were flushed with youth and their hearts pumped with renewed vigour, but they couldn't remember where they were going or why they were going. Popping up on the corner of Padova Drive and Arno Way, they stood quivering in the sunlight, completely unaware that they were a lot younger than they'd been before they'd quenched their thirst on that strange milky liquid underneath the Perrys' house.

14

"Jesse, hey Jesse, come see these," called James Jackson to his twin brother, not so loudly that their mother would turn, but loud enough for his mirror image to hear and come running.

"What've you got" asked Jesse Jackson, a complete clone of his brother. Their mother made no effort to differentiate them and only she could tell them apart. The boys had identical temperaments and leveraged their alikeness to their advantage.

"Baby rats, look!"

"Cool! Put them in my bag quick, before Mom sees them." Jesse opened a schoolbag adorned with images of the Incredible Hulk and a collection of key rings from various family friendly restaurants where the over-priced nutrition-deficient food was disguised with free gifts and bottomless soda cups.

The rats were deposited into Jesse Jackson's schoolbag, to await a fate worse than the sewers they'd come from, and both boys scurried after their mother as she carried on towards their school. The boys exchanged gleeful looks, today was turning out to be better than expected.

As THE FAMILY walked past the Rose Haven Retirement Resort, their mother cast a nervous glance towards the blank windows following them. Amber Jackson had a decision to make and it didn't sit comfortably with her. She was embarrassed to be contemplating it, but with three children, an almost full-time job, and no husband, she didn't have the time or energy to care for her ailing father, which made her feel like a failure. The longer she put off the decision, the worse she felt, but she needed to move somewhere cheaper and smaller, and fast because she was falling behind in her payments. She couldn't manage any longer with her father holding them back. He was an extra mouth to feed and he took up a whole room which the baby needed. *She* needed the baby in his own room so she could finally get a proper nights sleep. It'd been forever since she'd had an uninterrupted sleep, so long ago she couldn't even remember it. Maybe she should move into the old folks home and leave her dad to raise the boys?

The gussied up face of the Rose Haven Retirement Resort followed her harried progress. Amber quickened her steps, barking at the twins to hurry up or they'd be late for school. Little beggars were whispering about something and once again she felt like an outsider within her own family, shut out of their secrets and their play. It had been that way since they were old enough to open their eyes.

"Come on boys, stop dragging your damn feet or we're going to be late and you'll have to explain to Miss Barnett why you're late," Amber chastised, turning for them to see that her face had an *I'm not messing about* look on it.

As she turned, the stroller went over the lip of the sidewalk, its front wheel catching in a stormwater drain missing its protective grill. A grill which hadn't been replaced despite more than one concerned citizen ringing the authorities about the hazard.

Amber Jackson's forward momentum propelled her into the stationary stroller, the weight of her body knocking it into the path of a monster of a Mercedes, a gleaming white beast hurtling towards the screaming baby and his stunned mother lying dazed on the sticky bitumen.

The Mercedes driving mom slammed on her brakes and the smell of burning rubber filled the air as the German engineering kicked in and the brakes did their job, stopping the car an inch away from Amber's head.

Amber Jackson never saw the car in the other lane, the one driven by a learner driver whose boyfriend had just broken up with her via text. Amber never saw the tears streaming down the young girl's face as she read her boyfriend's pathetic excuse for the breakup. She never saw the girl take her other hand off the steering wheel to type an angry reply. And she didn't see the little blue car pull slightly to the side now the driver had both hands off the steering wheel. But Amber Jackson did hear the little blue car clip the side of the stationary Mercedes at just the wrong angle, which shunted it over her terrified face.

Amber's face didn't stay terrified for long; the rubber of the huge tyres stripped the skin from her face and crushed the cartilage of her nose and her worries fell away with her skin. One of the diamond earrings her husband had given her on their wedding day was pressed into the hot tar of the road, the other one was caught in the ridges of the tyre. Later, a mechanic would pull the tiny gem from its rubbery grave and slip it into his pocket. From what he'd heard, the woman who'd been wearing the earring didn't need it any more. Hard to wear earrings when you don't have any earlobes.

———

THE TWINS WATCHED the whole thing unfold in a surreal haze. And for the first time in their lives, they thought about someone other than themselves. What would they do without their mom?

Eventually someone noticed them, a woman on her way home from a long nightshift at a chemical plant. She ushered them away from the carnage, and in a daze they allowed themselves to be lead into the Rose Haven Retirement Resort. The Good Samaritan thought it was the best place for them given the nature of the accident, and she left them with the receptionist, who'd been loitering in the doorway watching the proceedings the same way you'd watch a dog fight between two strays on the street — with interest, but with no intention of getting involved.

The receptionist had no idea what to do with the two identical faces in front of her. The boys seemed content sitting in the waiting room, swinging their legs, looking neither upset nor happy, but bored, which was how she would have described them if anyone had asked her.

The twins had considered asking about their baby brother, but they hadn't known him that long, only a few months, so they sat, silently waiting for their mother. By the time anyone thought to check the stroller, their baby brother was dead. He'd suffocated on the plastic cover their mother had placed over the stroller to protect him from the flying midges which annoyed everyone at this time of year.

And after the other witnesses had left, and the first

responders had done what the state paid them to do, and after the tow trucks had hitched both vehicles onto their rigs, there was no one left to consider the whereabouts of the two young boys waiting patiently for their mother in the reception area of the Rose Haven Retirement Resort.

When Doctor Perry showed up at eleven o'clock for his regular clinic, the antsy receptionist pounced on him. Asking Tracey Chappell for advice wasn't something she wanted to do.

"Excuse me Doctor Perry, but I need some advice about the boys."

"The boys?" Doctor Perry's brow furrowed. He didn't like being asked questions outside of his clinic; there was no money in free advice.

The receptionist inclined her head towards the twins, explaining in a theatrical whisper why they were in the waiting room. That the mother had been taken away but not in an ambulance with its lights on, which must mean that she was dead. And how she'd waited for someone to come and collect the boys, and how it seemed that they had been overlooked.

Doctor Perry carefully arranged his face. "That's terrible," he commiserated, casting his eyes over the boys.

So enraptured with retelling the lurid details, the receptionist didn't notice the change in the doctor's demeanour, she only felt a wave of relief when he offered to deliver the boys to the *relevant authorities*.

"Sadly I've dealt with many children orphaned by the untimely death of a parent, so I've a number of contacts with the local child welfare office. Leave it with me. Keep an eye on them for a few minutes more while I have a quick word with Tracey."

The receptionist nodded, her blonde ponytail bouncing in agreement. The sooner the boys were gone, the sooner she could ring her girlfriends to tell them all about her traumatic experience. Those cars could have even hit the front of her building. She was seriously lucky to have escape unharmed herself.

Doctor Perry emerged from Tracey's office and bundled the boys into the back of his sedan, marvelling at their identicalness. Neither child had questioned what was happening with them. They were the most compliant children he'd ever encountered. Perfect children.

Driving home, he observed them in his rear vision mirror. They both sat looking out the windows, school bags clutched in their laps. Yes, they were perfect in every way. He'd already fired off a text to Myra warning her to prepare another room for their new guests.

He'd never had a pair of twins before and he was tempted to experiment on them with different doses but deep down he knew he wouldn't. There was too much money involved to ruin the appeal of twins. He allowed himself to daydream about the profit they would fetch. With that money, it would definitely be time to move on.

Pulling into the driveway, he drove straight into the garage, closing the cedar door behind him. You never knew when prying eyes might see something they shouldn't. Myra was waiting at the back of the garage, a forced smile on her face. Doctor Perry frowned. Myra's face hadn't changed in the slightest. If anything, the lines between her eyebrows looked deeper than they had this morning. He questioned the dosage he'd left for her on the kitchen bench. Perhaps she'd built up a tolerance? He made a mental note to increase it next time.

THE TWINS CLAMBERED out of the car and stood shoulder to shoulder. They'd expected to be taken back to their grandfather, but obviously that wasn't the case. At least they weren't going to have to share a bathroom any more with a stinky old man who couldn't hold his bowels.

The woman ushered them inside with the promises of banana cake after they'd eaten some lunch. Cake! They never had cake at home so trooped behind her to the kitchen, climbing up onto the stools. They ogled the expensive appliances on the bench and the vast lawn they could see through the window complete with a large ginger cat challenging them from under the tree. This adventure was turning out to be better than expected.

After a mumbled thanks, they ate the sandwiches Myra had prepared. The doctor followed them into the kitchen and they squirmed under his scrutiny, Myra's promise of banana cake keeping their manners in check.

"I'm going to leave you in my wife's capable hands and I'm sure you boys will be on your best behaviour while I'm gone. Myra will show you which room will be yours until the State sorts out some official care for you-"

James started to interrupt but Jesse kicked him in the shin, out of the doctor's sight.

"Pardon?" Doctor Perry said.

"He was just going to say *thank you*," Jesse replied.

"Yes, good manners are essential, your mother has raised you well," Doctor Perry smiled at them. "And your father of course..." he added.

"Our father died," James added. "In the war."

"War is a terrible thing," the doctor replied.

The boys couldn't tell that the doctor's heart started beating a little faster and they couldn't see the dollar signs dancing in the man's eyes. They nodded at his sympathy. He'd responded the same way everyone did when they found out their father was dead. He'd spent most of their short lives stationed overseas and on the few occasions he came home, he either slept lots or spent his time behind the locked bedroom door with their mother. He'd never done any real fathering.

"Right, well I must go back to the Rose Haven Retirement Resort now, there are patients relying on me. I'll see you all tonight," the doctor said before disappearing back down the hall.

With the doctor gone, the boys finished their sandwiches and devoured the banana cake, practically inhaling the moist slabs of cake. James licked the crumbs from his plate and would have looked for more but Jesse read his mind and shook his head. The woman offered to show them their room.

They followed her down the hall towards an open door.

"This is your room, I'll leave you here to get settled in while I sort out the baby, so I'll check in on you shortly then maybe we'll have afternoon tea outside? Okay?" Myra said.

Jesse and James nodded silently. They didn't need to talk to communicate. Today was turning out to be one of the best days ever.

"It could be worse," Jesse said.

"Yup, could be worse," James replied.

"Is your knife in your bag?"

"Of course."

"Where shall we do it?" Jesse asked.

Both boys looked around the room. Fairly spartan with two beds, one bedside table, a bookcase filled with the complete works of Charles Dickens bound in faux leather and a dozen or so Readers Digest books. Tucked away in the corner was an old dining chair, an ironing board and an ugly set of plastic drawers filled with life's detritus.

"On the ironing board, but look in the drawers for something to put them in," James directed.

Jesse rifled through the drawers before settling on an old tobacco tin. It hadn't held any of the evil weed in it for at least a century but still reeked of tobacco. It was filled with old buttons, bobbins and needles. Jesse's face glowed as he carried the tin over to his brother.

James set up the ironing board in the middle of the room and took the tin off his brother. "Perfect," he said, tipping the contents onto the bed. "You sort out the pins, we could use them for sure."

Jesse smiled, he'd had that exact thought himself.

James shoved his hand deep into his school bag and pulled out a handful of squirming baby rats. The whole time he'd been sitting in the foul-smelling reception of the old folks home, the knowledge of the rats in his bag had kept him quiet. He didn't want a suspicious adult going through the bag and taking their rats away.

The little boy placed the rats carefully in the tobacco tin, like treasured possessions, and stepped away to admire his handiwork.

THE RATS HUDDLED TOGETHER in a corner, their pink eyes darting faster than a hummingbird, seeking out the threat, sniffing the air. The brothers and sisters clambered over each other using barely formed limbs.

The bottom of the school bag had been a smorgasbord for their palates — bread crumbs and mandarin peel, raisins and popcorn kernels and a sliver of luncheon sausage caught in a seam right at the bottom, the green hue not a deterrent to the rats' voracious appetites.

"PASS ME THE PINS," James instructed, his hand outstretched.

Jesse straightened up the selection — a darning needle, a fine embroidery needle, and a thick crochet hook which looked like a miniature hockey stick. He'd wanted to play hockey at school but there was no money for the gear, so Mom had said no. She always said no.

He fussed over the selection of pointy needles — the darning needle would be too quick, so he chose the thin embroidery needle with a thread of red silk looped through its eye. *That would be pretty* he thought, and passed it to his brother.

James transferred the nearest rat to the solid surface of the ironing board and holding the squirming body flat, he took the needle and plunged it through the rat's tiny paw, pinning it to the ironing board.

"I need another one like that needle. They should all match don't you think?"

Jesse nodded, he had them all lined up ready. He knew what his brother needed, he always knew, that's what made them such a good team. He passed another needle over, no thread this time, so it didn't look as joyous as the first one. There were dozens of thread fragments mixed in with the buttons so while James was pinning the second limb of the rat he licked the end of a blue silk thread and passed it through the eye of the needle, just like they'd been taught at school.

"You can do one if you like?" James offered. They shared everything.

Jesse took the embroidery needle with the blue thread and instead of pinning the rat's third paw to the ironing board, he passed the needle straight through one paw, once, then twice, before pinning it down tight. *There, that was better, much prettier.*

The animal's only free paw scrabbled at the floral fabric cover of the ironing board, frantically trying to escape, like swimming one handed.

The boys stepped back, heads cocked to the side, as they surveyed their efforts so far.

"Not bad," James said. "Now we need the knife."

Elijah had watched the whole event unfold across the road. He couldn't see what it was that the twins picked up but if they were anything like he'd been as a child, it was probably a nest, a python skin, or a lizard's tail to throw at the girls. Whatever it was they'd stopped to pick up, he was grateful it delayed them long enough that they hadn't been close enough to see their mother's head pop like a balloon.

The two boys had stood bewildered on the sidelines as people flocked to the scene, no different to vultures circling high above a dying buffalo. Humans gravitate towards mayhem as a way of assuring themselves that they're still alive, a reminder that there is always someone worse off than them.

Elijah didn't own a cellphone any more, there was no need, he had no one to ring and no one wanted to ring him. He did have an emergency call button which he'd never had cause to use before, but today he was seconds away from using it, to summon someone to rescue the twins. If the scene outside was as bad as the faces of the onlookers, it would haunt those boys for the rest of their lives. Elijah knew boys, he knew how damaged boys grew up, angry at the world. Elijah knew what made boys tick, and what made them explode.

Before Elijah could persuade his grotesque fingers to press the bell, he spied the good samaritan hone in on the twins and in a carefully orchestrated move, wrap her arms around them and hustle them into the Rose Haven's reception before they even had a chance to protest.

Elijah lost sight of them after that but at least his own pulse returned to normal knowing someone was caring for the boys, someone eminently more suitable than him. He tried not to think about his own accident. The sudden screams cut off. A heady mixture of rum and oil — a sickly sweet Caribbean flavour remembered from a holiday long ago in another life. Elijah's ears buzzed with the memory of the ticking of the cooling engine. Overwhelmingly, mostly he could only recall the stickiness of the rum dripping from his hair, and the utter confusion of how rum got into his hair.

A KNOCK on the door interrupted Elijah's reminiscing, plucking him from the fitful doze he'd fallen into, the sweet smell of alcohol fading like a photograph in the sun. The knocking grew more insistent and Elijah struggled to get up from his chair, engulfed by the fabric and cushions. He clawed his way out of the fog of sleep, the stuff of his nightmares clinging to him, as he tried to escape from the car... no, not the car, that was his old life, his other self. Then the pain hit.

Clambering up from the chair without his usual careful ministrations sent shockwaves of pain coursing through Elijah's fingers and hands, radiating up his arms. Worse pain than his accident. Worse but deserved. The pain was his punishment.

"Hey, Mister Cone, you okay?" Benson Flag let himself into Elijah's room after hearing him cry out. He lead him back to his chair, lowering him like you would transfer an invalid from his wheelchair to his bed.

"What did you do Mister Cone?"

"I didn't think, Benson. It's a bad habit of mine, not thinking. Jumped out of this damn chair without thinking about my hands. So much for being a damn easy chair. The pain hit me a bit, but I'm okay now," Elijah said. He didn't want to look at Benson's face. He was a nice kid, but he was an efficient kid, and this would end up in his notes. He was on track to be a fine doctor one day, after he paid his way through medical school, or nursing school, or whatever school it was he was at. Elijah didn't care any more. He wanted to be left alone with his thoughts or with a bottle of rum and a handful of pills.

Benson backtracked to scoop up his folder from the bed. "It says here you're to see Doctor Perry today, I came by to say there's going to be change cause he's taking some kids to the child welfare people so your appointment will be after lunch now."

"I didn't make any appointment, Benson," Elijah said.

"No, Mister Cone, you didn't, we did. It's our job to look after you folk, you know that. You aren't going to give me a hard time now are you?"

Elijah shook his head, it was the only part of him which didn't hurt.

"Do you mean the boys from the accident earlier?"

"Yup, if I'd heard about it I would have been over there myself but I was on the other side of the building. Didn't even click that the sirens were so close. Someone should have called us to help. But Doctor Perry is a good man to look after those boys. Hope their momma is okay."

"It didn't look so good from here," Elijah said. If Benson trusted this doctor, then he could too. God knew he deserved the pain he was in, but some relief so he could hold his own cock without grimacing when he went to the toilet would be welcome.

"What time do I go see the doc?"

"You need to be in his waiting room at one o'clock. He's a bit funny about patients being on time."

"I'll be there."

Benson raised one eyebrow.

"When I say I'll be somewhere, I will be. I don't need babysitting," Elijah replied.

The orderly shrugged, "They're your hands, I'm here to look after you, it's what I get paid for."

"You're the only one," Elijah muttered and returned his gaze to the window. The road was empty of any evidence of the crash. Even the broken glass had been swept away by an overly energetic County employee. Most times accident debris was left in situ, waiting to be washed into gutters by the rain, saving on manpower. Elijah imagined portions of brain tissue tumbling through the city's sewers. A bizarre art project gathering momentum underground.

The image of another morbid art installation detached itself from the recesses of his memory. Another woman's head, crushed in a car accident. The smear of the lipstick she'd been applying streaked across her face from the corner of her lips, if she'd still had them. Her lips sliced off by the metal sign they'd hit. The County's health and safety advisor could not have foreseen that eventuality.

"I think I'll have a rest now. I'll be in the doctor's waiting room at one o'clock, you can count on me."

Elijah imagined he could still smell the scent of rum long after Benson had left the room. Perhaps it was the other man's aftershave. Perhaps it was his guilt. Tears fell from Elijah's face. There'd been a time when his tears were more rum than water. If only he could forget that time and wind back the clock. He'd do anything to have a second chance.

17

Seven elderly patients sat in the waiting room, two chatted happily in the corner — their ailments not immediately obvious to the casual observer. The others flicked through magazines deemed too ancient or too dull for the staffroom; Nancy Brood leafed through a June 2006 issue of *Florida Sportsman* and Jennifer Withers, a retired botanist who'd once worked for an international fertiliser company, was reading about Princess Diana's latest landmine eradication campaign despite the Princess having died twenty years ago. Elijah Cone held a tatty *Readers Digest* but made no move to read it. Next to him sat a woman he didn't recognise who'd pulled a paperback from her handbag and was engrossed in its pages. Leaving Polish Rob sitting alone in the corner, jiggling his legs.

Polish Rob wasn't his real name, but one given to differentiate him from the four other Roberts who lived at the Rose Haven Retirement Resort. They'd named him Polish Rob for the obvious reason that he was Polish, and despite having lived in America since 1946, his accent was as strong as the vodka which had decimated his liver. Polish

Rob had moved into the Rose Haven a month earlier and the strict no alcohol policy had sent him into a detox hell only death would cure.

The seven old folk sat on old board chairs with fraying arms, reading magazines well past their shelf life, waiting to see a doctor they'd had no choice in choosing. There was no relaxing mood music or calming colour scheme, the waiting room had been shoehorned into the old fitness centre of the resort, where dusty exercise equipment still adorned the space. The residents had given up asking if they could use the equipment, management claiming *health and safety* was a factor, as there weren't sufficient funds to employ a qualified physiotherapist, to oversee the use of the equipment. Avoiding lawsuits seemed to be one thing the management of the Rose Haven excelled at. Beige paint plastered the walls, the remnants from a cancelled commercial order the owners had got cheap at auction, with gallons of the stuff festering in the basement.

When Doctor Perry first set up in town, establishing a relationship with a suitable old folks home was a key business decision. In his experience, most businesses catering to the elderly didn't do it out of altruistic tendencies but out of a deep love for the bottom line. Old people didn't complain, their families weren't interested in their welfare, they didn't eat much and couldn't remember what they'd eaten anyway. They didn't need as much space as the mandated square feet prisoners were allocated, and their population turned over faster than a rollercoaster at Disneyland. All in all, working with the elderly was a cash cow. And the State subsidised it.

After much research, choosing the Rose Haven Retirement Resort had been an easy decision. The owners favoured profit above all else, and how they made that profit didn't really concern them too much. They were open to suggestions, which made it the perfect business relationship.

Doctor Perry opened his consulting room door and counted the bodies waiting for him — seven, as per his appointment schedule.

"Good afternoon," he announced, causing six out of the seven heads to pop up. Polish Rob didn't look up, eyes downcast, hands shaking in his lap.

"Sorry for the delay," Doctor Perry said. He had no intention of elaborating as to the reason for the delay. That was the good thing about the elderly, they believed their doctors and rarely, if ever, questioned them. Doctors were important people and if they were delayed then it must have been for something important.

"Miss Withers, please come through."

Jennifer Withers, the retired botanist with a penchant for English royalty, shuffled into the office and Doctor Perry closed the door behind her.

"How are you feeling today?" he asked.

"Oh a lot better since I last saw you," Jennifer said, "but I'm still getting these headaches, makes me so tired, and well, I was wondering if perhaps another dose of your tonic might be just the thing I need?"

Doctor Perry made a show of looking over his notes but he'd already seen the improvement in Miss Withers, her skin was smoother and she walked with more agility than she had a month ago. With some patients he kept their dosages low enough that they'd feel better but slowly the effects would wear off and their problems would return, and thereby they'd return to him. A money-go-round if you like; their money went to him, over and over and over again.

"Hmm, it's been a month since I last saw you and the headaches haven't improved? Have you been drinking water like I suggested?" He raised a practised eyebrow, he knew this party trick always got a giggle from the older ladies.

As predicted, Jennifer Withers tittered before droning on about her hydration regime. It didn't matter to Doctor Perry whether she did or didn't hydrate her body efficiently for her age, she had a prosthetic leg which made her unsuitable for anything other than a small dose of his tonic every now and then. Just enough to make her feel like Wonder Woman briefly before the same ailments took hold of her decaying body.

He might as well string her along for as long as he was still in town, it was all extra dollars in the coffer. "And you call yourself a scientist? You of all people should know the benefits of hydration. Miss Withers, if you are not drinking water with every meal, and a glass before bed at night, I will hear about it. I will only prescribe my tonic if you can find a way to adhere to that health advice?"

"Yes, I'm sorry, Doctor Perry. I promise." Jennifer said, like a child being told off by a favourite teacher. "But these headaches, I can't think straight…"

"That will be dehydration. Trust me, Miss Withers." He passed a medicine cup across the desk and watched Jennifer gulp it down, the untamed whiskers on her chin dancing up and down as she licked the inside of the cup.

"It won't be long until that takes effect and as long as you drink plenty of water, in conjunction with gentle walks around the halls, you will see an improvement. You must trust me, Miss Withers. I am your doctor."

She limped out of his office smiling. It was a shame

she wasn't a whole woman, and an even bigger shame he hadn't worked out how to regrow limbs, yet. He closed the door and returned to his desk. He had to write up his notes before the next patient. That was the way he worked. One patient in, one patient out, write up the notes, put them away, next patient in. That way no one got confused. Medications weren't mixed up. No one died.

Doctor Perry checked his watch, half a minute to spare. He stretched and did a couple of deep lunges to keep his legs limber and the blood flowing. Exercise was just as important for one's health as hydration.

The next patient was a new resident, so he spent most of the session ascertaining her medical history and personal circumstances, as any doctor should with a new patient. The patient was an eighty-one year old spinster from California, who'd initially moved to Florida to care for an elderly aunt and had never left. With no close family, few friends, or acquaintances at the Rose Haven, she was a perfect candidate.

Doctor Perry made sympathetic noises as he made notes in his own inexplicable shorthand. "It must be very hard for you, all on your own?"

Frances Merriweather smiled, "I don't mind so much. I never argue with myself, I always get to eat the last chocolate in the box, and I can watch whatever I like on TV without having to compromise. It's just now I…" She didn't need to finish the sentence, Doctor Perry already knew why she'd moved into the Rose Haven Retirement Resort; why she couldn't live on her own any more. It was a sad story, sadder than most to be fair, but she was his now.

"Being married has benefits, but I understand what you mean, Miss Merriweather. I'm not one for prescribing medications willy nilly, but without running any further tests-"

"I'm not having any tests-"

"Yes, well, you've already made that quite clear, but it goes against my better judgement as your doctor. I was about to say, I can offer a natural tonic to ease the symptoms you're experiencing. I would normally recommend a higher dose, which would have a much better chance of alleviating them faster and for longer, but again, without those tests…"

"I'll consider it but I'm unlikely to change my mind. As I said, I'm old, and old people get sick and die. That is the natural way of things. It is not for us to play against the hand we've been dealt, Doctor."

Doctor Perry had no answer for the feisty woman in front of him. Instead he motioned towards the scales and noted down her weight as Frances Merriweather slipped off her slippers and stood lightly on the digital scales.

"May I ask, have you recently lost weight, or is this your normal weight?"

"Not being able to keep down most meals generally leads to acute weight loss, don't you agree, Doctor?"

Doctor Perry bristled. It wasn't a surprise she'd never married, with a tongue like that in her head she would have driven any man into an early grave. "I should like to see you again next week and then we can have that discussion about those tests. I'll add your name to next week's appointment schedule but for now I'll just measure out-"

A commotion interrupted whatever he was about to say, the walls rattled and screams filled the small consulting room. Doctor Perry didn't move. He'd invented most of his reputation and wasn't the right sort of doctor for an emergency. He froze.

Frances Merriweather however leapt up from her seat and threw open the door. The scene in the waiting room was like a mosh pit at a concert. Polish Rob was thrashing around on the ground and vomit decorated the walls. On the floor with him was one of the male orderlies riding him like a bucking bronco at a rodeo. The other patients waved their arms around in horror, too afraid of the vomit and the flailing limbs to get any closer.

Eileen Hislop threw up discreetly into one of the fake pot plants. The mere scent of vomit was enough to get her started. She pulled a tissue from her voluminous bosom and dabbed at her mouth.

Elijah Cone wanted to help, but when he'd tried, Polish Rob had grabbed his hand so hard, Elijah almost blacked out, which would have added to the disaster unfolding in the waiting room, so he'd retreated to the corner, cradling his hand protectively.

Frances Merriweather may have been small but vomit had never bothered her and she waded into the fracas, cooing to the man on the floor, pushing the nurse out of the way, surprising him with her strength. She knelt down on the floor by Polish Rob, taking his hand in hers.

Polish Rob's enforced detoxification had broken him and his liver had closed up shop while he'd been sitting in the waiting room. One by one his other organs went out on strike causing his body to convulse. The useless orderly supervising the doctor's clinic thought Polish Rob was playing up and had tried subduing him, which only aggravated the situation. The dying man lay on the ground, holding the hand of a woman he'd never known, surrounded by people who didn't speak his language. It mattered not — he had no words left inside him, none that he could coherently form. Blood tainted vomit soaked his chest but he couldn't smell it and couldn't see it. But he could hear Frances Merriweather's voice and knew she was holding his hand. She sounded like such a nice lady, with a voice like an angel. As that final thought pulsed through the dying synapses in his brain, Polish Rob slipped away to join the real angels up in heaven.

Doctor Perry hovered at the door. His hands were shaking and his breathing shallow, the fear of being unmasked hit him like a freight train and he broke into a sweat. Struggling to control himself, he pressed his nails into his palms. Half moons of blood bloomed as he pushed his nails harder and harder, until he felt his self control return. Taking a deep breath, he rushed out of the room, professional concern plastered all over his face, Frances Merriweather's glass of tonic abandoned on his desk.

The first thing he noticed were Frances Merriweather's stockinged feet as she sat on her knees next to the man on the ground. Then he noticed the audience, watching him, waiting for him to step up, expectation written all over their faces.

"Move away, move away," Doctor Perry blustered.

Frances Merriweather ignored him.

"Miss Merriweather, could you please let me see to my patient?"

She turned to look at him, dismissing him with her ugly old eyes he thought. His temper threatened to give way but he was better than that. He was better than all of them. They had no idea what he could give them, another life, a second chance. Fools, they were all fools. He couldn't wait to be rid of them all. The twins would be his ticket out of here. Then he'd be done with all this, and not a moment too soon.

Miss Merriweather closed Polish Rob's eyes, and asked for some assistance to stand, her face suddenly representative of her age now that the adrenaline was wearing off. Gentle hands reached towards her, old hands, but they did the trick, she was as slight as a ten-year-old girl.

"If you'd let me get past Miss Merriweather, I could have helped the man," Doctor Perry pontificated, reclaiming the moral high ground he was so used to.

Frances Merriweather, former Air Traffic Controller and long time volunteer Coastguard, didn't give him a second glance as she limped off. She didn't drink the tonic he'd prescribed either. He watched the tiny woman march off. She wasn't the only one to slink away, and within the space of a heart beat, he was alone in the waiting room with an orderly, a dead patient, and a vaguely familiar man cradling his arm in the corner. For the first time in a long time, he wasn't sure what to do now.

18

Elijah watched the doctor struggle with the scene. Cone was as good a reader of people as you could be without having a psychology degree; you had to be in the game and be able to predict the next move based on physical clues — the holding of hands, the itching of the nose, the ruffling of the hair. Years ago he'd sat in on an interrogation course run by the FBI. It wasn't as in-depth as the real thing, but for the group of them who'd been locked into a gymnasium for the session, it had been a windfall of useful advice, and it had done wonders for the team's performance over the next decade. Half remembered snippets came back to him as he observed the sheen on the doctor's forehead, the clenched fists by his side. The guy hadn't even bent down to look for a pulse on the poor sod on the floor, he'd left that to the orderly to check. Benson trusted this man, but Elijah was having doubts.

"Doctor Perry?" Elijah stepped forward.

The doctor turned to look at him, dark eyes flashing across Elijah, dark eyes with nothing in them. There wasn't shock or sadness or even an obscene joy at the death of a patient. The nothingness forcing Elijah to step back. His movement jolted the doctor from whatever private hell he was in because a man appeared within those black eyes. Elijah now saw a deep sadness and compassion in the doctor's eyes.

"So sorry about this, I should have seen him first. Addiction is a relentless tsunami, almost impossible to escape without assistance. You are…?"

"Cone, Elijah Cone," Elijah said, waiting for recognition to cross the doctor's face. Surprisingly there was no reaction from the other man.

"Mister Cone, please come through, they don't need us here to… well, to tidy this up," and the doctor ushered Elijah through to his consulting room without any last glance towards the body on the floor, eager to escape the stench of released bowels mingling with the vomit in the stale air. The air conditioning system was only suitable for aftershave and perfumed lotions.

If Doctor Perry recognised the name he couldn't place how he knew it. Whether it belonged to an actor or a politician, although it was unlikely any American politician would ever end up in the Rose Haven. Politician's squirrelled their money away from their constituents as if preparing for the final apocalypse.

"Please take a seat. I'll need to run through some standard questions, to ascertain your medical history, to see if there's anything I need to know before I start treating you. Shall we begin?" Doctor Cone said.

Elijah nodded, keen to avoid making waves. Back before the shit hit the fan, he would have been furious at Doctor Perry's handling of the events in the waiting room, but not now, now he just wanted something for the pain and to go back to his room to wait for the sweet release death would bring. Hoping that his death would be pain free, not like the death which had taken... no, he would not think of her. Of them...

"I'm here about the arthritis in my hands. Benson said you'd be able to help. There's no family history of arthritis. I was told it's the case of too much sport when I was young so now I'm paying the price."

"You may think that your medical history is of no concern but I need to know about allergies and such and I do need family background. I need to know who to contact if you have a reaction to the medication I prescribe and-"

"There's no family to contact," Elijah interrupted, his voice louder than he'd anticipated. "I'm not allergic to anything, I just need something for the pain because I can't even hold my own cock without passing out in pain." The look on the doctor's face was gratifying and Elijah didn't regret cussing in front of the other man. Give a man a title like *doctor* and they thought they had to know every inch of you. How hard was it to prescribe pain relief?

"Mister Cone, I assure you I'm here to help but to do that I need some personal information. I'm not employed by the government, I have no other partners in my medical practice save for a woman I employ to do the filing. Whatever you tell me in this room goes no further. I don't share it with the management of the Rose Haven Retirement Resort. I am your doctor first and foremost. You can trust me."

"Doctor, I trust you to listen to why I'm here and then prescribe me some pain relief. I'm here about the arthritis in my hands. I've seen every specialist under the sun. I know what it is, so all I need from you is some pain relief stronger than *Tylenol*. Ideally something for arthritis which is subsidised , but if you can't help me, please say so and I'll go back to my room."

The doctor steepled his hands on his desk, exposing a

set of bloodied half moons on his palms. To Elijah, it looked like the doctor quickly hid his hands when he realised Elijah had seen them.

"I have something we can try," the doctor finally said. "It's not subsidised-"

"I can't afford..." Elijah interrupted.

"Please, Mister Cone, let me finish. It is not subsidised because it is not a restricted medicine, it's a natural remedy I would like you to try first. If your insurance won't cover the copay charges for the accepted arthritis drugs, then I expect you know there's not much else I can prescribe other than exceptionally high doses of over the counter pain relief, which at your age is likely to play havoc with your stomach lining. So let's try this alternative and if, when I see you next week, you haven't noticed any change in your condition then we can try something else?"

Elijah almost stopped listening when Doctor Perry had said *natural remedy*. Pure quackery, the flake was probably going to prescribe medicinal marijuana or deer velvet or rhino horn or whatever the current cool aid flavour was deep in the rolling meadows where the doctor learnt his trade. But then again he didn't have anything to lose and swallowing whatever placebo it was might keep the staff off his back for another week, leaving him in peace.

"Whatever you say, you're the doctor."

Elijah watched on as Doctor Perry scrambled through his notes. He had no idea what the doctor was looking for. He was pretty proficient at reading upside down but couldn't make any sense at all of the squiggles and lines in the doctor's notes. He wasn't surprised Doctor Perry couldn't fathom them either.

"I, ah, after the commotion I've muddled up my paperwork, very unlike me, bear with me..."

The doctor only had seven folders on his desk so Elijah

couldn't understand the confusion but it was an interesting observation of human nature regardless. Doctor Perry kept checking his watch and tutting to himself, a vein pulsating rhythmically in his forehead, bulging out of his skin. Elijah imagined the vein popping like a balloon... That Doctor Perry was flustered was obvious to Elijah, as the doctor checked his watch again, shuffling through the paperwork and muttering to himself until he finally swivelled around in his chair, grabbed a medicine cup from the bench behind him, and thrust it towards Elijah.

"This is the tonic I was talking about. Precisely measured for you, for your, ah... age, yes. I have your file here so it's all fine, this is the right amount for you. Yes, yes."

As the doctor talked, he appeared to be persuading himself, and Elijah, that all was fine whilst rechecking the time and peering at the measurements on the side of the cup before pushing it into Elijah's hand.

"You must drink it all and you should feel some relief in the next day or two. And I'll see you again next week, at the same time."

Elijah had barely finished tipping the viscous liquid down his throat before Doctor Perry grabbed the medicine cup from his hand, oblivious to the pain he caused Elijah by knocking his fingers. Elijah recoiled, but Doctor Perry was too busy gathering up his folders and shoving them deep into his leather bag.

"Yes, I'll see you again next week. If you have any concerns before then, I'm sure the nursing staff can see to them. I really am running very late now."

Before Elijah had even finished swallowing the chalky tasting concoction, Doctor Perry swept from the room, not even glancing at Polish Rob's body which was being attended to by a pair of orderlies. Elijah stood in the doorway of the consulting room, the stench of vomit reminiscent of college football parties where the over imbibing of liquor resulted in the ruination of many a scholarship. On this occasion, booze had been the ruin of a man, and the doctor hadn't given him the slightest thought.

Elijah ran his tongue over the velvety liquid coating his teeth. Not unpleasant tasting, but not something he'd choose to drink. Whether it worked or not remained to be seen.

19

Jesse and James spent a pleasant hour playing with the rats with their pocket knife — a multipurpose tool which they'd taken turns with trying out the different implements, comparing their effectiveness with their ease of use. An innocent game of doctors, if a little messy, leaving both boys splattered with blood and the ironing board looking like a horror movie prop.

A knock on the door made Jessie jump but James didn't even blink, instead he wiped his hand through the blood on the board and smeared it under Jesse's nose and down his chin, then shoved the dismembered carcasses into his pocket. A glance at his brother warning him to stay silent.

The door opened and the woman walked in. The blood on the ironing board looked more like a red scarf or a shawl, but as her eyes travelled to the faces of the twins she screamed, a rasping bleat, like the strangled cry of a fox caught in a trap.

"It's all right, miss. He had a nosebleed and we tried not to get it on the floor. We were playing with the ironing board and he banged his nose but we couldn't stop the blood. Our mom is going to kill us, making such a mess, but we didn't get any on your carpet..." James burbled, his innocent face curiously blank of anything.

Jesse nodded, screwing up his nose as the drying blood tickled his face. He pantomimed holding the bridge of his nose, like how he'd seen his grandfather do it. Grandad had weak blood his mother said; she also said it wouldn't stay in his body properly which was why it leaked out of his nose and his bum when he coughed. He coughed a lot. All through the night sometimes, keeping them all awake.

The woman's scream dialled down to a murmur of distress and she fluttered about them like a moth around a church candle. "You boys should have come to get me, you didn't need to go through this alone. Come through to the bathroom and I'll get you cleaned up. Leave all that there and I'll sort it later. At least you found something to entertain yourselves with," she said, running her hand through the upended buttons on the bed. "Ouch!" she said, jumping back.

Hidden amongst the buttons, a darning needle had speared her hand causing a bead of blood to blossom. The boys watched as she brought her palm to her mouth to lick away the blood, leaving behind a tiny smear.

"Are you all right, miss?" asked Jesse. Of the two, he had the greatest capacity to show empathy. Except he wasn't empathetic, he was a talented mimic. He would make a great Shakespearean actor if he ever decided to channel his talents in that direction.

"I'm fine, it's a tiny prick. I should've remembered the needles. I'll be more careful when I clean it away," and ushered the boys from the room. If she noticed anything strange about the dark stain spreading on Jame's shorts pocket, she never mentioned it.

As Myra ran the bath, she instructed both boys to strip

and to put their clothes in the hamper, explaining that while they were in the bath she'd hunt out something suitable for them to wear. There was a stock of clothes for situations just like this as foster children invariably arrived without any belongings and Myra was expected to dress and care for them using whatever was available in the wardrobe in the far bedroom.

Once the bath was full, and the woman had left the bathroom, James fished the rat carcasses from his pocket, dropping them one at a time into the toilet, their congealing blood turning the water red. He flushed each rat individually, imagining the tiny bodies going on the best waterslide of their life. Down to the sewers to rat heaven. He didn't know he was sending them back to where they came from, back home. Home was such a foreign concept. Sure he and Jesse had a home, a roof over their heads, but a *real* home required you had someone to love you, to take an interest in you, and their mother had never been like that, nor their father or grandfather. They all just existed in the house, living side by side but as strangers, treating the boys as mere inconveniences to their own small lives. The boys knew they were better than their mother. Better than their father and grandfather. And better than the woman who'd just run the bath. They could tell by her voice that she viewed them as a chore, as part of her job as a wife. That's how they knew they were better than her. She clearly didn't have the intellect to be anything other than a modern house slave. Although unspoken, the boys knew the doctor was different, that he was cleverer than the others. He had taken a special interest in them so he couldn't be like the others — their teachers, the children at school, their neighbours. So small minded, none of them aiming for greatness, settling instead for mediocrity. Yes, they'd have to be careful of the doctor. And then they hopped into the bath and scrubbed away at the rat blood under their fingernails and staining their faces as if they knew the doctor would be able to tell the difference.

OUTSIDE THE BATHROOM Myra listened to the toilet flushing, once, twice, three times. There was no talking but she did hear the hamper lid lift and fall, once, twice, and then the thud of feet on the enamel bath followed by the slashing of water. She leaned against the wall and stroked the bridge of her own nose, broken umpteen times playing field hockey at school. She was as familiar with blood noses as she was with broken fingers. It worried her that they were such little boys but lying little boys grew up to be lying older boys, then men. Evil didn't differentiate when it came to age. Evil was within so when it came to nurture over nature, nature always won. She could only trust that her husband would find a home for them sooner rather than later.

"Come on, Tom," she said to the cat weaving himself in and out of her legs, "Let's get you some food." She sucked on her palm, the site of the needle stick, the taste of iron in her mouth reminding her of her own humanity.

20

"People don't just disappear. We're not talking about scary clowns hiding in drains or people being sucked into their televisions, we're talking about normal people living normal lives. So where are they?" Clive Jeffries' moustache bristled as the words shot out of his mouth. Fourteen years he'd been a police officer and in that time his ability to believe in the fantastical had all but petered out. There was always a logical explanation and nine times out of ten it involved a family member. It didn't even matter what the crime was, it was invariably a family member or friend. Nine times out of ten. It was a bit like the kidnapping they'd dealt with last week; the media sensationalised it — the kidnapping of a baby, but in the end it all boiled down to drug debts and the family being paid a lesson by their supplier. It had never been about the baby, the baby was only a conduit for the message. But here today, he had on his hands two separate files for missing people, adults, elderly adults.

The rest of the people in the briefing room shrugged. They were all just as disillusioned with life as Clive. Theirs wasn't a small town but they weren't New York or Los Angeles so you couldn't hide people for long without a neighbour getting suspicious or a jilted girl friend narking on her ex. They would find them.

"How do we know they're even missing? Maybe they don't want to be found," Emily Jesmond offered, doodling in the margins of her notebook, instead of writing down the names of the missing men.

"We know they're missing because their families have reported them missing," Clive snapped back, his words as sharp as the cuffs he wished he could slap over Emily's mouth. The most annoying member of his team, she never went far enough to be disciplined but flew very close to the wind with her laziness and backchat. If she didn't want to be on the force, he wished like hell she'd bloody well leave and go write books or chant Buddhist hymns or whatever it was that she enjoyed doing because she clearly didn't enjoy policing.

"They could have gone on holiday and not told their families," she offered back.

Clive turned back to the whiteboard, fists at his side. *Two deep breaths* he thought to himself. *In and out.* She was an idiot but for the time being he was stuck with her so he had to deal with it. Taking up the marker pen, he started writing names next to tasks. The squeak of the pen on the board as calming as the reciprocal sound of the other people in the room copying the information into their notebooks.

"Right, these are your taskings. Both men have been gone over a month, give or take, but neither family is entirely sure-"

"So you're saying that their families didn't bother worrying about where they were until, what, someone else said they were missing or until the money ran out?" Emily interjected.

"As always, following the money is a given. Emily, you can liaise with the banks and credit card companies. Pull their records. I can prepare any warrant applications you need for that data. Gary, you and Tony can visit their houses. Go in under the auspices of a welfare check at both addresses. See what you can find. Check the mailboxes too. Burton, you and Michelle can interview the families. We only have their missing person reports but the men live close to each other, so let's see if they know each other in any way — clubs, memberships, golfing, that sort of thing. You know what needs to be checked. Right then, all of that, on top of everything else. And that fatal this morning, we still need some witness statements tidied up for that." He smiled, "Emily, you can run by the rest home across the road from the accident site. Some of their residents might have seen something other than vague stuff we got already."

"Seriously? She tripped over into the road and her head was run over. And her baby, I guess that was pretty unfortunate but we're not charging the driver with murder, or manslaughter, so why do we need to bother?" Emily said.

Snickering from around the briefing room greeted her statement. Not the sort of snickering done in agreement with her comments but more the sound a group makes when an annoying team member is about to be slaughtered.

Clive ignored her. One day she'd overstep the mark just enough that he'd be able to deal with her, for now it was good enough that the rest of the team were serving up their own form of punishment: exclusion and derision.

"The name of the place is the Rose Haven Retirement

Resort. Make that your first port of call today. That's it everyone, good luck and keep me posted about any developments." Clive Jeffries dismissed them all, turning back to the board to reread the plan of attack. He waited until he was sure everyone had left the room before slumping into an empty chair and jotting down some quick notes about Emily's latest insubordination. The list was getting longer every day and he was slowly building an overall picture of her performance. That's what the HR people had told him to do when he'd gone to them for advice. He should have started earlier because now it was as if she knew she was under scrutiny and had toned back her more usual argumentative backchat. She was a pain in the arse but he couldn't fault her success rate. If anyone was going to track down their two missing octogenarians, it would be Emily. And that killed Clive more than anything else.

Most families lived with some version of disfunctionality so he hadn't been surprised to hear that it had been over a month before the two families realised their elderly relatives were missing. Hell, it had been at least two weeks since he'd spoken to his own mother.

Pulling out his phone, he dialled home.

"Hello?"

"Hi Mom, it's Clive."

"Hello, Clive dear. Sorry sweetheart, now really isn't a great time, Judy and I are off to the movies and they're offering a special today which includes a free coffee. It's lovely to hear your voice, but can I ring you back tonight, Judy and I don't want to be late? Okay? Lovely, take care, bye bye."

Yes, most families lived with some version of disfunction. His mother had a far more active social life than he'd ever had. Even though she was in her mid-seventies, he could never rely on her being at home on the few occasions he'd swung past on his way somewhere. Most times he'd resorted to wedging his business card in the fancy trellis of the insect screen over the front door to prove he'd tried to see her. But at least he'd rung and knew she was alive and healthy. *Healthy.* That gave him pause for thought. Maybe the two men shared a doctor? Clive fired off a couple of texts to the team, asking them to find out the medical practices the missing men belonged to. It was entirely possible the families didn't know, and in that case the team searching the houses would need to look for any relevant paperwork. But it was another track they could take. Serious crime in their part of Florida was rare which was why he could devote so many people to two missing persons files. He imagined his counterparts in Chicago or Dallas laughing at them even bothering to investigate two missing grandfathers. But that's what they were paid for, so that's what they would do. And in between they'd fit in investigating the fatal accident this morning, an assault charge which had come in the night before from one of the bars alongside the river, and a couple of other minor complaints which made up the majority of their workload. He was happy that this was their reality. He had no idea how soon that reality would implode.

21

"Good morning, Mary Louise, how are you today?" Doctor Perry smiled at the woman who'd opened the door.

The woman standing in front of him was a far fitter version of the woman he'd met only a week earlier. She appeared taller, her eyes clearer, the smile on her face stretching from one side to the other, a pale pink gloss highlighting lips fuller and younger than the last time he'd seen her.

"Good morning, Doctor Perry, please come in," Mary Louise replied.

Doctor Perry followed Mary Louise to the kitchen. "Your range of movement has improved," he said, watching as she sat in a normal dining chair. The hospital's invalid chair abandoned in the corner, a pair of crutches leaning against it.

"I feel amazing," Mary Louise replied. "I thought I could return to work. It's not that hard managing with the casts now and I feel so much better in myself. I'm going crazy here, there's only so much daytime television I can handle," she laughed.

"I'm pleased your recovery is going well but you don't want to overdo it," Doctor Perry counselled. "Another week at home and I'll reassess you. Let's have a look at you."

Doctor Perry calculated the next dosage for Mary Louise based on her reaction to the amount he'd administered last week. Her high level of fitness made her more susceptible to the effects of the tonic and the doctor didn't want to admit that he'd made a dosage error but he'd spent so long now working with the elderly and infirm, that he'd miscalculated last week's dosage. Her recovery should have been much more incremental, that way he'd avoid questions from the hospital who were paying him for this service, and earn her trust. Avoiding questions from other medical specialists was key to his ongoing success.

The scarring still marred her abdomen. He'd been unable to produce any form of tonic to solve that problem. Not that his clients cared too much, they were happy with what they got. Clients who had exhausted all official channels. Some used their funds to trek across the world to acquire the rarest of trophies. Clients for whom even the costliest of medical treatments had failed. Clients who paid whatever they needed to, to get what they wanted with no questions asked. Those were his clients.

Doctor Perry's name was traded through whispered back channels and quiet internet chat rooms. Not that his name had always been Doctor Perry. He'd had many names and Doctor Perry was his latest incarnation, and the one he was about to retire.

A baby with abdominal scars was almost as desirable as a child with no scars. He provided every child with a thorough medical history explaining away the scars and any injuries he couldn't reverse. He wasn't a god, but he played the part well. Despite the scarring, re-homing Mary Louise was going to be easy, he even had a couple in mind — their religion dictating no medical interference in the pursuit of fertility, but buying a baby, that was fine. Doctor Perry knew they'd ask no difficult questions about the scars on her stomach or the old breaks of her limbs, because God would save her if she ever got ill, which he knew she wouldn't, based on the medical history provided by the hospital. He'd stumbled onto the most perfect of careers — a matchmaker of sorts, one which could assure any new parents that their child would never contract cancer or develop MS. He smiled as he listened to the healthy sounds in Mary Louise's chest. She was perfect. Just the way he liked them.

"You are recovering well, but I stand by my initial assessment you can't overdo things or you'll go downhill and be back to where you started. One more week, Miss Jackson, and we can reconsider your status. You must trust me, I am your doctor."

Doctor Perry measured out a dose of his tonic. Not as much as last time, he didn't want her recovered by next week. He needed her well enough to come to his surgery and from there he'd administer the final dose. It wasn't sensible to administer it to her at home, it might raise too many awkward questions if the neighbours saw him, or heard her.

He passed the medicine cup over to Mary Louise, who swallowed the liquid and then stared at the empty cup.

"What's in your tonic Doctor Perry?"

He wasn't fazed by the question. Most of his patients asked him, eventually.

"I spent time in the Amazon in my younger years," he said, before explaining how he'd learnt the healing properties of the common rainforest plants the local tribes people had used for generations, which the pharmaceutical industry still tried to dispute, claiming the indigenous people were putting themselves and others at risk. The pharmaceutical industry would say that until they'd figured out a method of monetising the plants themselves.

Mary Louise lapped it up, nodding at every accented syllable. *So docile*, perfect.

"You can see how the pharmaceutical industry don't want people knowing this because it would decimate their profits by putting a virtual end to the money-go-round of expensive treatments every physician prescribes, coerced by massive bribes from the industry. No, I'm happy helping my patients where I can. I try to stay under the radar, lest the big corporations catch a whiff of the results I get with my patients, with patients just like you." He smiled and fancied he could see her growing younger in front of his eyes. The smoothing of fine lines, the erasure of sun damage, freckles fading away to nothing.

"I'm sure I'd be fine at work this week, if I took it easy."

"No!" Doctor Perry shouted.

Mary Louise's eyes widened, her youthful, line free eyes.

Doctor Perry smoothed out his own features and lowered his tone. "No, it's the tonic masking the pain, you can't overdo it. Next week come to the office for a final check. You'll be fine going out by then but *not* before, you must promise me that. It's for your own good. If you catch a virus from someone else, you'll delay your recovery, and you don't want that do you? You must trust me, Miss Jackson."

Mary Louise nodded at him. Had his outburst scared her into silence? If it meant she didn't leave the house till next week, he'd be satisfied.

Doctor Perry wondered if using his tonic on younger people was too dangerous. Most had lives and jobs. The elderly were better — forgotten members of society, thrown on the scrap heap by their families. Considered a burden by society. He shook his head. Mary Louise was a bonus addition to his treatment programme, together with two other patients from the clinic he'd been cultivating, the twins at the house, and a handful of residents from the Rose Haven Retirement Resort. After that he'd be done and gone. He'd take his cash and move. With Myra? He'd think on that later. The thought of the furrow between Myra's brows niggled at him. Time for a younger model? And Doctor Perry added his faithful wife to his ever lengthening list.

22

"What do you mean my food ain't right? I've been here twelve years and they wouldn't keep me on if my food ain't any good." Pauline blustered about the kitchen, trailing the faint scent of cigarette smoke behind her.

Benson leaned on the counter and waited out her tirade. Pauline had a heart of gold and she did her best with the things she had. He also knew her expletive laden response was bravado and she'd get over it, but he still hated having to pass on a complaint from a resident.

"Who does she think she is, waltzing in here and complaining about my food, eh? Miss High and Mighty, that's who she is. Does she get waited on hand and foot at home, like? Something with curry in it? We're not the Taj Mahal here. If I served up a dish of curry, you'd be dealing with a flow of shite bigger than the Tyne River, like. Curry." Pauline shook her dyed blonde bob, shoving packets around in the pantry. "Ooh I'll need a fag after this, eh?"

Benson cringed at the English slang. You could take the

girl out of Northern England, but you couldn't take the Northerner out of the girl.

"Sorry, Pauline. I know you'll sort something out for her."

"Oh, I'll sort something out for her, you mark my words. Sort something out for her right where the sun don't shine."

Benson laughed. Once Pauline got back into slinging insults, all was well in her world.

"Been here one week and already complaining, eh? What's she like with everything else then?"

"She's okay. Seems quite taken with Elijah Cone. Livens up the dining room. I'm sure half the residents think she's the paid entertainment."

Pauline muttered a random Northern expression under her breath, the sort which defies translation into any other language.

"Can you do it Pauline? She's missing her curry dinners, and she's on her own. Can you rustle up something to make her happy?"

"Course I can. What do you take me for? She'll get her curry, I'll make sure, eh."

"Thank you, Pauline." Benson turned to leave Pauline's gleaming domain. "Sorry, one last thing, keep this between you, me and Sulia Patel?"

"Oh, aye, course I can. Can't have the boss getting a whiff of something not on the menu like. If I get caught…"

"You won't. Thank you, Pauline. I owe you one."

"Oh aye you do. I'll remember. Now get outta me kitchen."

BENSON HURRIED DOWN THE HALL, clipboard under his arm. He had two more residents to check before his tea break and then... He pulled up outside the room which had until today belonged to Johnny Paulson. Johnny's few belongings were in a cardboard carton in the hall and inside the room, two big men, their butt cracks showing all their hairy glory, were trying to manhandle Paulson's old arm chair through the door. Either the chair had grown, or the doorway had shrunk because the men were swearing like seamen as they shoved the chair fruitlessly into the door frame.

"What's going on?" Benson asked.

"It's not rocket science is it," countered back one man.

"Nothing is going on, Benson. Paulson's health has taken a turn for the worse and he has had to move to another facility, a *secure facility*. A sad time for all of us here at the Rose Haven Retirement Resort as I'm sure you'll agree." Tracey Chappell said, sailing into the hallway, her lipstick impossibly bright under the florescent lights.

"Tracey," Benson greeted his boss. "It wasn't on the charts."

"An oversight I'm sure, but as you know sometimes these things come upon us." She cast her powdered eyes over the removal men, who'd become a hundred times more efficient than they had been before her arrival. "There's a new resident joining us tomorrow, so this room needs to be spic and span before then. I'm sure I can leave it in your capable hands, yes?"

"Yes, but Paulson's things?"

"No need to concern yourself, Benson. It's all taken care of. We'll forward them to his new home, trust me."

Benson nodded again. It wasn't his place to question Tracey but he couldn't help feeling that there was something amiss with the whole situation. Not a single one of the other residents moved to secure facilities were transferred with such haste or without their paperwork forming a trail worthy of Hansel and Gretel. Among the staff, Tracey's reputation was that she was at the Rose Haven for one reason and one reason only, to feather her personal financial nest as abundantly as possible.

Tracey barked at the removal men, who'd finally squeezed the chair through the doorway, sending them scurrying down the beige hallway, the chair held awkwardly between them.

"The room needs cleaning, Benson. See to it."

The tap, tap, tap of her heels against the linoleum floors echoed in Benson's ears, long after she'd disappeared, leaving him to survey the barren room. Crumpled sheets on the bed the only sign anyone had been there.

Benson stripped the linen, it was easier than waiting for someone else to do it as part of their shift later. As he gathered up the sheets, a page of notepaper fluttered to the floor, wedging itself under the industrial wheels of the trolley bed. Furtively, Benson looked around, unaware he was subconsciously worrying about someone watching him pick up the paper.

Benson rescued the standard sheet of notepaper smothered with ink, crumpled from being caught up in the bedsheets. There were dark, cramped words, filling every line. Some words underlined once, twice, three times even. One word written in capital letters, half a dozen times, jumped out at him - PERRY PERRY PERRY PERRY PERRY PERRY.

A cry in the corridor made Benson start, and he shoved the note deep into his pockets, guilt stealing over him. Benson checked past the doorway but there was no one in the hall, the crying was moving away from him. A distressed resident. They were all distressed in one way or another although he tried to make their lives better, to make them more comfortable, connected. But it was so hard with so few resources and without the support of management, who viewed every resident as a number, awaiting their turn, their death.

Paulson's sheets under his arm, Benson hurried off to the laundry, the notepaper in his pocket burning through his trousers. He'd have to read it at home, he couldn't risk reading it here, too many eyes. Surveillance was one thing management didn't mind investing in. *For the safety of the staff and residents*, was their line. The staff knew it was so they could be picked up slacking off or stealing. There'd been a bit of that; a Lladro figurine, a brooch, a silver topped walking stick. Things easily bundled up in bedding, so the surveillance system didn't achieve much there.

The crying restarted, reverberating around the hallway, bouncing off the industrial beige paint. Benson frowned, someone should have investigated by now. Rounding the corner, he stumbled across the issue.

"What you doing, Ginger?" Benson asked the woman cowering on the floor.

"They're trying to take my boy."

"No one is trying to take your boy, Ginger. It's just us. Come now, I'll get you back to your room. How d'you end up here?"

"They were going to take my boy, but I chased them off," Ginger said.

Confused, Benson didn't know how to answer her, instead he helped her to her feet and walked her down the labyrinthine corridors until they reached her room, a room full of sepia toned photographs and trinkets. Benson watched Ginger unfurl her arms and place the china statue she'd been holding in the centre of the shelf. Benson settled her into bed, covering her frail legs with a crocheted throw. He cast a long look back at the statue of the boy, Ginger's boy, before closing the door behind him. If Ginger was wandering, becoming confused and forgetful, Tracey would have her moved out of the Rose Haven as quick as a flash. Ginger was a kind soul — a former pin up girl and a successful pageant competitor and model. Even before she'd moved into the Rose Haven, she was still a sometime catalogue model for retailers catering to the older shopper. A series of poor investments had frittered away her money and her confidence, leaving her withering away in a room a thousand times beneath her, surrounded by long forgotten moments of her life.

He should have made a note on his clipboard. He always made notes on his clipboard. He was renowned for making notes about everything to do with the health and welfare for the residents here. But today he wouldn't be making any notes about Ginger Bruce, about her cowering in the corridor. If the cameras picked it up, he'd be questioned later, but until then he'd keep his own counsel and there wouldn't be any notes. At that moment Benson decided that there'd be a lot fewer notes in his daily reports, if any.

23

"One boy had a blood nose today," Myra told her husband, jiggling a young baby on her lap, a bottle thrust into his mouth.

Doctor Perry looked up from his dinner. "Which boy?"

"One of the twins. He's okay, I cleaned it up but maybe you should examine him?"

"Yes, right after dinner. Thank you for telling me." Perry flicked his eyes from his wife's forehead back to his plate of spaghetti. He hated the stuff and spent more time moving it around the plate instead of shovelling it into his mouth. He watched his wife feeding the baby, her frown line spectacular now carving her face in half. Doctor Perry puzzled at the obvious degradation to her looks. *Was the tonic losing its effectiveness?* He tried to remember how long he'd been administering it to her. Other than himself, there was no one else on his books who'd been taking it as long. He'd have to write up these observations later tonight, he was meticulous with his note taking. You needed to be in his profession. Federal investigators didn't worry him, he needed to record the successful and the unsuccessful dosages he administered. He'd try a stronger dose on Myra tomorrow because he didn't think he could bear to look at her any more.

"Aren't you hungry?" Myra asked, her plate wiped clean with a piece of garlic bread, the crumbs adorning her chin, her hairy chin.

Doctor Perry's stomach churned.

"I ate at the retirement home, they were celebrating someone's birthday so there was plenty of food laid out." The Doctor laid his fork on his plate, pushing it across the table, the scraping sound echoing in the kitchen. The baby slurped on, oblivious to the surrounding action.

Myra ducked her head towards the baby, ignoring him. This was becoming a trend. She made him feel unwelcome in his own home, the home he provided her. Her gave her everything she wanted. Why didn't she know he didn't like spaghetti? He suspected she did but served it to him, anyway. To spite him? Why did she do that? Why do things to annoy others? Wasn't it easier to bend like grass in the wind, to make life easier, happier? He existed to make people happy, this was his role. He'd lost count of how many dreams he'd made come true. The childless couples he'd made whole and yet his wife couldn't find it within herself to serve him a dish he liked. Why had it taken him so long to realise the level of spite she harboured for him when he'd done everything to keep her beautiful?

"I'll check on the boy," Doctor Perry muttered, averting his eyes from the woman he'd married, the woman turning into a grotesque version of the one he'd married, and who he'd kept, catering to her every need. And this was the thanks he got.

AFTER HER HUSBAND left the room, Myra cooed to the baby in her lap. This one was cute despite his funny shaped shoulder, giving him a slight hunchback which appealed to her. There was no beauty in symmetry, life's beauty was in the odd and misshapen. Trees weren't judged by the smoothness of their bark but by the canopy of their leaves or their proclivity to fruit. People judged trees by the stoutness of their branches and how easy they were to climb. There was nothing perfect in nature but nature itself was perfect.

Myra shuddered as she heard her husband's heavy tread retreat down the uncarpeted hall followed by the opening and closing of the twins' bedroom door. He didn't slam it, that wasn't his style, but the solid shutting of the door was enough to tell her he wasn't happy, inferring that she had contributed to the boy's blood nose.

With the baby in the high chair she cleaned up the dinner dishes. She licked tomato sauce from her fingers as she tipped the leftovers into the trash, the spaghetti snaking around empty packets and discarded mushroom stalks. In her youth, she'd helped her mother collect wild mushrooms from the field behind their house. Mushrooms were tricky, eating the wrong one could kill you. Today's fungi were harmless portobello mushrooms, yet she daydreamed that one poisonous variant slipped through the food safety check and that her husband had eaten it. She imagined him writhing in agony on the kitchen floor as she clutched her metaphoric pearls, and the smile widened on her thin lips, a smear of burnt tomato paste streaked across her chin, like war paint.

The baby cried and the moment burst like a sudsy bubble in the sink, oil floating on the surface corralled by a single strand of white spaghetti. Myra gazed out the window towards the lawn, her world. There were no fields, or long bike rides and raucous games here. She'd been imprisoned in a velvet covered box.

The baby cried again, his volume rising with her misery, sensing her unhappiness. Outside on the lawn her old cat joined in, his yowl full of urgency trying to tell her something, something important.

DOCTOR PERRY STOOD by the door looking at the twin faces. It was as if there was a full length mirror in the room reflecting the image of one boy. They were in different clothes now than the matching outfits their mother had dressed them in when he'd first brought them home. A mother now laying in a mortician's drawer, her shattered head concealed behind a chiller door.

"Hello boys," Doctor Perry said, still marvelling at their identical features.

"Hello," said Jesse.

The boys had been doodling in their school books, swirls and spheres danced across the pages. Childish handwriting marched down the edges of the book, nothing which made any sense, odd words and snippets of phrases — *ashes, mother, dust, pretty girl, mommy, ice, open the door, get out, family, get out, stop, get out.*

"Are you hungry?"

"No, the lady gave us dinner, thank you," Jesse answered again while his brother concentrated on drawing long entwined tails, or was it a jumbled morass of spaghetti strands? James didn't offer an explanation, intent on his charcoal pencil scratching across the lined paper.

"Myra said you had a blood nose…"

The boys looked at each other, a mute conversation passing between them.

"We're okay now. We didn't get blood on the carpet, we were careful." Jesse looked towards his brother as he answered, seeking confirmation that he'd answered the right way.

"The state of the carpet doesn't matter, just your health. I need to make sure we return you to your family as fit as we found you," Doctor Perry explained.

"Is our mother dead?" James asked, looking up from his workbook.

His brother froze cross-legged on the opposite bed, his breath as still as an icicle hanging on a winter's branch.

Doctor Perry nodded. This made things easier.

"I'm sorry, but yes, your mother did not survive the accident. I'm so very sorry."

"Do we have to go home?" James asked, scrawling through the words he'd written out around the edges. With the words *family* and *mommy* obliterated, he chose another coloured pen, a red pen, and circled the words *get out* over and over, until there was only a red circle. The black words smudged beyond recognition.

"Tell me about your home," Doctor Perry countered.

Another look passed between the boys which said *should we tell him the truth or a version of the truth?*

Perry hadn't questioned patients for so long without learning how to read body language - a better yard stick of human thoughts than written words. Words can deceive. Body language was the subconscious's way of communicating with the world, nuanced and delicate, flighty and humourless. And these boys were holding something back. Something he couldn't pinpoint. Something which made him feel uneasy.

"We don't have a home now so can we stay here? We promise not to bleed on anything."

Doctor Perry had no words. How to handle these two?

Everyone had a home. Part of his procedure after signing up the patients he only ever had come in late at night was disposing of their belongings. In the beginning he'd left loose ends, untidy edges, and there had been moments where he was nearly burnt. He was more cautious now. People packed up all the time, running from rent arrears, from angry partners, from poor financial decisions, from life. Tidying up behind them was easy now he had a process, and one didn't deviate from a system protecting a successful enterprise. Even his system required cogs and wheels, other people — an unfortunate downside. He'd tried doing everything himself but that was too visible, so now he had a small stable of contacts who worked on the dark edges. Like rats they scurried behind him, cleaning up behind him. Undoubtedly these boys had loose ends he'd need to consider — school, grandparents, nosy neighbours, babysitters. And he needed the loose ends tidied up before he could sell his newest acquisitions.

"Child Welfare has directed that you stay here until we can sort out a permanent placement. They need to contact your family, your grandparents—"

James interrupted, "We don't have any."

"Our grandfather—" Jesse started.

"Our grandfather is dead too," James finished.

Doctor Perry tilted his greying head, his own dark eyes taking in the talking heads in front of him. Older than their years, these boys were speaking untruths, a dangerous prospect. Only the truth allowed him to work without suspicion falling on his shoulders.

"You should get ready for bed now. I'll see you in the morning."

The boys' blinked, their long eyelashes exaggerating the movement as if blinking in slow motion. Doctor Perry's heart skipped a beat, and he fumbled at the door.

Something wasn't right with those boys, he couldn't put his finger on it. Perhaps it was his own imminent escape weighing on him, tainting everything else around him, or perhaps it was something more. He'd look into the boy's history and consider his options. He'd need to get them to his clinic sooner rather than later, that was something he was sure about.

Once in the kitchen he let out the breath he'd been holding. Myra had gone off to the nursery to change the baby who would be gone soon and after that, well, then it would be time for Myra to go. He had a long list of willing clients who'd take her, given how fit and healthy she was. All his wives had been, that was a requirement, because when he tired of them, they had to be suitable for trading.

He opened the fridge and pulled out his bottle of tonic. This was the same batch he'd given Myra which hadn't had any noticeable effect. He sloshed it around, the viscous liquid inching its way up to the rim. He was careful not to spill any because replacing it was proving to be more difficult. Another reason to pack it in and retire to enjoy the fruits of his labours, but not with Myra. Her time was over.

24

Mary Louise stared at the reflection looking back at her in the bathroom mirror. Wiping the steam from the glass she peered closer, closing her eyes and opening them again. She'd never considered herself beautiful, it had been an aunt who'd told her when she was young she'd been standing behind the door when God was handing out the good looks, but the face staring back at her now was the face of a forgotten stranger, a beautiful but forgotten stranger.

Tugging her towel tighter around her middle, she traced the face in the reflection. It was a face she barely remembered. A face she remembered spending more time studying than partying, more time babysitting than dating, and more time sleeping than dancing. A face which should have been told to have more fun and stop worrying about the future. A face which didn't yet understand that Bobby Sharpe would never be interested in her because he was a loser, destined to end up working in the local Bed King Supermarket as the weekend manager... hardly the most illustrious career for the best-looking boy in high school.

The face looking back at her wasted so many days dreaming about someone who didn't matter, frittering away a life full of promise.

On the toilet seat Mary Louise gathered her thoughts. That she could sit on the toilet seat without lowering herself using the edge of the avocado-coloured sink for support, was a miracle. Her recovery had been quick, faster than she'd expected, and she had been eager to get on with her life before her employment was ended. But now... now she felt a certain reluctance to leave the house. Reluctant to do anything other than stare at herself in every reflective surface in the house. She'd caught herself admiring her reflection in the range hood, the kitchen window, the television screen. Each surface showing the same youthful face and lush dark hair, hair she'd given up caring too much about before, allowing long silvery strands to slither past her shoulders.

Ever since swallowing the doctor's chalky tonic, she'd recovered from her horrific injuries with ungodly speed and it seemed she was growing younger by the hour. She didn't know how or why, but lines which crisscrossed her face for years had vanished. A frown line cultivated by years of union negations at work was nothing more than a ghost of its former self. It was as if she'd stepped out of her college dorm room as a fresh faced eighteen-year-old and not as a woman in her early forties recovering from an accident which most people would never recover from. She didn't want to squander this opportunity, but she was almost too scared to leave the house in case the fantasy dissolved.

Walking to her bedroom, she tried not to glance at her reflection in the brass shades of the wall lamps, and assessed her wardrobe. She was slimmer than she'd ever been before, despite all the running she did, and she hadn't even set foot in a gym. She hadn't paid for a gym membership for over a decade, couldn't abide donating money to a giant concrete box filled with vapid people preening themselves in front of each other, which is why she ran, thrusting her into this situation. Mary Louise couldn't get her head around it.

Pulling a pair of ripped jeans from the bottom of her drawers, she pulled the faded denim up her smooth legs. It had been forever since this pair of jeans fit so well. A siren outside disturbed her silent musings, the strident sound filling the space with its self-importance before it faded down the long street. Zipping up the fly, she let the towel fall as she stepped in front of the mirror.

A jagged scar traced the bony steps of her ribcage and time passed like a lumbering bear, slow but steady as she examined her youthful skin, until she shivered and pulled a sweater over her unrecognisable body. The rough fabric tickled her skin. She had to go out, to the supermarket or for a walk, with sunglasses and a cap on, no one would stop her to ask her how she was. Anyway, the neighbours had shown little interest in her over the past ten years and she doubted that would change now.

With the front door open she breathed in the heady scent of... a new life or freedom from the old? Whatever it was she allowed it to fill her lungs, her fully healed lungs, and stepped off down the path. With no destination in mind, she walked without purpose engaging only with the birds and the bees on the street. She didn't see the curtains twitching behind the windows of the red brick house across the road nor the masculine face behind the yellowing net curtains following her every step.

"Hands up everyone, that's right, up to the ceiling. Arms straight. You can do it. And, stretch. Okay, now we're all going to stand up. Take it slow folks, feet apart and now we will stretch up again. To the ceiling. Fingers apart. Don't worry if you can't stand up, yes you can do it sitting down. It would be nice if you could try standing up... yes, perfect. Okay team, now shake out your hands, gently at first and then copy me. Imagine you've walked through a huge spider web, shake it off, make that blood flow."

The excitable woman at the front of the lounge babbled on, cajoling her reluctant audience to push and fold their elderly bodies into poses better left to lithe yoga aficionados. All the residents had to attend the weekly exercise classes, part of the Rose Haven's wellness campaign. Whether the instructor noticed the misery on the attendees' faces was a subject much discussed over tea every week. The consensus was that she was happy being paid to show up but had no real interest in whether the elderly residents got any benefit out of her programme. Sure she tried to encourage those taking part in her class and who put up with her condescending comments about how well they were doing, but she never acknowledged the high number of frowning residents who sat in their armchairs watching the proceedings. It was as if eighty percent of the residents didn't exist for her. Perhaps Jules the instructor, was too strung out on a homeopathic stimulant to notice anything around her.

"She like this all time?" Sulia asked, her dark face incredulous at the travesty underway.

Elijah shrugged, never taking his eyes off the thin Agatha Christie paperback in his hands. Given he had to attend, he came prepared to these god-awful sessions. For the first few sessions he'd tried to participate but had now found the solace he needed... hell, he'd lived and breathed exercise for more years than this hippyesque instructor had been alive and he'd come to the realisation she lacked complete understanding about fine motor skills or even gross motor skills.

"Are you going to read?"

"Ah huh," Elijah responded, trying to ignore the woman who'd deposited her bulk next to his seat at the back of the overheated room. He almost felt fit enough to take part in the class although he still wouldn't because he had standards. But whatever had been in the doctor's tonic seemed to have oiled his joints and eased his arthritis. It had mostly worn off but for the first time in years he'd slept through the night and now this woman was ruining his day.

"It's good for you, exercise. You should give it a go, might help with your hands, get the blood flowing. You don't need to be embarrassed cause you got a disability. I'm not."

The woman was like a high speed freight train hurtling towards a washed out bridge. Elijah tried turning away but as she gabbled on she grabbed him by the hand. Elijah screamed, the scream tearing at his throat, ricocheting off the other residents, racing around the walls of the lounge before settling back in his throat, replaced by a solitary sob as he cradled his hand against his chest.

The crying broke the trancelike state of the residents and an excited clamour filled the room. Sulia fussed over him mother-like and the instructor snapped out of her reverie, or her drug-induced calm, and flew to Elijah's side. He was oblivious to the surrounding noise, to the accusations fired at the woman of colour sitting beside him - a larger-than-life enemy, a new face, therefore an easy target.

"Hey, can you hear me?" Jules asked Elijah, her hands fluttering over him. "Hello? Are you okay? Was it the exercise? Oh don't say it was the exercise. They're all gentle exercises, that's all I'm allowed to do. Don't say it was the exercises." Her voice lowered to a whisper, "I need this job, please don't say it was the exercises. Are you okay though? Can I help?" Jules looked terrified and her eyes darting between him and the crowd, expecting accusations of torture from the residents at any moment.

"I'm fine. It's arthritis, nothing to do with your class. Leave me alone, please." Elijah replied. The relief on her face as bright as the sun. She fluttered around him for another moment, her desire to help at odds with the way she ran the moronic exercise class. Perhaps she had more of a clue than he'd given her credit for. Perhaps, perhaps, perhaps. Life was a litany of perhapses and maybes. But none of them turned the clock back.

His fellow residents returned to their positions, the show over. Sulia remained by Elijah's side — the person responsible for plunging a barbed dagger into his hand.

"Sorry, shouldn't have grabbed you like that. I didn't

know you was in such pain. Do they have any idea here?" Sulia said, her tone lower than the ocean at low tide.

"A couple of them. I don't shout it out from the roof top. They don't like the *residents* to have problems. Problems are costly so they move those residents off site. Don't know where they go, but given how bad this place is I can only imagine how bad it must be in comparison."

Sulia nodded, taking it all in, the bangles on her wrists clinking with the movement. "They give you anything for the pain then?"

"Tylenol mostly, can't afford anything else. No healthcare package, I lost all that when... well, lost it anyway. No coverage now and couldn't afford to keep it even if I had it. Shit country we live in. The Doc gave me some holistic stuff, but it didn't last too long."

Sulia's cloudy eyes looked into the distance, past Jules who was trying to get back into the swing of things by jollying the residents into an organised shuffle around the room.

"What if I could get my hands on something for you, for the pain?"

"What sort of something are we talking about?" he queried.

"Something for the pain and trust me when I say you won't be asking any more questions once that pain disappears like rain on a summers' day. You come see me when you're ready."

Sulia heaved her bulk out of her chair and waddled from the room, her bracelets providing a tinkling backdrop to the grunts and moans from the rest of the room. He considered his options as he waited for the pain in his hand to abate. It had taken every ounce of his strength to downplay the agony he was in. Even now, waves of pain were making him dizzy and there was no way he'd be able to stand up and leave the class without passing out. Leaving him here with only his pain and his thoughts to occupy him. He'd dropped his book when Sulia had grabbed him and it had fallen face up. The empty pill bottle on the old fashioned cover seemed to be a sign that whatever pain relief Sulia was alluding to couldn't be worse than the pain he was in now.

The familiar voice in the back of his mind, the one telling him he deserved the pain, was curiously silent.

26

"How much do you want for this?" asked the man in the grubby jeans, his stained hands caressing the back of an oak rocking chair, its polished arms bright through years of use.

"They're a dime a dozen, nothing special. I'll offer forty for it."

"Forty! You're dreaming, this here's a nice piece. My uncle loved it like it was one of his damn grandchildren-"

"Come off it Nate, you and I both know the closest your *uncle* got to this chair was that someone the same age as him once sat in it. Forty dollars, take it or leave it."

"Fine. Forty it is, but throw in another five for the cushions and you've got yourself a deal."

Tom Williams, the waistcoated dealer pulled a wad of cash from his pocket and peeled off two twenties and a ten dollar note, handing them to Nate Blackwell, a player in the local secondhand trade. Dealing with people like Nate was distasteful but an essential part of the trade. They say every antique has been stolen property at least once in its life, even half a dozen times depending on what it is, but he didn't want to think Nate sold him stolen goods. Given the age and quality of the stuff Nate sent his way, he had his suspicions as to the source of an unending supply of Lladro, rocking chairs, walking sticks and silver photo frames. Only one sector of society owned that many silver photo frames and cane walking sticks - the surplus of old folks who retired here for the weather. Whether Nate tricked them out of their treasures or whether he was a financial saviour to every pensioner within a fifty mile radius, Tom didn't want to think too much on.

Tom's normal clientele came from the well-heeled side of town and having someone like Nate Blackwell flogging his wares in his elegant and air conditioned store wasn't the look he desired. He'd started out just like Nate, turning up to every yard sale, scouring the smaller auction rooms for gems hidden in box lots, buying direct from the classifieds in the local paper, but now he did most of his buying at more prestigious auctions, where being seen to bid was as much a part of his persona as the huge premises on the high street in the best part of town.

Tom Williams massaged his reputation like a cruise ship masseuse, and courted publicity, good publicity, so getting tied up with anything shady would be the death knell to his business. And yet he still bought off Nate, because he did well out of the stuff Nate sold him, mainly due to the silverware. His clients had the appetite of a bear preparing for hibernation. They devoured anything sterling silver, as if owning silverware was a badge of rank, a requirement for their entry into the upper class. Anyone could buy a flash car — second hand or on finance, but not everyone had mantlepieces stuffed with family photos grinning from polished silver frames, nor could they serve their Canadian salmon on silver plates underneath gleaming silver candelabra. What Nate sold him flew out the door which is why Tom asked him what was in the box on the floor.

"Ah, there's good stuff in here. The best stuff. Thought about keeping it for myself. Shame about the lady who owned it, had a bad fall and has to move into a home so can't take it all with her. Hospital bills are a killer." Nate tried to put on a sad face but the dollar signs in his eyes made him look like a speed addict as he hiked the box onto a gleaming rosewood table almost sighing with pleasure as he opened the lid.

Tom pushed his glasses further up his nose and peered into the box. Nestled amongst layers of old newsprint lay a fine Georgian tea service, complete and in perfect condition. Tom purred. More than any cameo brooch, or eclectic sword stick, these old sets were impossible to get in such good condition.

"It's a nice one, eh?"

"It's okay, a little dated compared to what I'd prefer, but it's okay," Tom replied, his glasses slipping back down his nose as he looked at Nate over the frames.

"Dated? Come off it, Tom. It doesn't get any better. Two hundred dollars and it's yours. A bargain. I've done my homework see. The lady who's selling needs the cash, you know what healthcare is like, worse than the roads."

Tom mulled over the other man's offer. Two hundred was a bargain. He didn't for a moment buy the story about the woman and her healthcare bills but it was part of their dance. But this time Nate wasn't lying, he was telling the truth — the truth as far as the good Doctor Perry had told him.

"Two hundred is a little steep but I'll pay it this time,"

and pulled out a wad of cash. He knew it was worth at least five times what he was about to pay, possibly more depending on the maker's mark, but he'd check after Nate took his filthy self out of his shop.

"As always, it's been a pleasure, Tom. I'll be by again next week. Any requests?"

Nate always asked. In the beginning Tom hesitated to ask for specific items, worried Nate was stealing to order. But their relationship had been going on for years with no interest from the law, so he'd got into the habit of obliquely asking for items which Nate produced, sooner or later.

"Cufflinks, preferably gold, Father's Day is coming up, so some of those would go down well…"

Nate nodded and the cash in his hand vanished into his already bulging jeans pocket and sauntered out the door.

NATE CAST a quick glance up and down the street. He didn't expect to see a stream of cop cars or a detective dangling a pair of handcuffs, but he always checked. A steady stream of blonde diamond-bedecked women flitting in and out of the high end shops littering the street and not a single one of them looked his way. To them he played no part in their perfect world. Although he was the one who sourced all their fancy antiques and jewellery, he was as invisible as the gardener and the nanny and the housekeeper. He was nothing to them, but the cash in his pocket was real enough, a security blanket. Underneath his filthy jeans and faded sweatshirt he had a head for numbers, which he always made work for him. He was careful with his money and his accounts. The taxman got you in the end, not the local sheriff, just ask Al Capone or Bernie Madoff. He declared enough to keep the taxman happy and hid enough to keep himself comfortable in his retirement. He had enough to keep him out of those godforsaken waiting rooms they called old folks homes; God's Waiting Room is what he called them. He would retire somewhere flash, somewhere five star, that was his plan, and the good Doctor Perry was his meal ticket. So far the clients the good doctor sent his way had been more than enough to finance his retirement plans. That was Florida in a nutshell, you were either retired or planning for your retirement.

He whistled to himself as he walked down the road satisfied with his efforts for the day. The rest of the stuff he'd picked up from the old lady's house was on its way to Havisham's Auction House, all rubbish from Walmart and Ikea. Cheap junk. Pointing his keys at his beat up Land Rover, the beast beeped satisfactorily, and he slid into the drivers seat. He couldn't see out the rear windows due to the mountain of boxes in the back. He had a big job ahead of him farming this lot out, all the boxes earmarked for the right dealer. It never paid to put all your eggs in the one basket which is why he spread the love around. Kept them all happy and hungry for more. Sure the best stuff went to Tom Williams because he had the most money, but others would spend just as much depending on what it was he was selling, stuff Tom wouldn't even give a second glance to — medals, linen, old records. He couldn't believe the price old vinyl commanded now. He used to chuck the stuff into the trash, but he'd paid a little more attention to record collections he bought after reading a few articles online and had held a couple back here and there, so had a nice selection in his storage locker, the one no one knew about, the one he paid cash for no questions asked.

Changing his whistle to a decent David Bowie melody, he drove off to his next appointment, another house clearance from Doctor Perry. This first visit just an appraisal — he had to see how much time he'd need to clear out the estate. Being a doctor to old people paid off, for him anyway, although he didn't want to be a patient of the good doctor's — they tended to die with great regularity.

27

Myra stood at the kitchen window, a feather duster in her hands watching the twins climbing the tree. They weren't yelling or screaming like normal little boys but communicated silently with knowing looks, which made her uneasy. Instead of climbing or swinging on the branches they'd settled together on the branch brushing against the upstairs corner of the house. Myra twisted her head to see what they were looking at and her blood ran cold — the boys were watching the window of the nursery, as still as statues.

Myra filled a glass with water, chugging it back to quell the nauseating thoughts running through her mind. Just little boys playing in a tree, making faces in the window, playing their own little game, inventing a world far more exciting that the one they inhabited. They were just little boys she told herself again. Still, she turned from the window and dropping the duster on the table, hurried to the nursery, taking the stairs two at a time, her breath coming in ragged gasps as she stumbled into the quiet room.

The sleepy snuffles of the baby in the crib met her winded gasps, but she still placed her hand on his chest to feel the rise and fall of his breaths for herself. Satisfied, she turned towards the window. She'd left it open a fraction, to allow the breeze to circulate but now she shut it, sliding the bolt. The boys had vanished from the branch.

Myra pressed her face against the glass, scouting the lawn for any sign of the boys. Two pairs of shoes remained at the bottom of the tree, so they hadn't gone far then. She turned back towards the crib and tumbled backwards into the window with a cry.

The twins stood either side of the crib, hands by their sides, watching Myra as she struggled to regain her composure. How had they made it upstairs so fast and so quietly?

"Hello, boys," she said, the windowsill pressing into her back, too unsettled to move away from the wooden support.

"We're hungry," said one.

Myra still couldn't tell them apart so nodded, her mouth dry. She didn't trust trying to answer them coherently.

"Why is the baby still sleeping?" asked the other one, reaching out to poke the sleeping child.

"Don't touch him!" Myra shrieked, darting forward.

The boy dropped his hand and tilted his head to the side.

"I wouldn't hurt him, he reminds me of my brother. He's dead too."

He'd said it so honestly that Myra questioned her irrational fear. Just little boys who'd lost their mother and a baby brother. Her husband had said nothing about a brother but maybe he didn't know? Had she misjudged them? Guilt stole over her. She wasn't herself since she'd tipped out the tonic her husband left on the bench for her. Was the paranoia a result of not drinking it? Either way she felt her grasp on life slipping away bit by bit.

"I didn't know, I'm sorry. What was his name?" She still stood over the crib not trusting the innocence she saw on the face in front of her.

"His name was Peter, he cried lots, not like this one. He's quiet for a baby," Jesse replied.

"Peter is in heaven now with your mommy and as sad as that is, at least they're together, with your daddy too."

"Our daddy is-" Jesse started until James elbowed him in the ribs.

"Your father is what?" Myra asked.

"Gone," James replied, taking his brother's identical hand in his and walking him downstairs. The clicking of their bedroom door sounded more than ominous to Myra. *Gone* wasn't the same as dead. What were the boys doing in her house when it sounded like they had a father? She couldn't leave the house but she had access to the internet and until the baby needed her, she planned to do her own research.

MYRA NEVER GOT ROUND to searching the internet. The baby woke up screaming, the twins turned up hungry, and her husband came home earlier than usual. Myra prepped snacks and dinner and bottles and baths and changed sheets and wiped up spills and a hundred other things a mother normally did. She wasn't a mother, had never been a mother. They'd tried but she'd never conceived and her husband had suggested fostering children as a solution to her barrenness. They'd fostered dozens of babies, the occasional toddler, but this was the first time they'd fostered children who didn't rely on her for their every need.

"Why are they still here?" she asked her husband after settling the children for the night. Myra wished there was a lock on the twins' bedroom door but had persuaded herself she was being foolish so tried not to think about the baby alone upstairs in its crib while the twins were asleep in their room. There'd been no more blood noses or anything else of concern. She'd rescued their shoes from under the tree, sliding them into the shoe rack in the laundry. She might not have been so relaxed if she'd seen the spread of feathers decorating the lawn under the tree, or if she'd noticed the wad of feathers stuffed into the toe of Jesse's trainer, put there for entertainment later. Feathers plucked from the breasts of the chicks the boys had found in a nest high in the tree. No, she wouldn't have been sitting tucked up in the armchair talking to her husband about the boys sleeping in the room down the hall.

Doctor Perry sighed, turning his dark eyes towards his wife. She'd interrupted his viewing of a wildlife programme and she could tell he was less than pleased. He was busy, with little downtime, but she was more responsible for the boys until the child welfare people found a new home for them.

Myra always found saying goodbye to the children they fostered difficult. Her husband took them away and they never spoke of them again. She'd tried remembering their names, but there were too many, so she kept a journal recording their names and the dates she'd cared for them and important milestones she'd been privileged to witness, in case their adoptive parents ever asked. Also for her own gratification. She knew she was a great mom and her journal reassured her of that. Some babies had only been with them for a day or too which she'd forgotten to add in, but overall she'd kept a comprehensive record of all the babies who had passed through their home. She'd long given up any thought of persuading her husband they should adopt one. She'd raised it several times in the beginning and his response was almost violent.

Her husband didn't answer her straight away but she could see him weighing up his answer. He chose his words like a chemist dispensing pills, never saying any more than he needed to, as if each syllable was a treasure, as if he only had a limited supply of words and refused to spend more than necessary.

"It is complicated. The coroner hasn't released their mother's body. After that, the child welfare agency will step in, but until then they will stay here. Are you having trouble with them?"

Myra shook her head. She'd long given up wasting words on her husband as well. She spoke more to the cat and the babies than she spoke to her husband.

"I'll need more things for them if they're staying with us a while. Toys and clothing, I should take them to the mall…"

"No, order what you need online. There's no need to take them out, they need stability not crowds of shoppers jostling them in a Walmart aisle."

"But they should choose what they want—"

"Online, Myra. There's no need to go out. I won't discuss it any more. I think I'll head off to bed, today was long, and a patient died. Goodnight."

She watched her husband retreat. He never spoke about his work so it was a surprise he'd mentioned the patient dying. Myra presumed every doctor had patients die during their careers, but if her husband's patients ever died, this was the first she'd heard of. She sipped the cooling cup of tea she'd made — camomile, although now the brew tasted foul, like cold dish water mixed with turps. She'd make a fresh one because she needed all the help with sleeping tonight. Staying in the nursery tickled at the back of her brain. Her husband wouldn't appreciate that, he liked her in his bed or he had, now she wasn't so sure.

Waiting for the kettle to boil, Myra peered out the kitchen window. The yard was pitch black, the surrounding neighbours choosing to be as parsimonious with their electricity as Myra and her husband. No point paying for electricity you aren't using he'd told her from the moment she'd first crossed the threshold. That had been in a different house in a another state but it was a lesson she hadn't forgotten. If she'd been able to see the lawn in the dark, she might have seen the wind picking up the downy feathers and dancing them across the lawn. A macabre dance of many.

Taking her camomile tea to the nursery, Myra didn't see the desecrated nest slip from its precarious perch spilling its decaying contents onto the lawn. Four freshly plucked chicks, two with a noose of woven wool around their necks. The other two had no heads.

If Myra had known the two missing avian heads were wrapped in plastic and hidden in Jesse's pocket for further investigation, she'd have barricaded the twins' bedroom door. And it was fortunate James hadn't told her he wanted to see what connected the sparrow's gelatinous eyes and what would happen if he poked Myra's sewing needle into them...

MYRA'S GINGER cat padded over to the nest and flattened himself to the ground, ears back against his head as he smelt the boys — the stench of evil enveloping the broken nest and its mutilated occupants.

28

Pungent gasoline filled the air and the *drip drip* of water echoed in his ear together with the cries of the night birds. With his arm numb, he couldn't feel the shattered glass embedded in his skin. The ticking of the cooling engine added to the evening's symphony. They'd won the final and the post-game celebrations were massive but he was getting too old to party with the players and the hangers-on. So many sycophantic girls, who got younger and prettier every year, and the way they threw themselves at the boys... Elijah hated to think how many fathers his players would be by the end of the year. He stayed at the party to chaperone, even though the players were old enough not to need a one, but the parents laid their trust on his shoulders and he took that seriously. He'd only had one bourbon, just a small nip, half a cup, he could handle it and it made the torturous party bearable.

Elijah woke up with a start, sweat plastering his hair to his face and his body to the sheets, his arm tingling with pins and needles from sleeping on it. He struggled to sit up, the memories of his dreams strangling him as much as the sheets were. He didn't realise he'd cried out in his sleep — crying for a life he'd lost and the lives he'd destroyed. The dream was nothing new; he had it every night, a hellish reminder of the end of his life. Only half remembered, other than the smell of fuel mingling with bourbon, and the blackness. A blackness which swallowed him whole and then regurgitated him like the figurative Moby Dick, leaving him to relive the night over and over. A purgatory only death would release him from.

Disorientated, he struggled to climb back into the present. Nothing in the room made sense, and it seemed smaller, as if the walls had shrunk overnight, closing in on him, entombing him in a living coffin. Then reality broke through the walls and crashed upon him. He didn't want to think about the kids he'd put in coffins, their names forever carved on his every waking moment. The sooner he was in a coffin, the better.

He was suffocating in his room; he needed to walk, to purge the demons from his mind. Reaching his door, he twisted the handle which didn't budge, locked from the outside. He hammered against the door before the arthritis made it known he wasn't to try that again. He kicked the door and the flimsy hollow door shuddered in its frame but didn't open.

Elijah cried out, for what, he couldn't say. One final kick and he slumped against the door, his age forgotten. He was a child lost in a grown up world with no one to help him. Memories crowded in on him like the fans and his colleagues and the players all had. They'd put him on a pedestal. If only they knew how far it was to fall from that lofty perch.

At the sound of a key turning in the lock, the door opened onto Elijah, flinging him to the ground. Light fell into the room illuminating Elijah cowering on the floor and the angry orderly at the door.

"What the hell is going on? You trying to wake up the rest of the residents? Calm the fuck down or I'll give you something to make you sleep. Tracey don't put up with this shit."

"I wanted a drink. Why was I locked in?"

"We always lock you in, can't have a hundred old farts roaming the corridors, you'd all end up in the wrong rooms. Health and safety man, look don't make my job any harder. You get back into bed, there's water in the bathroom, you can help yourself. You've been here long enough to know the rules. No one gets out of bed at midnight unless you're dying, and even then Tracey'd prefer you died quietly in the night and we dealt with the mess in the morning. Saves a ton of money that way."

"I needed a coffee. You've got coffee, hell I'm paying for coffee and I want my coffee." Elijah's voice rose. He realised he was being belligerent but night after night of interrupted sleep and living a never-ending nightmare forced him out of accepting the status quo. He was past the point of no return.

"You fuckwit, there's no coffee for residents. There's no getting out of bed at night, and there's no fucking making my job harder than it is. Get the fuck into bed, old man."

Elijah stood his ground. "I want a coffee. I'm not a prisoner, I am a paying guest. And if you think I need to discuss this with the manager, you go wake her."

"Lay back down old man, you're nobody here. You're not a big shot coach any more. Get that, you're a nobody. No one cares if you want a coffee, no blonde cheerleader will deliver you a latte with a happy ending afterwards. Get into bed. Or I'll put you there myself, old man."

Elijah almost responded but the futility of the situation

swamped him and like the old man he'd become, he slumped on the covers, hanging his head in defeat.

"That's better, old man. No more noise from you tonight or I won't be as polite next time," said the orderly before slamming Elijah's door and locking it behind him, the fall of the hammer absurdly loud in the night.

The orderly was correct, he was a nobody. He'd been a somebody once, but that all changed on a road next to a tree after a game. A game they'd won. That was the last thing he'd win. It wasn't a surprise he couldn't even persuade the staff to let him have a coffee. A nobody, nothing.

His thirst deserted him and a great lethargy overtook him. Elijah folded himself into his blanket and waited for sleep to come, a sleep without pictures or memory, but like the coffee, that too was unobtainable.

29

"You having trouble sleeping, Elijah?" Sulia asked over breakfast.

Elijah paused, a slice of toast halfway to his mouth.

"I can give you something to help with the dreams. What I got will make those dreams disappear just like your arthritis pain."

"I'm fine." Elijah carried on eating his toast with margarine. The budget honey barely making it any more edible than cardboard. Breakfast was toast or a thin porridge resembling the detritus at the bottom of a stadium urinal on a Friday night.

"Suit yourself, but I'll be here when you want to come calling." Sulia tucked into both the toast and porridge, and great slurping noises dominated the table. "Damn this needs sugar," she announced, after emptying her bowl.

Dread settled over Elijah as Sulia's gargantuan arm beckoned the closest orderly. Not the same one who'd come to Elijah's room, but he knew from experience that this one was trouble, and he didn't look pleased.

"Have you got any sugar, dear?" Sulia asked, her voice itself dripping with honey.

The rest of the room sensed the conflict and the hubbub of conversation petered out, the residents lowering their spoons and mugs and toast. Like an Oliver Twist parody, everyone knew not to ask for more; everyone except Sulia.

"What?" the orderly asked, his grasp of the finer points of the English language lost between his mother's womb and his last day at high school.

"Sugar, for the porridge. There's none on the table, and a woman can't have porridge without a ton of brown sugar and fresh cream. I sure don't need the cream, look at me, but I need the sugar. Helps keep my energies up."

Watching Sulia, Elijah thought he saw a flash of something there. As if she knew she was playing with fire but wanted to test it.

"You think you're in Trump Tower? The only cream you'll be getting is cream of sweet corn soup for dinner. If you've finished breakfast, get back to the lounge so we can clean up after you."

"Oh I haven't finished, I'm having more porridge."

"No you aren't, you will take your fat arse back to the lounge and play kiddy games with the nurse and try to remember your own name if you can. That's a good game to play. Think you're above the rules, you fat—"

At that, Elijah stood up. An unplanned, impulsive move. He'd been thinking about Sulia's sugar, which made him think about sugar in his tea, which led to imagining sugar in his coffee, in the coffee he wasn't allowed. Stale coffee tainted the breath of the orderly, and one thing lead to another and he confronted the other man.

"Apologise. Apologise to Sulia for your rude comments

and we won't make a complaint about your behaviour," Elijah said, not as the introverted old man he'd become, but like someone used to being understood and obeyed without argument.

Elijah stared into the man's bloodshot eyes. Eyes surrounded by an infinite number of blackheads, with a day's worth of stubble and wheat-coloured hair plastered back with a chemical smelling gel. So entranced with the sudden euphoria of standing up for Sulia, Elijah never anticipated the orderly's next move.

Oomph

The orderly threw a hefty punch into Elijah's stomach with the power of a well fed younger man and Elijah folded, the shock and the pain taking him to the ground. The room erupted. Crying women and decrepit old men pushed back their chairs ready to enter the fray.

Nursing staff and uniformed orderlies appeared from nowhere as if they'd squeezed through the cracks of the sewers the residents suspected they came from.

On the ground, his breath knocked out of him, Elijah had no idea of the surrounding commotion, and he couldn't have said who tipped their bowl of porridge over the head of the pugilist but the orderly reacted by firing a boot into Elijah's side, cracking a rib. Toast and mugs flew and cutlery clattered to the ground. Octogenarians tussled with men a quarter their age whilst others cheered them on from the sidelines.

The dining room was a complete disaster. Broken crockery, brought for its indestructibility, lay shattered on the lino floor. Congealing porridge dripped from the wall and coated the residents and the staff. One benefit of the fracas was the disappearance of sachets of honey from the tables, sachets secreted into voluminous pockets and bags of innocent knitting, to eat at leisure in the safety of their bedrooms with crackers. Sulia herself had collected a handful of honey pouches, and a knife and a side plate. She didn't expect the staff to bother with a stock take when they cleaned up, but then again she wasn't yet aware of how the Rose Haven operated — any loss or destruction of Resort property was deducted from wages and Tracey was nothing but vigilant when an opportunity arose to save money, money which disappeared into her pocket.

An eery quiet descended as the residents slinked away in pairs and alone. No one wanted to be there when Tracey arrived, and she would... she could sense trouble.

IT DIDN'T TAKE Tracey long to appear in the doorway, her high heels tapping on the linoleum as she approached. Tracey had watched the fight unfold on her surveillance system, on the cameras she loved. She'd have more if it was legal — in the bedrooms and bathrooms, the kitchen and staffroom. She hadn't seen the orderly's punch, but she'd seen Elijah stand and then an image on another screen distracted her - the image showing another orderly ducking into one resident's room - an orderly who shouldn't have been in that corridor then. *What was he doing?* By the time she'd looked back to the dining room camera, Elijah Cone was on the ground, the giant Indian woman next to him, and the roomful of pensioners were on their bunion-clad feet protesting. She'd stayed in her office until the staff had it under control; she was wearing a new suit and the last thing she wanted was slop thrown over it.

With her hands on her hips in the doorway, Tracey looked the part of a successful lawyer or accountant, but up close she looked more like Miss Hannigan from *Annie*.

"Preston, over here," she called to the orderly at the centre of the maelstrom.

Slinking over to Tracey, Preston Sergeant hung his head.

"What happened?"

"He threatened me," Preston mumbled.

"Threatened you? We can't have that behaviour now can we?" Tracey replied. "Was he posing a risk to the other residents?" The clipboard under Tracey's arm complimented her officious tone and with manicured hands she marched a pen across the paper on the board, her chicken script impossible to decipher. She didn't wait for Preston to answer. "And when you realised he was a threat, you did what you had to do? To protect the other residents?" Tracey said, revelling in placing the right words into Preston's mouth, dictating the tone of the exchange. Power had been denied to her when she was young so now she coveted it, brandishing it like a weapon. The power warmed her and filled the void inside her heart.

Preston jumped on her words. "I subdued him because of the threat to the other residents from his behaviour. Their safety was my only thought."

Tracey smiled, showing a set of surgically whitened teeth. "I'd have expected nothing less from you, Preston."

"He caused a ruckus last night too. Pedro told me at changeover. I expect it's in the notes. Pedro said he wanted coffee in the middle of the night and damn near broke his door trying to get out."

Tracey's pen wavered above the page. She read the handover reports which hadn't mentioned a disturbance in the night. Preston had just blackened the name of Pedro Levi, the night orderly. Tracey surrounded herself with those less competent than herself, they were easier to manage, and to fire, but she needed them to abide by the rules. One rule was that any instance of the residents straying outside the accepted behaviour parameters had to be in the handover reports, which she used to flush out difficult residents, identifying who to move on. Churn was good for business… her main business, and the profitable sideline she had going with Doctor Perry. The rules were there for a reason.

"Help the others clean up and I'll handle Cone," she said to Preston, dismissing him. Pedro she'd deal with later.

Tracey picked her way through the mess towards Elijah, who was still on the ground, leaning against a chair. Her high heel slipped on a smear of porridge on the polished lino, and cursing under her breath, she made a mental note to ask Pauline to cost out a new breakfast menu which excluded porridge. Not serving it would reduce their electricity usage as a start. A smile played across Tracey's painted lips.

"Mister Cone, let's get you up off the floor." Tracey offered her hands to the man on the floor, well aware of his crippling arthritis. That at least was in the handover reports.

Elijah ignored her and Tracey spread her smile wider, twisting her face into a death grimace. "Mister Cone, we need to get you up so the orderlies can clean up the mess. It pains me to see one of our residents on the floor. Come, let me help you."

Still the man ignored her and Tracey watched as Elijah rolled to his knees with glacial speed and stood on his own. Oh how far the mighty had fallen. When he'd first moved in, she'd watched old YouTube footage of him on the sidelines, hollering at his players and being interviewed on TV. And now he floundered on the floor at her feet.

Tracey's eyes widened as she watched Elijah lean on the substantial arm offered by the sari-clad Indian woman beside him. As far as she knew, Elijah had shown no interest in connecting with anyone at the Rose Haven Retirement Resort, other than Johnny Paulson, but he wasn't an issue any more. So what was this? A friendship? Whatever it was, it could be problematic.

"That orderly punched him, it's assault. You should call the police, not send him to clean up the mess he caused," Sulia's voice rose with every word.

"I don't know what happened, other than a group of senior citizens started a food fight. A food fight in a home for retirees. Can you imagine the police response? We'd be a laughingstock. No, I suspect Mister Cone here slipped over in the fight, which will be an expensive exercise to clean up and to replace the broken crockery. I'll watch the security tapes because someone started this and they will be billed for the mess. Was that person you Mister Cone?" Tracey was on home territory with money. Billing the residents for replacement crockery was a genius decision and smug conceit wormed its way onto Tracey's face.

"Elijah was standing up for me. He did nothing wrong. It was the orderly," Sulia insisted.

"Leave it, Sulia," Elijah wheezed.

He wouldn't look Tracey in the eye which she found satisfying. He looked guilty which made it an easier decision to add the cost of the replacement crockery to his weekly account. If he was going to be trouble, she'd consider handing him over to Doctor Perry, but only after he'd paid his bill. She couldn't abide outstanding accounts. She couldn't hand him over to Perry until after she'd bled him dry. Given his former high profile career, it was a sure bet he had cash salted away for a rainy day. Hiding it from the families of the kids he'd killed. He'd have to pay her though, they always did. She laughed.

AT THE DOORWAY, Sulia and Elijah looked back at the sound of Tracey laughing amid smashed bowls and abandoned slices of toast. Both felt an icy finger of premonition up their spines. Sulia tugged gently on Elijah's arm, pulling him away from the dining room and the painted woman's piercing eyes.

Sarah Miller coughed discreetly into a tissue at the counter but to the rest of the waiting room the cough sounded more like a colony of seals clamouring for attention. She was sick; she knew she was sick, and to her utter annoyance she had to see a doctor or she'd end up on a hospital respirator, that was how sick she felt.

It had been at least twelve years since Sarah had last stepped foot in a doctor's surgery. She preferred holistic, and her regime of daily vitamin C tablets and a clean vegan lifestyle, combined with a spoonful of honey, cured any ills. But her cough had worsened, and she didn't want to die alone at home for want of antibiotics. She'd fought the idea for a week but she knew she was running out of time.

The receptionist handed her an enrolment form for new patients. Hopefully she wouldn't need to see the doctor again, which she explained to the girl, but the receptionist was insistent she complete it. With an impatient sigh which turned into a hacking cough which threatened to send her lungs up through her throat and out onto the floor, Sarah retreated to one of the plush armchairs and filled in the form. The waiting patients shrank away from her, their own woes not as bad as Sarah's cough.

She got as far as the next of kin question before her heart twisted with a pain worse than the coughing. A pain deeper than anything she'd experienced. Even death wasn't as bad as the heartache overwhelming her as she considered what to write. The emptiness of the line was as empty as her life and her heart. The utter rejection she'd received over the phone still as crushing now as it had been then. How long ago was it now? She knew within the fraction of a second how long ago it had been - four weeks, five days and seven hours ago. Her life shattered with one phone call, breaking her heart with no possibility of ever picking up the pieces. There was no one to add for *next of kin*. She had no one, so left it blank.

The receptionist took her form whilst chatting on the phone about her weekend plans. It would be nice to have weekend plans, or any plans at all. Sarah was an artist and worked at home, at one with her oils and watercolours. Her brushes and liniments were her true friends. Most of her old friendships had fallen by the wayside when she'd immersed herself in her relationship. They'd given up on her after she brushed them off one too many times so it was only karma she had no one to make plans with, to dream about the future with, to grow old with. Her debilitating cough took over again and the waiting patients flinched away from her.

Spitting into a handkerchief, tiny droplets of blood appeared on the stark white fabric. This was it, she'd left it too long and now she would die. Her eyes welled up, and the congestion worsened in her sinuses until she couldn't catch her breath. The years of clean living were no defence to the pneumonia attacking her lungs. Coughing and wheezing, she struggled to get enough oxygen, and clawing at her throat Sarah collapsed to the floor.

SARAH's fellow patients jumped out of their chairs, and Molly all but leapt over the reception counter after pressing the emergency call button. She didn't have the skills to do anything other than push the patients out of the way, making room for Doctor Perry.

Summoned by the panic button, Doctor Perry appeared in the waiting room, striding to Sarah's side. His calm demeanour doing more to help Sarah's panic subside than anything else. Doctor Perry smoothed her hair back and loosened the shirt from around her neck. The cool air soothed her ragged throat, and the doctor counted her breaths in and out, in and out, until she found her breathing back to normal.

"That's it, concentrate on taking slow breaths, slow them right down, that's right, breathe with me, in and out. In and out. Don't worry about anything else, breathe in and out. I'm the doctor here, you can trust me." Doctor Perry cooed to Sarah like a mother settling a newborn.

Sarah's breathing evened out but even the other patients could hear the rattling coming from her chest.

"Molly, help me get, ah-"

"Sarah Miller," Molly said.

"Yes, help me get Miss Miller into the consulting room, then you must reschedule these appointments, with my apologies."

Molly rescued Sarah's form from the floor, before helping the doctor move Sarah into the consulting room and onto the hospital bed in the corner to the room.

"Here's her enrolment form. She hasn't filled in the next of kin details. Should I ring for an ambulance?"

"No thank you. I'll sort it from here. I'll need those appointments rescheduled now."

Annoyance fled across Molly's face before she walked out of the surgery, slamming the door harder than normal behind her.

"Are you feeling better Miss Miller?" Doctor Perry asked, wheeling his chair over to the bed, he read over Sarah's enrolment form. The form was a wealth of information, most of which a normal doctor didn't need, but these questions were a necessary part of Doctor Perry's business. The next of kin question in particular.

Sarah stared at the doctor, her eyes wide.

"Miss Miller, you realise that you are ill, yes?"

Sarah nodded, a tiny movement given the pain in her throat.

"You haven't filled out the next of kin questions, and I need to ring your next of kin because you're looking at a lengthy hospital stay. Do you understand what I am saying?" Doctor Perry kept the searching eagerness out of his voice. He tried not to get excited. She probably just forgot to fill in that section. The most important section of the whole form.

"There's no one," Sarah whispered, the words barbs in her throat, and her heart.

Doctor Perry smiled a sad smile, "There's always someone. An aunt or a girlfriend?"

"There's no one any more. No one to call."

The doctor sniffed as he made his own shorthand notes in the margin, running his eyes down the page until he came to the section on medical insurance. Again, empty.

"And your medical insurance provider? You haven't filled that in either."

Sarah shook her head and closed her eyes at the futility of her life.

"Ah, that makes it more difficult doesn't it. Never mind, we will sort something out, even if we have to send you back home and manage your recovery with house calls. That's a more affordable option given the circumstances. But first I'll have a proper listen to that chest."

Sarah closed her eyes as Doctor Perry pressed his stethoscope to her chest, rolled her to her side and listened to her back and palpated her stomach. He checked her eyes, her ears, her throat, her glands, and the whole time she wanted to scream at the man that the infection in her lungs was a symptom of her broken heart and nothing would fix it.

31

Doctor Perry drove Sarah Miller home. It turned out she'd taken a taxi to the surgery that afternoon, so as a gesture of goodwill, and with more than a small measure of curiosity, the good doctor drove his newest patient home.

Home wasn't a romantic bohemian garret room, instead an old apartment block suffering from neglect and a transient population. Doctor Perry shrugged off a flash of concern about the safety of his car. There were no obvious undesirables hanging around, but he locked the sedan as he helped Sarah into the building.

"The elevator works," Sarah said, the corners of her mouth turning up as she pointed to the elevator doors. Someone had graffitied the doors and although the offending words had been scrubbed off, like the damage to Sarah's lungs, the shadowy swear words remained.

The numbers above the doors counted down from seven. Seven, six, five, four, three, two, and without hitting one, the doors opened. An oily stench fell out of the elevator. Doctor Perry had expected worse, much worse.

"Which floor, Miss Miller?"

"Six," Sarah rasped.

Doctor Perry pulled his sleeve over his finger before pressing the button for the sixth floor. You never knew what germs abounded on elevator buttons.

The elevator doors opened reluctantly as if sand oiled their runners. Doctor Perry escorted Sarah along the corridor, the linoleum squeaking under their shoes — the doctor's leather brogues and Sarah's vegan leather sandals ordered direct from the Netherlands, until they came to door 613, which differentiated itself from the other apartments with a large PETA sticker on the cream-coloured door.

Sarah's hands shook so badly that Doctor Perry eased the keyring from her fingers and slid the key in himself. Sarah faltered at the threshold so Doctor Perry half carried, half dragged her to the couch dominating the room. A mountain of pillows covered with sequins threatened to engulf her and the doctor flung them to the floor, keeping the least decorative one to place under Sarah's head.

Doctor Perry watched Sarah shrink into the couch, her eyes closing. Her coughing had subsided although the rasping from her chest was audible in the quiet apartment.

Satisfied Sarah Miller was comfortable, he checked out the room. Exotic trinkets adorned every shelf — a Cuban baseball, a Tibetan ceremonial bell, a jewelled box from the Middle East, an assortment of polished wooden statues; dust collectors all.

Tiny snores emanated from the couch, allowing Doctor Perry the freedom to explore. Apart from the trinkets and the art on the walls, the apartment was impersonal and devoid of photographs. Doctor Perry ran his fingers along the spines of the books in the bookcase - travel guides, autobiographies, dog-eared Agatha Christie paperbacks, and a full set of the Harry Potter books. Ah, on the bottom shelf. Sarah's photo albums.

Doctor Perry lifted the albums from the shelf, and settled himself at the small dining table noting that there were only two chairs, not big on entertaining then. Home visits were so important in his line of work. Vitally important…

The first album held a series of familiar shots — children's birthday parties, outings to the beach and awkwardly posed adults with beer bottles or wine glasses. Cookie-cutter images from a middle-class family. The photos thinned out as he flicked through the pages and the children got older, the parties smaller. One girl emerged as a younger version of the woman sleeping. The older people from the earlier photos disappeared, and then the father figure vanished from the photos altogether. A dozen teenaged photos of Sarah and her friends filled the back of the second album, complete with graduation photos. Moving to the last album, he thought three albums seemed sparse given Sarah's age, but there could be valid reasons there were so few albums — a family break up, a fire, theft.

The third album told a contrasting tale, with the woman in these photos different from the one on the couch. The album version of Sarah glowed with joy standing beside a striking taller man in every photo. Skiing, sailing, hiking; they lived for the outdoors. There was even a photograph of them holding a gleaming tennis trophy. That was the first half of the album, the second half told an inconsistent story. There were still the outdoor shots, but most of the photographs were of the man on his own, posed on the beach, on a camel, and not beside Sarah.

If the photos of Sarah showed a woman in love, the photos at the end told a different story from her boyfriend's point of view. The light in his eyes dimmer, his smile smaller. In the last shot, he held out a hand out towards the camera, pushing the camera away. Half a dozen scenic shots followed and then nothing. Empty slots.

Doctor Perry replaced the albums and continued his inspection of Sarah's apartment. A tidy kitchenette, its cupboards well stocked, and in the sink one glass, one mug, one plate and one knife. The dishwasher held the same - clean, but needed emptying. The refrigerator a cornucopia of veganism — leafy vegetables filled the chiller bin. Containers of nuts and seeds lined the shelves, and the milk was of the almond variety. Doctor Perry sniffed the container, recoiling at the sour scent.

Pushing the door open to the only bedroom, he stepped into a room decked out like a Bedouin tent. Incense and perfumed oils filled the room and Doctor Perry gagged at the competing scents. How anyone could sleep in that miasma was beyond him. He tugged the curtains open revealing a bed, a dressing table, and an Ikea wardrobe rack. Underneath the window sat Sarah's art desk, her equipment arrayed at the top of the desk. Rainbow-coloured paints filled every shelf of the unit which served as a room divider, breaking up the workspace from the bedroom.

Leaning over the workbench Doctor Perry's breath caught. In front of him lay a fine sketch of the tall man from the photo album but a sketch of happier times. Drawn with an easy smile, his eyes laughing out from the canvas, the likeness uncanny. The sketch was the only masculine thing in the house and well satisfied, Doctor Perry moved on. He'd found no sign of men's toiletries, or shoes, or shirts, or any sign that Sarah Miller had any relationship or family in her life. The temptation to dose her with his tonic overwhelmed him and he returned to the lounge to watch the sleeping woman.

He cracked his fingers as he considered his options. First, he had a full house at home, second, he had other patients close to receiving their final treatment — and clients lined up to receive those patients. And although he had a list of clients waiting for the fresh stock only he could provide, he didn't have many on his waiting list as he'd reduced his workload to prepare for leaving town.

Doctor Perry prided himself on making quick decisions based on the evidence. He had a head for numbers and incredible recall, but he dithered over this decision. If he was being honest with himself the sticking point for this decision was Myra. There was something happening under the surface, something he couldn't see. He'd been in this business long enough to heed his own sixth sense, which was why he moved often, and traded in wives. He had no real affection for Myra, she was a tool — something kept in the garage on the workbench, useful when required, but redundant at other times. Doctor Perry again considered adding her to his growing stock reserves; she was healthy, he'd made sure of that. *Damn*, there were too many variables at this stage in the game.

He decided. Sarah Miller would be a valuable addition to his stock list. She was a good looking woman, but in no fit state to go anywhere. He needed her healthy, so he'd schedule the required house visits and dose her slowly, his preferred method. He'd shuffle the transfers around for some patients on his list, bring a couple forward, but that wouldn't be an issue. Doctor Perry always delivered. He was a doctor and everyone trusts their doctor.

32

"She's disruptive, not a good fit. God knows why I accepted her application," Tracey huffed into her cellphone, with her back to the wall, watching the door. This was not a phone call she wanted someone to listen to. The answer on the other end not what she expected.

"She's upsetting the other residents. No, I can't *have a word with her*, I want her gone. I want you to come now and deal with her. No one will miss her if she goes today. The longer she's here, the more trouble she'll be and I'll have a riot on my hands. When that happens... that's when the County officials get involved... How? You know how it works, they hear things. Not all the staff here are trustworthy. No one is, you taught me that. Now tell me you'll be here soon to remove the problem?" Tracey swivelled back to the computer, tapping with her free hand pulling up the file for the newest resident at the Rose Haven Retirement Resort - Sulia Patel. She parroted the information into the phone, her voice curt and to the point until she was interrupted.

"What do you mean you won't take her because she's

Indian? What on earth does that matter?... So it's because she's female then? Because she's Indian and female? That makes no sense... how the hell do I know why she's blind, I don't have her full medical records here, she's blind... surely you can still use her? Ask, because I'm telling you now, if you don't sort this out, I won't play this game any more. It's too risky. If you can't find someone to take her, then you can, you know... sort her out the other way. Her eyes won't be any good to anyone else, but the rest of her might, so fix it for me."

After ending the call, Tracey Chappell slumped to her desk, massaging her temples with manicured fingers — the dark red polish looking like rivulets of blood seeping out of her skull as her fingers moved through her bleached blonde hair.

"Miss Chappell?"

The voice sent Tracey's fingers hurtling to slam the laptop shut, she hadn't heard her door open. She spun round, heart in her mouth, to face whoever was there, relaxing a fraction when she saw Tala in the doorway.

"Sorry, is now a good time to go over the medical schedule?"

Every week, Tracey and Tala, the head nurse, discussed the scheduled doctor visits, hospital appointments and medication requirements for the week ahead. How Tracey had forgotten was a worry, but what was even more of a concern was whether Tala had overheard her conversation.

"What's on the list?" Tracey blustered.

Ever efficient, Tala spread out her notes and without referring to them she reeled off the residents who had regular check ups scheduled, followed by the people who needed appointments with specialists or had new health concerns and needed a care plan. She charged patients for appointments but preferred keeping medical appointments to a bare minimum and in-house. Far more time efficient, and it kept nosy outsiders out of the Rose Haven. Having a facility full of healthy people was more cost effective than caring for sick people, and Tracey couldn't stand wasting money on the old and infirm. She couldn't abide the elderly. If aged care wasn't so lucrative, she'd be happy never having to smell colostomy bags and soggy vegetables again.

"Why do they have to see a psychiatrist?" Tracey asked, pointing to a separate list of three people, her eyes as wide as the Botox would allow.

"They're veterans, and it's a new recommendation from the Health Department. I've checked, and they all expressed an interest in talking through-"

"What utter rubbish. We're not facilitating that. Henry Marchant can't even walk to the dining room unaided. He's coped this long without talking about whatever imaginary problems he has. Make them sit together at dinner and they can talk among themselves." Tracey drew a line through the appointments with her pen. The cost of the gas to take them to see a shrink was unacceptable, and she smiled as she calculated the saving she'd made. The van looked good outside the Rose Haven. Made it that much more appealing to potential *healthy* residents. The last thing she wanted was the van being absent for unnecessary reasons.

"And what's this one?" Tracey said, stabbing at Sulia's name.

"She has a regular appointment with her eye specialist, once a month according to her admissions paperwork. It's part of an ongoing insurance payout, so there's no cost to the Rose Haven…"

For the second time that day, Tracey regretted letting

the partially sighted woman move in. She refused to facilitate things to suit the woman; she wouldn't be there long. From the file, regular appointments with the optometrist or ophthalmologist or whatever the bloody eye doctor called himself wouldn't save the woman's sight, so it was prudent to drop any unnecessary appointments, which would just become a drain on her staffing resources, a cost she'd have to account for. She kept those thoughts to herself though as Tala was likely to protest, not much, but Tracey didn't want to draw any more attention to her dissatisfaction with the woman being a resident at the Rose Haven Retirement Resort.

"And Elijah Cone, you've got him down to see Doctor Perry?"

"Benson made two separate notes detailing Mister Cone's arthritis, but after what happened with Polish Rob, his appointment needs rescheduling."

Tracey massaged her head again. The death of the Polish man was unfortunate and messy but easy to tidy away. Their vetting should never have allowed an alcoholic into the Rose Haven. At least his untimely death had freed up another room, so with a slight price change, her profit margins would increase. The Pole had a paupers funeral, care of the local coroner, so she had incurred no costs there, a small mercy.

Cone's worsening arthritis needed to be addressed. He was another one she should have turned away. She wasn't interested in sports, so when he'd first applied to the Rose Haven, his high profile reputation was unknown to her. The staff had been quick to educate her though. Hard to dispose of a celebrity.

"Is he incapable of caring for himself, do you think?" the pitch of her voice rising like a child wheedling an answer out of a parent.

If Tala caught the question in Tracey's voice, she didn't answer, retreating to that peculiar medical void where health practitioners retreated to when they didn't want to impart uncomfortable information.

"He's uncomfortable at the moment, but he'd managing fine. The doctor should be able to prescribe something for the pain," Tala replied.

Tracey sniffed, signing off on the care plan. She'd bill Cone for the appointment, but it was the staff resources these appointments took up which was most annoying. She was here for the money, and the money alone, not to improve the health and wellbeing of the residents.

"That's all, Tala," she said, dismissing the smaller woman.

Tala gathered her notes and left, leaving Tracey to daydream of a carefree life well away from cabbage and urine and stale sweat. Even the nurse had a peculiar odour. Tracey opened her handbag and spritzed her office with a small bottle of perfume, and the room filled with the refreshing notes of jasmine and summer roses.

OUTSIDE THE OFFICE, Tala shuffled her notes back into order. If she didn't need this job so badly, she would have left months ago. Years even. But she needed the regular income to support her own family. Her daughter was at college and that didn't come cheap. Tracey made her insides curl up in disgust. The way Tracey referred to the residents, the way money was the single deciding factor over the wellbeing of the people in her care. And now, adding to her disquiet, was a suspicion about the level of *churn* at the Rose Haven; it wasn't natural. She'd been working in aged care since she first qualified as a nurse in the Philippines. It was her speciality, so when she immigrated here, with her engineer husband, it was natural she went into aged care here. The Rose Haven was the first place willing to employ her, so she had no other American experience to call on, but she *heard* things. She occasionally attended workshops, only when Tracey begrudgingly allowed her to, only if it was something the State declared as a necessity for registration. Most of the time Tracey made her pay for it herself, which Tala did. She expected to move on one day, and she needed all the western credentials she could get to improve her salary and her work placement. Listening to conversations at those workshops, which invariably concerned pay and conditions and employers and general workplace gripes, led her to believe that no other aged care provider in the local area had as much *churn*, as much turnover, as the Rose Haven Retirement Resort, and that scared her.

Jasmine and roses seeped out from under Tracey's office door, making Tala gag. It was the scent which followed Tracey around the Rose Haven, so strong it almost preceded her as she stalked around the halls, hoping to catch one of the staff slacking off. One of the staff except for Ricky Donovan, who no matter how many times Tala wrote him up for laziness and incompetence, Tracey ignored. Newer staff called him *Teflon Don*. The longer serving staff knew it didn't pay to complain, so they kept their gripes to themselves. It was safer that way. It wasn't only the residents of the Rose Haven Retirement Resort who had a higher than average level of turnover.

Tala scurried away before the overpowering floral smell threatened to bring her breakfast back up. The doctor visits wouldn't book themselves.

33

Elijah leaned on Sulia, holding his ribs in one hand and her solid arm with the other. He forgot Sulia didn't know where she was going and so they stumbled down the corridors with Elijah muttering a *left* or a *right*, whereupon Sulia would turn like a gargantuan ocean liner steering around an iceberg looming in the dark.

The corridor lights flickered as they passed by as if they too were giving up the will to live. As if life at the Rose Haven had just become unbearable, unliveable.

"It's here, this is my door," Elijah managed, his breathing shallow. Every movement, every breath paining him more than he could have imagined. A memory emerged of instructing one of his boys, a promising player called Jimmy Hunter, to harden up and get back out on the field after a hard hit from a solidly built Midwest opponent. It turned out Jimmy had broken three ribs and after another tackle on the field, the broken ribs lacerated his liver. He'd come off the field at full time throwing up blood. He'd sat on the bench for the rest of the season until his liver healed, but it was the end of his career. Until now, Elijah hadn't known broken ribs would hurt this much.

Sulia leaned him against the corridor wall and opened his door. Easing him off the wall, he let her slide him into his armchair by the window. Better than trying to get him into bed on her own.

"How you feeling, Elijah?" she asked, panting with exertion.

"Sore," Elijah replied, his eyes closed.

"You going to report him, the one that kicked you?"

"No."

"What! You should. No one should get away with what he did. It'll be on their cameras," Sulia exclaimed.

Elijah opened his eyes to watch Sulia as she gesticulated, punctuating her points with violent hand gestures and the shaking of her head. The woman had untold difficulty navigating the corridors of the Rose Haven and needed help to find the condiments on the table in the dining room, so how did she know about the security cameras?

"Stop looking at me. Just cause I'm blind doesn't mean I can't see," Sulia retorted, taking a break from chastising him.

"You're blind, how can you see?" Elijah asked, his curiosity piqued. Sulia was the first blind person he'd met. They'd asked him once to train a team of visually impaired players for a charity, and he'd laughed down the phone at the absurdity. As if he had time to teach blind kids how to play football, a stupid idea. His reaction to that old request now made him squirm.

"I've got ears haven't I? And I know how to use them, and they work better than the ones you've got plastered to the side of your head. Men, you're just a bunch of testosterone dressed in khakis and aftershave. Not one brain cell in amongst all those angry man genes running around inside your head. You need to report him. You need to or I will."

Elijah sighed, sending sharp pains through his chest, forcing him to think about Jimmy and his lacerated liver again. He sent the boy a silent apology. Elijah couldn't remember what had happened to Jimmy, he didn't keep track of his ex players. Once they left the game, they were of no use to him so he dropped out of contact. Which was why no one bothered visiting him here, not the main reason, but one of them.

"If you quit staring at me, I'll let you try my medicine," Sulia said, teeth gleaming as a smile split her face.

"If it's not illegal, I'll try it," Elijah agreed, figuring something was better than nothing. The pain forcing him to accept whatever it was Sulia was offering unless it meant prison time. He'd avoided being locked up for life, but his time behind bars during the court case was more than enough for him.

Sulia laughed, the booming sound rolled up from her belly and exploded volcanic-like from her mouth. "Oh you white men, you make me laugh. You think because I'm foreign I'm out to seduce you with my dark arts? I'm as American as you are, born and bred."

"What?"

"I was born in Chicago and lived there my whole life, apart from now. I should never have left, would have had myself a nice little apartment in a senior's village if I'd stayed. Still you learn," Sulia said, her milky eyes looking backwards.

"But the way you dress…" Elijah said confused.

Draped in an emerald green sari, the voluminous fabric barely restrained Sulia's girth. Her addition of a cable knit cardigan jarred with the rich fabric covering her.

"The sari? Hahahahaha, you think I dress like this because I'm Indian. Oh boy, hahahahaha," Sulia laughed and laughed, great guffaws which echoed down the hall through the open door.

Elijah watched her, perplexed, his energy spent trying not to move, to not jar his painful ribs. Sulia's jocularity exponentially brighter than her clothes and the gold bracelets tinkling on her arms. He'd never understood women, and this one was no exception.

"I'm lost," he admitted.

"It's the only thing which fits!" Sulia laughed again, slapping her thigh and Elijah's bed creaked dangerously underneath her as she jiggled.

A face appeared at the door, another resident, Elijah couldn't remember his name, but recognised him by the thick silver hoop he wore through one earlobe, as if he'd once dressed up as a pirate but had forgotten about his earring, leaving it to blend seamlessly into his skin, becoming part of him. The walking stick he leaned on could just as easily be a sword with a solid silver handle.

"You okay?" the jewelled pirate asked.

"Sore, but okay, thanks," Elijah replied, the first words he'd exchanged with the man.

"You wanna come in and join us, John?" Sulia asked.

The man shook his head. "Best not, on my way to my room. Thought I'd check in though," and he shuffled away, his slippers slapping against the floor in his haste.

"You know him?" Elijah asked. He'd been here four times longer than Sulia but struggled with the names of the staff and residents, preferring to keep to himself. Better not to form any relationships, that way no one would get hurt again.

"That's John Gallows, nice guy. Slippers are too big for him so I can hear him a mile away, but a heart of gold that one. You'd both get on well. He was something to do with sports. Not football, but something else, golf maybe?"

Elijah coughed, his normal way of changing the conversation, except he had forgotten about his ribs and the coughing turned into a painful experience. It worked, and Sulia heaved herself off the bed, rushing to his side to support him as he coughed his way through the spasm.

"You can't keep changing the topic..." Sulia said, pouring him water after the coughing had passed.

"I wasn't."

"You can't lie. I'm blind remember, I can hear the lies in your voice, I can feel them swirling around me. This room is full of them and they're eating you up. The lies you tell yourself will send you to the same grave those kids are in."

Elijah struggled to his feet, ignoring the pain, Sulia's words were the last straw.

"Get out," he said, pointing to the door. It took every ounce of energy not to succumb to the pain pouring through him. Pain not from his ribs but from his heart.

Sulia nodded, and shuffled out the door, arms outstretched. She didn't apologise.

Sulia had memorised her way around the Rose Haven, so made her way to her room, the twists and turns of the corridors no barrier to her prodigious memory. Elijah would come to her, she knew that. Sometimes people needed the truth because the truth set you free, and Elijah needed the truth to free him from his past.

In her room, she closed the door behind her. The lock was on the outside, the only real change from when the Rose Haven had been a reluctant three star hotel, but that didn't concern her. Before the door closed, she slipped a modified piece of hard plastic from her voluminous pockets and slid it into the keyhole from the inside preventing the door from being locked. Based on her observations, getting a locksmith in to fix the door here would take weeks.

Sulia shuffled to her chest of drawers, her own breathing laboured now. Tugging open the top drawer she rifled through her underwear until she came to a rolled up pair of bed socks, far heavier than they should be. She unfurled the knitted socks and liberated a bottle of milky liquid. A silly grin spread across her face as she twisted the metal top off. After sniffing the contents, she made her way to her bedside table, where she poured a measure of liquid into her drinking glass and swallowed the contents, wiping her mouth on the back of her hand — the slick on her cheek the only evidence of what had been in the glass.

Hiding the bottle back in her socks she hesitated before returning it to the drawer. The curtains in the room were thick blackout curtains, left over from the hotel's heyday. Once there had been tiebacks and fancy hooks, but those were long gone. What remained was an excess of fabric loitering at each end of the window. The staff cleaned the Rose Haven with as much effort as everything else, which meant little effort at all. At the window, Sulia shoved the socks into the far edge of the window sill, concealed from the cursory glances of anyone who might come into the room. She needed what was in that bottle, more than anyone else here. The bottle was almost empty. Sulia tried not to think about what she'd do when there was nothing left. It didn't do to dwell too much on the mechanics of dying. It happened to them all, in one way or another.

34

Pauline's hands hadn't left her hips for the entire time Tracey was talking to her, and she hadn't stopped trying to talk over the top of the other woman. For the staff listening outside the kitchen, no one wanted to place bets on the winner of this argument.

"I won't," Pauline said, her shoulders square, her chin set. The gleam of northern defiance in her eye.

"Work with me Pauline. You saw the mess the residents caused. It will make your life so much simpler if you don't have to prepare it every morning," Tracey explained.

"I don't need me life made any easier. My life's been harder than it needed, but it's me own life and it's what it is. What you're asking me to do is to starve those poor folk out there. Most of them ain't got their own teeth. The porridge stays."

"Pauline, I need you to prepare a menu plan which doesn't include porridge. Think of the money you'll save from your budget."

Pauline shook her blonde head. She was all for saving money, had been doing it her whole life, first with her parents when she got a job to help with the household expenses, then again after she'd left her worthless husband. She'd done it the hard way but at least the decisions she'd made were her own and made for the good of her and her kids. What she wasn't, was as cold-hearted as the woman standing in front of her.

"The porridge is the cheapest part of me budget," Pauline explained again, rifling through the folders she kept for her desk. Opening the folder marked *Breakfast*, she ran her finger down rows and rows of itemised articles, reeling off their individual costs until Tracey held up her hand. The evidence was irrefutable, the porridge was the cheapest part of any meal, let alone the breakfast menu.

"Is there a cheaper brand of bread we can serve?" Tracey said.

Pauline threw her hands up, the conversation at an end. Replacing the porridge with any other staple would double their costs, and Pauline knew Tracey wouldn't accept that. So as she returned the folder to its rightful place, she heard Tracey *clip clop* out of the kitchen and released the breath she'd been holding. It was a bloody hard job churning out nutritious meals day after day with the budget she had, but by god she managed it, and on the scent of an oily rag. If she'd been back home, she knew she'd have been able to supplement everything with eggs from her Mam, and veggies from her own garden, but here, that was a different kettle of fish. If something didn't have preservatives in it, she'd eat her own hat. It surprised her that the poor souls in the Rose Haven Retirement Resort weren't malnourished like those poor kiddies in the news. She had her suspicions some residents were, so she occasionally supplemented the menu with things from home. Strictly illegal, but what they made her serve to the old folk wouldn't be given to the worst criminals on death row. Pauline suspected that most of the folk at the Rose Haven would be a damn sight better off if they ganged up, robbed a bank and were placed behind bars. It wasn't as if any of them ever went out so it'd be no change from their day-to-day life, except they'd have better food and access to proper healthcare.

Someone entered the kitchen and Pauline spun round to tell them to bugger off, but stopped shy of that when she saw it was Benson and Tala.

"Here's trouble. What do you lot want then?" she asked.

Tala fiddled with the folder in her hands and looked to Benson, who held his own folder tight against his chest.

Benson cleared his throat, looking to Tala, who alternated between looking at the door and the floor.

"If it's trouble, I want no part," Pauline declared. To prove her point, she turned the tap on, running steaming water into a huge pot she slammed into the industrial sink. She could feel the gazes of her visitors behind her. She left them stewing in their own awkwardness. They'd tell her when they were ready, everyone did. Pauline acted as a quasi psychologist, someone others came to with their problems. Tala and Benson would spill the beans, they wouldn't be able to help themselves.

"We need to talk," Benson said.

"Do we?" Pauline asked.

Tala nodded, with somewhat less enthusiasm than the orderly.

"It concerns Tracey," Benson added.

Pauline twisted the tap further and water fountained over the top of the saucepan, filling the sink.

"You can talk, but keep it quiet," Pauline said, gesturing to chairs around the table in the middle of the room.

Benson and Tala both took a seat, moving aside the various packets Pauline had been putting away before Tracey had accosted her about the porridge.

"You mind you keep it quiet," Pauline reiterated, her hands straying to the packet of cigarettes she kept in her pocket. She was trying to give up, she was, but sometimes she needed a quick puff or two, to take the edge off of working in this place.

Benson opened his folder, he didn't need to, but it made him feel better about what he was going to say. He cleared his throat, the words so uncomfortable they almost choked him.

"We think Tracey is selling…," he looked to Tala for help, but she was examining the grain of the wooden table.

"Selling what?" Pauline asked.

"Um, parts," Benson replied.

"Her soul more like it," Pauline quipped, humour her usual response to awkward situations.

"Body parts," Tala said, without looking up.

"Eh, what?" Pauline replied, her voice rising.

Benson shushed her, checking over his shoulder.

"You're pulling me leg. I wouldn't put it past her, mind. Anything to make a quid or two and she's there with bells on. But body parts? This isn't a Stephen King movie."

"We're not joking Pauline," Tala whispered, pushing her notes to Pauline's side of the table.

Pauline's pale English face, paled even further under her foundation.

"Why are you telling me then? I've got naught to do with it." Pauline's pushed the folder back towards Tala.

"There's no one else to trust-"

"It was Johnny Paulson disappearing that made me think about it-"

"And the phone call I overheard-"

"Tracey is selling body parts-"

"In cahoots with the doctor-"

"Doctor Perry."

Tala and Benson talked over each other like a pair of nightingales, and Pauline held up her hands to stop them, her head spinning. For the hundredth time in less than an hour, she wished she'd never come to this country.

"As if! And if they are, what do you want me to do?" she asked. Whatever they wanted, she wanted no part in it, no part at all. If she read what they wanted her to read, she'd be an accessory or whatever it was they called it on the crime shows on tele.

"Help us get enough evidence so we can go to the police before any more of the residents are butchered," Benson mumbled.

"Oh aye, and how am I meant to do that when I'm here in the kitchen? I don't waltz round the place with a folder under me arm looking important. I'm in 'ere, working. That's what I do. I work, I go home, and I come back. I don't even take me holidays, cause there's never anyone to take me place. Now you lot want to get me tangled up in this… whatever *it* is. I'll lose me job and then what? Who'll give me a job at this age then?"

"Pauline, you will not lose your job, I promise. You only need to listen and watch, and we know how good you are at that. You know everything that happens here, everyone tells you stuff-"

"Because you're a good listener," Tala interrupted, smiling for the first time.

"Damn straight I'm a good listener," Pauline agreed, mollified by their platitudes. "If that's all I have to do, then yes, but so help me, if I get fired I'm coming to live at your house, cause I ain't got any savings to fall back on. I spend everything on me Mam, so she doesn't have to live in a place like this. She's in a proper old folks home, one where they get to go play bingo every week. Once they even had a stripper in for one of the girls on her birthday. Can you imagine that? That's the way I want to die, surrounded by oiled up young men, gyrating themselves against my wheelchair." Pauline laughed and demonstrated the gyrations she meant. "I still think you're barking mad, both of you. Tracey, selling body parts. She spends enough on fixing up her own parts that's for sure. But what would anyone want with the bits and pieces of the poor sods who live 'ere then?"

"You don't have to read our notes if you don't want, Pauline, but the evidence is in there. Almost all. We're certain that's what she's up to, it's the only explanation-"

"Stop your babbling, I don't want to hear it. La la la la la la la," Pauline sang, her fingers in her ears.

"You are the only one we can trust here. We need more time before calling in the police. More time and solid evidence," Benson looked to Tala. "We're only asking you to keep your eyes and ears open, and we need to keep our papers here with you, with your papers. It's safer in here than anywhere else," Benson finished.

"Fine, but I still think you've both been into the good stuff in the drug cupboard. Get off with you both now, I've work to do," and Pauline took the file out of Benson's hands, as if handling a contagious pathogen. She hadn't read Benson's notes and didn't want to but she *could* file it away. That was one of her problems, she was always the one people came to for help and she always said yes. Got her into miles of trouble - financial and personal, but she could never say no when someone needed help. Body parts, they were both dreaming.

35

Myra jumped as the doorbell sounded. She'd been on edge since her husband had called to say Social Services would be round to pick up the baby boy they were fostering, and that he wouldn't be there for the handover because he had an urgent patient to see.

Myra had been there for the handover of their fostered children several times, but always with her husband there to oversee things. But this time was different. She didn't want to give up the baby. He'd been with them longer than usual and they'd connected. He needed her.

The doorbell sounded again, chastising her for her tardiness. Myra brushed away the tears forming and lifting her chin she strode for the door. Papering over her heartbreak with a forced smile she opened the door.

Shoulder to shoulder on the front step were two tieless men holding badges. Her eyes blurry from the tears, Myra couldn't decipher the delicate lettering on the shiny badges nestled in well-worn wallets.

"Mrs Perry?" asked one.

Myra looked up from the brassy badge to the man's

face. Clean shaven, around the same age as her and as unremarkable as she was herself. A face made to blend into the background. Even his eyes were plain, sandy with lashes that were neither short nor long. Eyebrows which did nothing other than sit dutifully on his face, and hair which fell ordinarily upon his head. Why then did he make her step back? Why did her breath catch in her throat?

"Yes," she said.

"I'm Detective Gary Pemberton, and this is Detective Tony Street, may we come in?" The sandy haired detective waited.

Myra stepped forward, closing the door behind her. She hadn't looked down the hall before closing the door, if she had, she might have seen the boys poking their heads out of their bedroom before exchanging glances which would send shivers down any psychologist's spine.

"Sorry, but the baby is sleeping inside, can we go round the back to talk?" Myra tried to quell her rising panic. Maybe it was her husband? Had he been in an accident? Perhaps one of his patients had laid a complaint, a serious complaint? Regardless, she didn't want them talking where the boys might hear. They'd just lost their mother and didn't need any more trauma in their young lives. The sooner her husband found proper care for them the better.

Following Myra along the manicured path, the detectives took their seats at a table in the garden. The wrought iron chairs were never that comfortable at the best of times, and the two policemen did their best to make themselves comfortable in the breezy backyard. Myra saw them scanning the house and the garden and her, judging her. She felt their observations as keenly as the wind against her skin although the goosebumps on her flesh were more to do with the frank gaze of the first detective.

"Has something happened to my husband?" Myra

asked, the wind whipping away her words, and silence filled the void.

Gary Pemberton shook his head, running his hand through his hair. His partner had his black notebook open on the table, his pen poised like a snake ready to strike.

"Your husband is fine as far as we're aware, but it is your husband we'd like to talk to," Gary said.

Pale to start with, Myra paled even further. She looked nervously back at the house, "My husband?"

"We need to ask a few questions about his medical practice."

"I'm not involved with the practice, so won't be much help." Myra considered her husband's medical practice. She'd been there once, when they were first married, and after that he'd made it clear she wasn't to interrupt him there, ever. A doctor's surgery was a place of *serious* work and he didn't need his wife bothering the patients or the staff. Of the staff, there was only the receptionist. Her husband had on the rare occasion moaned about her capabilities, but maybe it was a different one now. She couldn't remember her name and rifled through her cloudy memory for the name of the receptionist she had met. *Rose*? No. *Jasmine*? No, but she was sure it was the name of a flower, *Violet*? Then it clicked, it had been *Lily*, she remembered commenting to the girl that she loved lilies.

Myra knew the detective was watching her as she trawled through her memory. That he sat there silently was even more disturbing. Myra was unaware he was letting the silence speak for itself; as per his training. People felt obligated to fill a silence because silence made them uncomfortable. And Myra rushed to fill it.

"I can't tell you anything. We keep work and family life separate. I've only met Lily once."

The other detective scribbled in his notebook and Myra paled further, worried what she'd said which caused him to write in his notebook. Myra babbled more, her unease taking charge of her mouth.

"I think her name is Lily, named after the flower, that's why her mother called her Lily, because she loved lilies. Nice girl, but I only met her once. My husband doesn't talk about his work but he works hard. I think he's been struggling with a patient this week, he's worked a lot of late nights, so I think someone is ill…" she trailed off, conscious that her mouth had run away on its own accord.

"And her surname?" Gary asked. His own notebook sat idle next to him, his long fingers splayed on the wrought iron.

Myra shook her head. "To be honest that was months ago, I'm not sure if she's still there. As I said, my husband doesn't discuss his work. And if I need to speak to him, I call his mobile."

"And his patients, what does he say about them?" Gary probed.

"He doesn't. He's not allowed to." His questions flustered her further, and she questioned herself. Why didn't her husband talk about his work? It was normal, to mull over the days happenings. He didn't need to give her specifics, but he didn't even pass comment on the smallest things. They talked about their foster children, or how busy he was, especially with all the work he did at the old folks home. "He does lots of work at the Rose Haven," Myra blurted out, filling the awkward silence in the yard. She need not have worried because chimes of the doorbell disturbed the silence, echoing around the garden. Myra and the detectives turned towards the sound.

"Oh," Myra said, her hands fluttering above the table. Social Services, she wasn't prepared for this right now.

"Are you expecting someone?" Gary asked.

"Yes, Social Services are here to pick up my... I mean, picking up *a* baby we've been fostering, and now they will have found a permanent home for him. Usually my husband is here, but he had an urgent call, so I'm to..."

"We're happy to wait here," Gary said. His partner hadn't stopped scribbling in his notebook, and spidery words marched across the pages.

Myra couldn't help thinking each of the pen strokes were spider steps down her back and she shivered. "I don't know how long I'll be, I need to spend some time with them for the handover. Perhaps you should go and I'll get my husband to call you when he's back?"

"I understand, of course. We'll be in touch," Gary said.

The bell rang again and as Myra dashed off, Gary asked another question.

"One last thing, Mrs Perry. Do you often act as foster parents for babies?"

Myra nodded. "I haven't been able to have children, so at least this way I get to experience being a mother. It really is the most amazing gift and I only wish we could adopt one ourselves. There have been so many, but this one has been special and I'll miss him. I've still got the boys to look after. We're just waiting for the child welfare people to find a home for them. I don't normally foster school age children. Sorry, but I must go," and Myra hurried away, leaving the detectives in the yard.

GARY PEMBERTON SEARCHED the windows of the house for any sign of Mrs Perry and the people at the door. They must be on the other side of the house for there was no sign of any life in the kitchen. A movement upstairs caught his eye, and two identical faces peered at him through a second floor window. He waved, and the faces vanished.

"Let's go, Tony," Gary said.

"That was odd," Tony replied, reading over his notes. "Them being approved foster parents wasn't in the file. Did you see that?"

"No, nothing I've read. We'll drop in and see the child welfare team on the way back. Did you see the faces at the window?"

"Yup, looked like there was a mirror up there. Kind of creepy, like those demon kids in that horror movie, can't remember the name of it now."

They climbed into their car and Gary started the engine. "Make a note of the number plate of that car and run it through the system. I've got a funny feeling."

36

Mary Louise made it as far as the grocery store and a quarter of the way home before feeling faint and stopping to rest on a park bench. The broken slat at the front of the bench dug into her leg but she was too sore to move. She'd overdone it — too far, too soon, too fast. The bench was uncomfortable and her ribcage threatened to poke through her barely healed skin and even taking the tiniest of breaths sent waves of nauseating pain through every part of her body. She'd wait a few moments to build up the courage to walk home again. She'd brought very little at the store, knowing she had to carry it home, so leaving the bag on the bench wasn't a disaster. It only held two oranges, a pint of milk, a packet of cereal and a microwave dinner for later. A normal person could carry the bag to the top of Mt. Everest and back, but she didn't think she could lift it off the bench.

The dizziness passed, and the world returned to normal... for a moment, her field of vision had narrowed to a tiny pinprick of light, which was when she'd flung herself onto the seat instead of decorating the pavement. Slowly colour returned, and the trees morphed from shadowy beige fingers to an artist's palette of twenty shades of green. Her lungs weren't threatening to explode and the dagger-like pins and needles in her legs had faded enough that she could gingerly test the strength in her reconstructed knee before finally standing.

Casting a longing look at her groceries, Mary Louise pushed off the bench and wobbled down the sidewalk towards home, a hundred times slower than when she'd set out.

Near the end of her street, Mary Louise leaned against a concrete power pole, the smooth lines reassuringly solid against her frame. It wasn't the pain in her legs or chest forcing her to stop, but her narrowing frame of sight, viewing everything in front of her through a pin hole camera.

"You okay?"

A disembodied voice came from behind and Mary Louise struggled to twist around. The face swimming in front of her eyes wasn't one she recognised. And her vision narrowed even further

"Miss?"

The face was talking to her, his mouth opening and closing, but she could only hear the giant roar of surf pounding the beach somewhere, which was odd because she lived nowhere near a surf beach.

Mary Louise opened her mouth to reply but nothing came out — that was usually the way of things when someone held a cloth over your mouth. She could hear herself screaming inside her head but no one came running to help.

The man faded like an old photograph until she could

only grasp at his blurry features. And then a nothingness swallowed her whole. No one saw and no one came to help. The curtains at the window didn't twitch but billowed slightly as the front door opened and closed and the lock slid home.

37

Molly held the off-white business card in her hand. What did the colour say about the owner? Did off-white say something white didn't? Was it cream or did the printers call this colour ivory? And was there a hierarchy to business card colours and where did that place the man who'd given it to her?

She slid the card onto the dining room table, lining it up against the piece of notepaper where she'd jotted down additional details — home address, weight, eye colour, allergies… all things she hoped to find out but she liked to know these things in advance. Molly refused to waste any more time on someone still living with their mother or had a strange cohabitation agreement with their ex wife and her new partner. She'd been there before and it was always far more complicated than her prospective partners tried to make out.

Molly eyed the phone. When should she ring? The perennial question for most teenage girls, but she was far from being a teenager and still suffered crippling angst about it. A recent read of Teen Vogue at the checkout counter had added no light on the subject. He'd handed her *his* card, so the ball was in her court. She'd already saved his number, so didn't need to dial anything — only one press of a manicured finger away. Still, she hesitated.

Pushing back from the table she hurried to the toilet. A nervous wee and then she'd ring him because heaven forbid if she needed to go to the toilet when he answered. Who knew what the etiquette was. On the porcelain seat, she examined her fingers and picked at her nails, rehearsing the potential conversation openers she'd fine tuned the night before whilst simultaneously planning their wedding and the names of their two children or three children, she hadn't decided. She was young, but maybe not young enough to pop out three babies in quick succession.

Being honest with herself, the only reason she hesitated was because of something she'd overheard after leaving the clinic. She'd walked as far as the corner of the block before realising she'd left her house keys in her desk drawer, or she hoped that's where she left them because they weren't in her handbag. And at night she preferred walking to the bus stop with her keys in her hand in case of any trouble — that's what her grandaddy had taught her. No one could accuse her of carrying an offensive weapon if she only carried her house keys, but keys could inflict real damage if you held them right. After locating her keys on her desk, she was back locking the door, chastising herself to add her work keys to her house keys, when she heard screaming. Sometimes patients screamed, she hated it but understood that not everyone's pain threshold was as high as others. She'd just not expected him to be a screamer, especially not just for a shoulder injury, one well on its way to being fully healed.

Molly had stood in the clinic's entrance for a moment, wondering if she should pop her head in and offer to help. Holding Don Jury's hand whilst Doctor Perry did his thing had its appeal, but his childish screaming was just so loud that she'd shuddered on the threshold of the office, physically repulsed by it.

And so she sat on her toilet, wrestling with the memory of the flirtatious moments they'd exchanged versus the sound of his troubled screams. She should have offered to help. She missed a golden opportunity to help him, her future husband. He was a better catch than anyone she'd connected with online; capable of actual conversation as a starter. So what if his pain tolerance was almost zero? She'd just have to make sure he never injured himself.

Her foot went numb, a sign she'd been sitting on the toilet for far too long. It was time to ring him, because even here in her bathroom, with its mouldy shower curtain and an array of half used skincare products, her biological clock was ticking.

Molly flushed the toilet and steeled her resolve. After checking her makeup in the mirror, her imaginary armour, she flung herself teenage-like onto her bed and hit the *call* button.

The tinny sound of electronic ringing echoed in her ear. She pulled it away and pressed the speaker button, propping the phone against her pillow. The answerphone clicked on in the background.

"Hello, you've reached Don Jury, leave a message and I'll call as soon as I can."

Molly stabbed at the phone, ending the call. She hadn't expected an answerphone. That required a different response than the one she'd prepared. Rolling onto her back she stared up at the ceiling, a ceiling she'd spent hundreds of nights staring at as she sketched out her life plan only to have it dashed by one man or another. Tonight would be another night on her own.

AND IN A DENTED skip behind Doctor Perry's clinic, the message window on Don Jury's iPhone lit up, illuminating the whiskered face of a large rat who'd chewed his way into the black rubbish sack, after sniffing out Molly's leftover lunch — tuna sandwiches garnished with cucumber. The iPhone went dark, a tiny beep showing he'd missed a call from an unknown number. A message Don Jury would never receive.

Elijah stretched his fingers towards the woman, her curly blonde hair a dull grey in the dark. His hands came away sticky as if someone had used too much hair gel without combing it through. Confused, he pulled his hand away. The darkness hid the stain on his fingers.

"Natalie? Natalie, are you okay?" his voice stumbled over the words.

No answer.

His nostrils flared as an unnatural wind shoved the mixed scents of rum and beer and oil and earth through the car.

"Natalie?" his voice small.

Still no answer.

Dancing torchlight bobbed towards the car. Weird how it was coming sideways towards him, such a realistic dream but weird he couldn't feel anything. He waited for his wife to wake him up with a nudge like she always did. But nothing happened.

"Natalie?"

ELIJAH AWOKE, Natalie's face blurry in his mind. Her blonde curls set like concrete in her coffin his overriding memory of her now after they'd washed the blood from her hair. His heart beat slowed as he struggled out of his sleepy haze. His memory of the accident fractured and no matter how he tried to piece it together, there was a void in his mind. An emptiness where he should have remembered what happened.

Experience told him there would be no more sleeping for him tonight. Since Natalie's death, he'd not made it through a whole night without waking. Her face had faded but the pain and the self recrimination remained.

Pulling his curtains aside, he searched the outside night for anything of interest. Even the road was devoid of traffic, normal people at home asleep at three o'clock in the morning. His body ached for a release from the pain consuming him. Not the pain from his arthritis but from being alive after causing the deaths of so many others. Sure, coming to the Rose Haven was a step below the luxury he'd enjoyed with Natalie, but it was more life than he deserved. The papers called him a killer. The parents of the boys had called him that too. And his daughter, Libby. He was unlikely to hear from her again. Lost to him in a way more final than Natalie. Words were said which couldn't be unsaid. Despite everything, he yearned for one more shot of rum. Or bourbon. Or gin. Anything to numb how he felt in the midnight hours of night.

Shuffling back to bed, Elijah sipped on a glass of water bedside his bed. They didn't even trust the residents with real glasses, but gave them disposable plastic ones which they had to wash and reuse — saving money on everything, everywhere. The stale water caught in his throat, and he coughed, and coughed, and coughed. Elijah massaged his chest, his broken rib aching with every cough. Again, the pain was nothing compared to losing Natalie. With his eyes closed, Elijah missed the flash of headlights of a dark sedan pulling into the driveway of the Rose Haven Retirement Resort, its engine silent as it coasted to a stop.

A hammering reverberated on the interconnecting wall and a muffled shout which Elijah ignored. Another light sleeper. They all were. You became old and suddenly a full night's sleep was as rare as a day off had been when you were working. Now he could sleep the whole day, but couldn't. Was it a lifetime of misdeeds which kept them awake? Or was that the punishment for becoming old? He needed a rum, to help him sleep. A final shot to force his eyes to close and his mind to quiet.

Just as his eyes drooped, Elijah's door crashed open.

"What the hell, old man? I told you yesterday to keep it quiet. You're upsetting the other residents so that means you're upsetting me. Just fucking hurry up and die old man, you worthless old cunt."

Dark stains ran down Preston's white orderly shirt and the foul scent of filter coffee and body odour filled the small room. The coffee stains jolted something in Elijah's mind, reminding him of the dark sticky stain on his fingers from Natalie's hair — her blood. Drenched from a can of bourbon and cola, or was it rum and cola? He couldn't remember, maybe straight rum, after all it had been a big celebration. State champions, seventh year in a row. The orderly kept up his rant, grabbing Elijah by the shoulders, but he wasn't listening, he'd zoned out, remembering Natalie's soft hand in his, the sounds of the boys in the back playing drinking games, being kicked out of the motel which meant they were on the road instead of partying in their rooms. His trousers marked with urine from the shock of the accident, the knowledge that Natalie had gone, that his life was over…

"Are you bloody listening old man? Get up," Preston said, yanking Elijah to his feet, shaking him.

Elijah lost control. The arthritic pain he'd numbed for years with alcohol disappeared as he fought back. He fought against his treatment since moving into the old folks home. And against a society which demonised him after the accident. He fought against the friendships which vanished as he went through the court system, and he fought against the loss of a daughter who couldn't forgive him. Elijah was a big man, Preston Sergeant was not.

The men raged across the small room, knocking into the single bed, its quilt slipping to the ground. They banged into the wall, Preston grunting with the unexpected exertion. Elijah had been publicly vilified, crushed by the weight of public opinion, and broken by guilt, but he had a reserve of strength he hadn't had to use before, until now.

The sound of the fight echoed through the Rose Haven Retirement Resort, waking its residents from their slumber and sending the skeleton night staff running to investigate.

———

DEEP in the bowels of the Rose Haven, Doctor Perry tapped the thin glass of a test tube and watched the viscous liquid bubble above the delicate sliver of flame underneath, oblivious to the ruckus above him. It was a tricky task distilling his tonic, and it needed every ounce of his concentration.

The Doctor muttered as he checked his calculations. He'd never let his stocks run this low before. Don Jury had needed a larger dose than he'd initially calculated, and this business with Myra had sent him back to his lab to tweak the strength of the formula. Myra resembled an old hag at bedtime, so much so he'd slipped out of the house coming to the lab to work instead.

In the chair, he closed his eyes, lulled by the humming of the high speed blender, the fine blades breaking up the fibrous membranes of the sclerotic and cornea, both parts of the eyeball. He'd sliced off the muscles first, discarding those in the medical waste bin. So far he hadn't found a use for the muscles, or the optic nerves, a frustrating but temporary waste. He was confident that with more analysis he'd find a use for them one day.

Complex equations filled his notepad. He'd always been good at chemistry, and if he'd applied himself more at college, he would have graduated top of his class. As it was he'd been sidetracked early on with his private experiments using tissue from both the living, and the dead, specimens the college kept on site. Conducting unsanctioned research on live rabbits after hours hadn't gone down well with the college and they'd warned him to restrict his activities to the normal course work. That's when Doctor Perry, or an early iteration of Doctor Perry, realised his professors didn't want the competition. He'd been more circumspect after that first warning but the spark was lit and he spent the rest of his time at college only half listening to his tutors and conducting his own experiments off site after hours.

The blender whirred to a stop, leaving only the hiss of the gas heating the batch he'd prepared. Doctor Perry stood up, the wheels of his chair squeaking on the old linoleum. Swishing the liquid in its container to check the viscosity, he decanted it into a glass beaker and positioned it above another element. The whole configuration took up half the room and navigating the convoluted coils and connections required a ballet-like grace.

Doctor Perry was separating out the unwanted sediment when there was a knock on his door. He dropped the beaker, spilling the precious liquid on the floor. Anger rose behind his eyes. No one knocked on his door. A strict *do no disturb* policy was in place when he was working in the lab. The beaker and the liquid it had held were beyond recovery, with the mess on the floor representing over twelve hours of lab work. Processing, decanting, distilling, binding, and the biotransformation, all that effort, wasted. And Doctor Perry didn't have time to waste.

He flung open the door.

"No one disturbs me," he hissed.

The scabby-faced orderly stepped away, and Doctor Perry stepped through the door, pulling it shut behind him. He didn't recognise the staff member which made it worse. The fewer people who knew of his lab the better.

"You're needed upstairs, Doctor," the orderly said, picking at a scab on his arm. Blood bloomed underneath the cracked skin.

Doctor Perry checked the door locked behind him and indicated that the orderly should show him the way. The pair made their way up the narrow stairwell, the doctor's eyes narrowed as he noticed the orderly glancing back towards the lab.

Even if Doctor Perry couldn't hear the commotion up ahead, the scared faces poking out from identical doors along the wide corridors lit the way. The stench of the elderly residents made his gut twist and his nose wrinkle. The patients he'd been cultivating called out a greeting, expressing their concern about the well being of whoever he needed to attend. Soon he'd leave all this behind him. And Myra. He had no need of the elderly any more, he had enough put away for a new identity somewhere not as *old* as Florida. Somewhere not at risk of being annihilated by the next extreme weather event. Changing countries was an option. With money, you could be anyone you liked. It was the one thought which kept him going every time he had to lance a boil or prescribe a fungicide for a hideous toenail infection. The memory made him shudder. He also needed to disappear because the demand for his private services was getting out of hand. There were too many people involved on the periphery now. His name too well known, which could end badly but backing out now wouldn't work either. One didn't just walk away from the people he supplied. Disappearing was his only choice. With no strings attached. No Myra.

Outside Elijah's room, he shook off the twitchy orderly, making a mental note to suggest Tracey fire him. Even with his forged medical degree, he could spot an addict a mile off. This guy was trouble waiting to happen.

The crowd outside Elijah's room parted, allowing Doctor Perry to see into the room. As first he saw nothing out of the ordinary until he saw an odd shape on the floor held secure by a pair of legs in flannel pyjamas.

Benson squeezed past him, bending down to the strange installation on the floor, lifting an older man up under his armpits and propelling him to the armchair by the window, before pulling the bedspread off the other man panting on the ground. Only then did Doctor Perry enter the room.

"What on earth happened here?"

"He attacked me, that old coot. Madder than a rabid dog," Preston Sergeant puffed, his eye half closed, the swelling obscuring his piggy-like eyes. An improvement Doctor Perry thought.

Muriel Lincoln pushed her way into the room, pearls nestled in her bosom despite being in her nightclothes. "I heard it all from my room," she announced. "He started it, he attacked Elijah," she said, pointing a bony finger at Preston.

"You're as deaf as a bat, you bloody well didn't hear a thing. Stupid old woman," Preston spat.

"Enough," Benson said, offering a hand to the man on the floor.

Preston ignored Benson and pushing himself up he addressed Doctor Perry, "That man's a danger to himself, Doc. You should sedate him before he hurts someone else. Look at what he's done."

Doctor Perry's well practised mask concealed his thoughts about the situation. "It seems that way, thank you for your help, Preston" Doctor Perry said to the sulking orderly. If Preston had planned to retaliate, he lost the opportunity when Doctor Perry continued, "Take yourself off to the nurses' station for someone to look at that eye."

Muriel Lincoln clasped at her pearls as Preston glared at her on his way past.

"Do you want me to take Elijah to your office, Doctor Perry?" Benson asked.

Doctor Perry considered the question, conscious of the beakers and test tubes he'd left unattended in his lab, and smiled as he considered the attributes of the man in the chair. Elijah Cone's arthritis notwithstanding, another physically fit patient would be perfect to test the latest batch on. The last batch of tonic had been too weak, meaning he had to administer a second dose to the poor unfortunate Don Jury, delaying Don's biotransformation, and apparently making it more painful than Doctor Perry could endure listening to. Whether his patients coped with the pain was of no consequence.

"Thank you, Benson. Take him to my consulting room and I'll meet you there, just have to go downstairs to my...," Doctor Perry hesitated, a corridor full of rheumy eyes following his every word. "I'll join you," he finished saying, swivelling on his polished heels and walking through the crowd of onlookers.

DOCTOR PERRY DIDN'T NOTICE the large Indian woman in the corridor. There was no reason for him to. Even if he had noticed her, he wouldn't have recognised her or spared her a moment's thought. Her milky eyes changing her into a different person from the girl she had once been, a long, long time ago.

"Our missing geriatrics, where are they?" queried Clive Jeffries. No answer came from the room, the heads in front of him bowed over hardcover notebooks and feet jiggled under chairs. "Anyone?" Clive tried again, his volume rising until he caught Gary and Tony exchange glances and Gary shrugging at Tony's raised eyebrows, as if to say, *you go*.

"Gary? You got something for us?"

Gary checked his notes before addressing the room which had brightened considerably once Clive pounced on someone else.

"We found that both men share the same doctor — a Doctor Perry, who has his clinic in Boynton Beach. He wasn't at his clinic, so we swung by his home. No sign of any missing grandfathers, but we found his wife there with a baby they're fostering."

Clive's brow furrowed, and he opened his mouth to interrupt but Tony continued the story.

"The wife didn't know the name of the Doc's receptionist, she thought it was Lily, but the nameplate on the desk at the clinic says Molly, and Molly looks the same age as my aunt, not the young woman Mrs Perry described. Then Gary got antsy about the car picking up the foster child — the wife said it was Social Services, so we ran the plates. And unless the Child Welfare ladies are borrowing cars from the Cavalletto Cartel, I don't believe it was Social Services ringing that doorbell. You could not make this stuff up," he concluded.

Clive's frown had turned into slack-jawed amazement.

"Have you two been helping yourselves to the drugs in the evidence locker?" he said, running his hands through his hair. "What the hell is going on here?"

"They've got twins there," Gary replied, as if that were the answer Clive needed.

"That's not a crime is it?" Emily Jesmond piped up from the back of the room.

"That's something we need to establish. Gary, check with the welfare people regarding Doctor Perry's status as a foster parent. I want to know how long he and his wife have been fostering in Florida, and how many kids they've fostered. And who adopted this last baby?"

"I understood we were looking for granddads, not grandkids. Shouldn't the priority be interviewing the doctor?" Emily asked.

Clive's rolled his fists into tight balls on the desk. Emily Jesmond would be the death of him or of his career.

"We are Emily, you and the rest of us too. But as you are more than aware, sometimes during an investigation, the evidence of other offences comes to light and we action that, Police 101. Your task will be to follow the Cavalletto angle, I'm adding that to your taskings."

Emily protested.

"And Emily, be careful, they can be pretty dirty to deal with," Clive said, satisfied he'd allocated her a line of enquiry to keep her busy and out of the way. The bloody Cavalletto Cartel, he doubted it. It was probably bad intelligence, a mixup with the plates or something. But that would be for Jesmond to work out. "We need to have a chat with Perry. He's the doctor of the missing men so out of anyone he'd have a better understanding of their mental wellbeing than their families."

"Yeah, well, we haven't been able to track him down yet. We went back to his surgery, and the receptionist said he was at the old folks home. That's the Rose Haven Retirement Resort, he has another clinic there. The receptionist at the Rose Haven said he was at work. His wife said he was visiting a patient. It's been lousy timing. He hasn't answered his cell either," Tony said.

"Bring him in for a chat, make that your priority," Clive directed. "Right, everyone else, we need statements from their friends. Ask around, they must have friends. Maybe try back at the Rose Haven, they could have some friends there. So everyone knows what they're doing then? Good?"

Dismissing his team, he checked his cellphone. His own mother hadn't rung him back. He supposed she was living it large with her elderly but socially active friends, he couldn't help but feel put out she hadn't bothered ringing him. If he'd thought about it a little deeper, he would have been able to draw parallels to how he'd treated her over the years, always too busy to give her more than a harried minute on the phone or an awkward family dinner where he couldn't wait to leave, too caught up in his own life to worry about her needs.

Clive wanted to call her back, but he had work to do. She'd call when she was ready.

41

Benson lowered Elijah into a high-backed chair in Doctor Perry's consulting room at the Rose Haven. It wasn't as comfortable as the Doctor's public consulting rooms because the patients he saw from the Rose Haven Retirement Resort didn't matter. They had no money and no choice. Doctor Perry provided care for almost ninety percent of the residents. The others still had medical insurance or a relationship with a former doctor they maintained. Doctor Perry had spoken with Tracey about making it a condition of living at the Rose Haven that every resident sign up to be on his patient books, but she'd refused the idea, considering it a step too far. He still thought it the best solution but had let it go for now. If he ever went back into this line of work, he'd definitely implement it at the next place. It made things tidier.

Doctor Perry arrived a short while later, and ushered Benson out of the room, before closing the door behind him. He sat on the desk in front of Elijah and stared at the other man.

They looked to be of a similar age, Doctor Perry and

Elijah Cone, but Doctor Perry's face was mostly smooth, although he'd allowed a few lines to peep through over time and had enough crinkle at the corners of his eyes for his patients to trust he knew his stuff. His cheeks sagged ever so slightly as if he'd once been fat and was waiting for his skin to regain its elasticity. His eyes were a deep blue and had the ability to charm, but tonight they showed nothing — only a blankness, as if the doctor was mere flesh with no soul, a walking cadaver.

Doctor Perry showed no emotion perched on the edge of the desk staring at Elijah, biding his time. Silence worked a treat and old people couldn't abide silence. It was as if they lived with the silence so much that they jumped at any opportunity to open their denture-filled mouths and share the minutiae of their lives. This man would be the same, he'd wait.

The room settled around them, the walls clicking in the cool night and from somewhere came the muffled sound of a phone ringing. Footsteps came closer, then receded. And still Elijah didn't speak.

The desk under Doctor Perry's backside was knifelike beneath his khakis and he leveraged himself off and around to the other side of his desk before sitting in his cushioned office chair. Concerned about the cooling experiments in the basement, he'd slipped back to the lab to turn everything off before coming to his consulting room. It shouldn't matter too much if the substance cooled as long as it didn't cool down completely. He needed to get back to this latest batch, and this patient wasn't playing by the rules. Time to get this over with.

"Mister Cone, you've caused a bit of disruption since coming to the Rose Haven. The staff are here to help you. To provide *you* the best twilight years. But you have to help yourself," Doctor Perry said.

Elijah had tucked his chin into his chest, lips pursed shut. Doctor Perry had forgotten all about Elijah's arthritis and didn't realise that it was all Elijah could do to stay upright in the chair; that even the smallest of movements sent slivers of glass through every joint and ligament in Elijah's hands.

Sighing, Doctor Perry pulled a prescription pad from his top drawer. He had none of his tonic available, none which he trusted, so the best he could do was to medicate the problematic man until he could dose him properly. He had no time for this carryon. Tracey needed to keep better control of her staff because he knew Preston caused the fracas, Cone just didn't have it in him. You only needed to look at Elijah to know he was broken.

"I'm not the enemy here Mister Cone, I'm your doctor and you can trust me. I've prescribed you a mild sedative. Benson is waiting outside and he'll take you to the nurses' station for them to dispense the drugs," said Doctor Perry.

"What about the tonic you gave me last time, can I have more of that?"

Doctor Perry froze, Without his patient folders, or Molly to schedule his appointments, he was flying blind. Had he given this man some of his tonic before? He looked anew at Elijah, how much had he given him? And from which batch?

"Did you feel any relief after taking it?" Doctor Perry asked.

"For a night, maybe a little longer," Elijah said.

Doctor Perry's shoulders slumped, and he shook his head. His tonic was losing its potency but he wouldn't waste any of it on this man, at least not without his notes to refer to. Didn't want to give him too much, and he needed his medical history - such an important part of the deal he had going with his other clients. Only healthy stock allowed.

He pulled open the door and waved the orderly inside. "Benson, this will tide Mister Cone over until I have had a proper chance to examine him, which will need scheduling, so if you could just…" Doctor Perry motioned towards Elijah, who hadn't moved.

"Of course, Doctor Perry," Benson said.

Doctor Perry strode off down the corridor, striking Elijah from his mind. He had an experiment to finish. That was his priority, not a man losing control of his mind.

BENSON STOOD in the doorway shaking his head at the Doctor's retreat. "Come on, Mister Cone, let's get you back to your room, and then I'll fill the script."

"Not sure I can go anywhere, Benson," Elijah winced.

"I'll get a wheelchair," Benson said, expecting Elijah to tell him to stop being so ridiculous, but Elijah didn't respond, other that to tuck his head further into his chest. It was as if the man was ageing in front of him. Sometimes it happened that way. When you worked with the elderly as long as he had, you could predict when they gave up on life. And that's what Elijah was doing.

42

Myra sat on the toilet, her eyes on the door handle, which she'd locked, but since the twins had been in the house, it didn't always engage and she didn't want any little blonde faces surprising her.

She wasn't using the toilet, instead she was making notes, getting her thoughts down on paper. She'd kept a record of the babies they'd fostered right from the beginning, and as she scratched against the paper it wasn't hard to notice she'd almost filled the notebook. Myra had given every child their own page and kept notes detailing their age, gender, disposition, likes and dislikes, in case anyone ever came back to ask about the baby they'd adopted. There was always a chance health questions might arise. They'd never fostered any children with health issues, only the last baby came to mind, baby Don with his funny sloping shoulder. Undoubtedly his new parents would get that seen to by an orthopaedic surgeon.

Myra's heart ached with the loss of Don. He'd been her dream baby and her heart broke handing him over to

Social Services. Her husband said nothing about the child. He hadn't even noticed that the baby had gone. He'd spent increasingly more time at the Rose Haven doing who knows what, but there was one thing she knew, her husband had stopped coming to bed. And when he looked at her, it was with such a level of disgust on his face she assumed he was having an affair which didn't bother her as much as she expected. He hadn't given her the one thing she wanted, so losing him was no big deal. They were financially comfortable, so she knew she wouldn't want for anything if, when, he left her. The worst part was she was too old to have a baby herself or even adopt one on her own. She'd wasted the best years of her life raising babies for other people.

Tears stung Myra's eye as she noted everything she could remember about baby Don and as an afterthought, she made detailed notes of the handover. She hadn't thought to do that before as her husband dealt with that part. She'd been there in the past, but mostly she was upstairs in the nursery, crying at the loss of yet another baby she loved.

Someone knocked on the bathroom door.

"I'll just be a minute," she said, her voice cracking. Myra shoved the tattered notebook into her toiletries bag, the old one she kept her sanitary towels and tampons in. She knew her husband wouldn't look in there but still left the zip open so anyone rummaging through would see an array of industrial looking tampons staring back and back off.

"Can we have something to eat," came a voice from behind the door.

"Please?" added an identical voice.

Myra expected they were standing side by side outside the door, their features set in the same expressionless way. Staying in the bathroom was more appealing.

The boys knocked a second time.

"We can't hear you peeing. Are you really going to the toilet?"

"Are you hiding from us?"

Myra swallowed. She was hiding from them. The boys scared her.

"No, I'm not hiding from you. I've just finished, see," she said flushing the toilet. Then ran the taps and washed her hands vigorously. Anything to delay having to interact with the boys for any longer than she needed.

Drying her hands, she examined her face in the mirror. The signs of advancing age were coming thick and fast. She didn't blame her husband for looking elsewhere, her face was a route map to the nearest interchange with a dozen different lines crisscrossing her face. Her forehead more like the Golden Glades Interchange. She traced the lines with her fingertip. Her skin felt soft and supple, but looked wrinkled and old.

They knocked on the door, again.

They might need her but the feeling persisted that something wasn't right about the twins.

WITH THE BOYS devouring slices of peeled apple and a blueberry muffin at the kitchen bench, Myra unpacked the dishwasher and dried the stuff the dishwasher hadn't, almost half the load. She looked out over the garden which formed the boundary of her world these days. When they'd first married, they'd go for long walks around Amelia Earhart Park, and eat out at the Garcia Seafood Grille, but it was years since they'd done that.

Once they'd established the medical practice, and started fostering babies, her life shrank into the reclusive situation she found herself in now. As she dried the dishes, seeking refuge in old memories, her eyes swept across the garden, pausing now and then as she added things to her *to do* list — prune the *Spiral Ginger* and check the *Crinum Lily* for rust spots. It wasn't one of her favourite flowers but not long after their wedding, her husband had edged the whole garden with them. In some light they looked beautiful, but the red centres looked as though the lilies were slicked with blood. She preferred its official name instead of what the locals called it — the *cemetery plant*. Myra was oblivious to how poisonous the lily was.

Myra's eyes moved on from the glorious display of lilies and passed over a small mound in the grass. They flicked back. The object on the grass made no sense, it didn't belong. Laying down the tea towel she opened the back door and stepped onto the manicured lawn.

On the grass was the carcass of a cat, or what used to be a cat. Unmoving. the ginger tomcat lay motionless with its paws oddly unattached to its body, as if it had taken off a pair of gloves, laying them neatly on the ground. Myra stopped breathing. The feisty cat had been with her for fifteen years. He'd comforted her, given her joy and kept her company on the long days at home. And now she was alone.

Myra threw herself beside the motionless animal and a scream escaped from her throat. Bundling the cat up into her arms as if that would reanimate it, oblivious to the faces pressing against the kitchen window, a smear of ketchup under the fingers of one boy.

The garden filled with ragged sobs and the metallic scent of blood as Myra stumbled to her feet, the tomcat limp in her arms, Myra's grief blocking out the mutilation — the horror of that would come later.

From the bushes, a rat scuttled from its hiding place and faster than lightning it stole one of the cat's paws, hurrying away with its prize before anyone else saw. Before it too became a living specimen to be experimented on.

The eyes at the kitchen window saw the rat though. They saw the rat and nodding to each other they hurried back to their seats at the kitchen bench, staring at Myra as she reentered the house, inconsolable with her grief. She disappeared down the hall, into the garage where the door closed behind her, cutting off the crying which filled the unusual silence the twins created wherever they were.

Alone in the garage, Myra laid the tomcat gently on the laundry bench, her mind refusing to process what was in front of her. Wiping her eyes on her sleeves, Myra searched the shelves for a suitable box for her dear old friend.

The shelves featured an assortment of gardening supplies, suitcases and a lifetime collection of containers, boxes and bottles — the detritus of the things her husband had owned before their marriage.

Myra viewed everything through a veil of tears, blurring the names on the containers as she searched for a box for Tom's burial. Despite the tears, her desire for order overwhelmed her and as she searched the shelves she couldn't help but stack the boxes in height order and twist bottles till their labels lined up. Myra picked up an ancient bag of powder, so old the label had worn away, and refolded the bag's top releasing a plume of white powder as she replaced in on the shelf. A fine dusting of powder settled on the floor.

Myra spied a perfect sized box jammed in behind a rusty tin of infant formula and an assorted lot of car windscreen cleaners and upholstery polish. As she reached through the jumble, Myra knocked the formula tin, tipping it off the shelf and onto the concrete floor. The tin landed with a deafening crack and the lid flew off, spilling the contents out onto the oil-stained floor, hundreds of tiny white pebbles.

Myra scooped the mess back into the tin, cursing her husband for storing such random trash. She cursed her life and the loss of her beloved pet. All she wanted to do was bury him and now she had to clean up another mess, someone else's mess. This was her life, cleaning up after other people.

"Myra?"

Myra looked up to see the twins framed in the doorway.

"We're still hungry. Can we have something else to eat?"

"Please?"

"Not now, please go away, just go away," she yelled, and the boys vanished.

Myra sank to the garage floor, crying among the detritus of the one room in the house she had nothing to do with. There was never any reason for her to come out here. She never used the car. Never needed to use the stuff stored in the garage. Like the surgery, this was her husband's domain.

Her responsibilities overcame her, and she wiped away the tears, shoving the remaining pebbles back into the tin, jamming the lid on tight and placing it back onto the shelf. She carried the cardboard box over to the bench, placing it next to old Tom. He wasn't a small animal, he was the sort of cat you needed two hands to pick up or risk breaking your wrist if you only used one, but now he looked small, diminished. As she scooped him up and nuzzled his ginger fur one last time, his leg fell loose from her arms and the reality of his injuries struck home.

The world stilled and her heart thumped in her ears drowning out every other sound. Outside, the crickets put aside their chirping, and the birds muzzled their song and the twins huddled together in their room, their communication as silent as it always had been. She knew.

43

Snot dripped from Sarah Miller's nose. She'd run out of tissues, so used the crusty sleeve of her sweater, a sweater stained with ketchup, pizza oil and several days' worth of tears as she hibernated on the couch.

The doorbell chimed, and for a fraction of a second, Sarah thought he'd come back, before the tinny voice of her doctor echoed through the intercom. The euphoric lift to her mood popped like a balloon on a thorny cactus and tore a fraction more at her damaged heart.

Sarah struggled off the couch to let the doctor in. Hopefully, he'd come with more medicine because she imagined the infection in her lungs trying to take hold again. And then, as if the infection heard her thoughts, her chest spasmed triggering another coughing fit.

Doctor Perry came in just in time to support her, as she doubled over next to the intercom, coughing up her lungs. She should give him the entry code, having to get up off the couch to let him in was far too tiring.

"Now, now, we can't have you hopping up and down, back to the couch," Doctor Perry said and pushed through the mountain of home delivery takeaway cartons, easing her onto the couch.

DOCTOR PERRY TRIED NOT to consider the state of Sarah's arteries as his stomach twisted at the sight of the empty soda cans in the bin and the takeaway filth littering her apartment. He held back the recriminations as he should have taken better care of her because she had no one else. He had too much on his plate at this late juncture. You had to take the good with the bad, and he hoped there was no irreparable damage. Fast food delivery companies would be the death of America if the trash littering Sarah's apartment was any sign.

He assessed the woman on the couch, she wasn't a pretty sight. He appreciated her illness, but he'd expected some improvement in her physical state. The furrows on her forehead looked deeper than they had the last time he saw her. Her lips looked like smokers lips — fine lines splayed out around her mouth, not the slightest bit attractive. And her cheeks, sunken and sallow, dropping like the beer gut on Homer Simpson. Unease crawled over him. *Was his formula losing its effectiveness?* He didn't want to believe it but the evidence pointed that way. Maybe a larger dose was the answer? He needed to get her out of here and to his surgery, or to the lab, somewhere where no one could hear her, although from what he'd seen of this place, a woman screaming wouldn't bring the emergency services running. No one would interfere, not in a place like this, somewhere abandoned by the civic authorities, ignored by town planners. Owned by parasitic landlords for profit and profit only. Dosing her here would be easier...

Doctor Perry cleared a space on the cluttered counter, ignoring the cockroach who scuttled out from under the trash and disappeared over the side of the kitchen cabinets. He searched the cupboards for a clean glass, choosing a Hard Rock Cafe souvenir glass at the back, and then pulled his tonic bottle from his battered leather doctor's bag,

Normally his doses were based on his patient's weight and wellbeing but time was running out. The walls were closing in on him. He could just leave Sarah Miller to succumb to her illness with no one any the wiser. The idea appealed but moving to a new state with a new identity was costly and lately his clients had been more pushy, more demanding, so the pressure was on to deliver. Adding Sarah Miller to his list might relieve the pressure, keep the wolves from his door a little longer, until he left.

Satisfied he'd made the right choice, he poured a liberal dose into the tacky souvenir glass. More than he'd poured for old Johnny Paulson from the retirement home, who, even though he'd only been skin and bones, required more than he should have. Paulson was the first one he'd messed up for a long time. An utter waste of tonic and disposing of him had been costly. Doctor Perry tried not to think about the mess it'd made in the surgery. He'd spent hours cleaning it up, and his clients weren't happy getting involved in that side of things. His formula was failing.

Doctor Perry carried the glass to Sarah, who resembled an opioid addict awaiting her next hit. Eager eyes and hands outstretched, she grabbed for the glass but Doctor Perry held on a moment longer.

"Now Sarah, this dosage is stronger than what I gave you last time, you need to understand that the side effects *might* be uncomfortable. Do you understand?" he asked, emphasising the word *might*. He knew full well what the side effects were. Her pain didn't bother him, only the potential noise she might make.

Sarah nodded, salivating at the sight of the milky liquid in the souvenir glass.

"Small sips then, Sarah," he directed, and as he loosened his grip on the glass, the doorbell rang and an unfamiliar voice shot out of the intercom.

"Sarah? Sarah, it's me, Gary."

If Sarah had resembled a drug addict in the late stages of withdrawal before, now she looked like a prima donna on a stage. At the sound of the man's voice, her face lit up, breaking into a beaming smile, her shoulders straightened and she glowed.

"It's Gary," Sarah gushed.

Doctor Perry snatched the glass out of Sarah's hand. He didn't care who Gary was but whoever he was he didn't want any questions being asked about his tonic or his treatment of his patient. An annoying interruption to his plans, to his delivery schedule. He preferred patients with no encumbrances — no family, no friends, no interferences.

He fumbled as he tried pouring the tonic back into its bottle, every drop was valuable since making more was becoming difficult.

The intercom squawked into life again.

"Sarah, please let me in. We need to speak. I'm sorry and I'm worried."

"Could you let him in please, Doctor?" Sarah wheezed, her lungs irritated by the sudden increase of her heart rate.

Doctor Perry ignored her, his mind racing ahead. It paid to prepare for all eventualities but for the moment he struggled to find a solution. He'd have to let him in and then leave. And abandon Sarah, which was a shame but sometimes you had to cut your losses and this was one of those times. It was probably for the best, the illness had weakened her lungs and his tonic had made no difference. She wasn't the best candidate for what his clients wanted. His line of work had been much easier in the days before technology. With so much connectivity in the world, finding patients who were truly alone was near impossible.

Snapping shut his leather bag, he pressed the intercom button. Turning to gaze at Sarah, he shook his head. Such a waste.

"I'll going now, Sarah," Doctor Perry said. "I'm sure your visitor can take care of you from here."

Sarah pushed herself up off the couch. "No, you have to stay, to tell him how sick I am, he won't believe me otherwise. He always accuses me of exaggerating, of being a hypochondriac. That's one reason we broke up, and if you don't tell him how sick I have been, he'll walk out again, I know it," Sarah said. "Please?" she begged.

Doctor Perry stepped over the door, and arranging the right words in his mind, he opened the door.

"Sarah—" said the man at the door before recognising Sarah hadn't opened the door.

Doctor Perry stepped back to allow Gary into Sarah's apartment.

"Hello Gary," Sarah said.

"Sarah, are you okay?"

"I'm fine, well I'm not fine, I've been very sick—"

Gary interrupted and Sarah shushed him. "But before you say anything, Doctor—"

At this, Doctor Perry himself interrupted. "I'm Sarah's doctor and can confirm that she has been suffering from pneumonia. She's recovering well so you're welcome to stay and help her. This will be my last house call. She'll need a check up in another week. You can do that at your local medical centre. She needs rest and good food. I'll be off, more clients to see."

Sarah tried protesting but a coughing fit took hold. And without a backwards glance, Doctor Perry slipped out the door and vanished down the emergency stairwell, not trusting that the elevator would turn up in time to remove him from the premises before Gary questioned him any further.

Locking himself in his sedan, he chanced a look up at Sarah's apartment window. As he suspected, Gary was standing at the window looking down. That wasn't good, not good at all.

Doctor Perry turned his car key and fighting the urge to gun the engine and drive away as fast as he could, he pulled out from the curb and drove off, never once looking back.

GARY WATCHED the sedan disappear round the corner, his gut humming with vague distrust. There was something off about the man, his manner, his flight from Sarah's apartment, he couldn't place a finger on it.

Sarah's coughing behind him broke the spell, and he turned away from the window, cringing at how he'd treated Sarah. He'd thought he was doing the best thing for them both by breaking if off but hell he'd missed her. Their long conversations on the most inconsequential things, walks through the park, ducking under trees and laughing at the crush of humanity sharing the world with them. It had been on his morning walk he realised why he felt low, he was missing Sarah and her weird and wonderful ways. He'd never get used to the smell of incense or the random meals she cooked, and how she blew small things up into giant mountains, but mostly he loved her, hence why he was here.

Gary rubbed Sarah's back until her coughing eased. He wasn't a doctor but even he could hear the rattle in her chest as she fought to control the spasming in her lungs.

"I don't think the doctor knows what he's talking about," Gary said, searching for a glass of water for Sarah.

"He's been great. I should have gone earlier, but I didn't realise how bad things were until it was too late, so I went to the closest clinic I could find online. Doctor Perry has looked after me well," Sarah wheezed.

"Doctor who?" Gary asked, his face a picture of surprise.

"Doctor Perry. You know I don't go to the doctor's, can't stand them being under the thumb of the big pharmaceutical companies, but he's not like the rest. His remedies are natural. He's been treating me with—"

"Sorry, but did you say Doctor Perry? So that was Doctor Perry just now? In your apartment?"

Sarah's eyes widened, "Yes, why?"

Gary's mind raced. He'd just met the man they were trying to interview. He'd been in the same room as him and he hadn't even realised. Admittedly, the man wasn't a suspect, so no one had bothered pulling up a photo of him but still.

"Will you be okay on your own for a while? I promise I'll be back soon. I have to shoot into work, there are a couple of things I need to sort out," Gary asked.

He washed out a Hard Rock Cafe glass he found on the kitchen bench. God knows what Sarah had been drinking out of that but whatever it was, the milky liquid clung to the sides of the tall glass and he had to use the sponge to wash it out before refilling it with fresh water.

Placing the glass on the table next to Sarah, he took her hands in his.

"I'm sorry for not calling, I am and I promise I will be back. I'm going into work, then I'll swing past the grocery store and buy you all the things you need. You stay here and sleep. He was right when he said you need to rest, but I don't think Doctor Perry is the right doctor for you. Promise me you won't see him again?"

Sarah tried protesting but lost herself in Gary's concerned eyes, eyes she'd dreamt about night after night. It was enough he was back, so she didn't want to upset him, but Doctor Perry was a good doctor and his tonic made her feel better. And she wanted to feel better now that Gary was back, for him. She smiled at him but in the back of her mind she was planning to ring Doctor Perry's office for an appointment to see him again. Gary deserved to have the healthy her.

44

Pauline stamped about in the kitchen, a small radio blaring out hits from the eighties. Normally the radio soothed her fiery temper but not today. Today she'd turned up at work at the crack of dawn, to find a note in the kitchen saying her budget was cut by a further five percent and that she had to find the savings by the end of the month. *Five percent.* She was bloody livid. No consultation, no discussion, it was a crime and without a doubt she'd be blamed for the rubbish food by the residents. The menu was already as lean as she could make it without putting everyone on a starvation diet. This was the worst place she'd ever worked at, with no humanity at the top. If management worked out a way to feed the residents remotely, like a cat feeder, they would.

Her mood deteriorated even more when after her weekly stocktake of the cupboards, she found some key ingredients depleted far beyond her expectations.

"Shit and bloody hell, who's been in here?"

Someone had been buggering around in her cupboards but Pauline couldn't imagine who'd want to steal any of the substandard ingredients they made her cook with, although *cook* was a loose enough term for what she did.

"Jesus bloody well wept, didn't he, eh?" she ranted, slamming cupboards and crashing drawers until she flopped into a chair. She flipped through her tattered recipe book trying to find something to cobble together for the lunch prep. She'd sorted breakfast, but for some residents, lunch was their main meal so it needed to be substantial.

Turning the pages, her frustration grew as she calculated how many recipes she'd had to ditch with all the budget cuts. More than half the recipes she'd started with were no longer practical because she couldn't buy in the ingredients she needed for the money she had. She'd quit and fly back home to her Mam if she didn't need the money this job gave her. Too old to start again now, no one would have her, not even the useless jazz-playing husband she'd followed here, to the end of the world. He was a player, no question. He'd played the bars round where she lived, touting himself and his band as the biggest thing since the Beatles. She'd fallen head over arse and then like a twit, had married the unfaithful bastard and gave up her life to follow him to America. She'd followed him round all the bars here too, she was being played as well.

As Pauline wallowed in her own private pity party, Benson's notes fluttered onto the floor at the same time as Bart Stubbs wandered into the kitchen.

"Any food going, Pauline?" he asked, leaning against the giant chiller, fiddling with a crumpled packet of cigarettes.

"You ain't smoking in here and get your filthy behind off my fridge," Pauline admonished, shooing him away from the gleaming white beast. Pauline kept it immaculate as she did everything in the kitchen. She had pride in her work and her workspace, unlike Stubbs - a filthy mess, a walking cesspit of disease for sure.

"Calm yourself, I only asked for something to eat, wasn't trying to get in your pants."

Pauline sniffed, it wasn't worthy of a reply. She opened the fridge and pulled out a plate of yesterday's brownies. Made with half the sugar the recipe said but still okay. She'd warm them through and they'd do for dessert.

"Here you are," and she tossed one to Bart, to keep him happy and quiet. From experience, that was the best way to treat him.

Between fiddling with his cigarette packet, and itching at the rash he'd developed on his upper thighs, he missed the brownie and it hit the floor next to the paperwork Pauline had forgotten to pick up.

They both went for the papers, heads colliding. Bart snatched them from Pauline's hands.

"Eh, you give them back Bart Stubbs. They're none of your business," Pauline said, trying to control the panic in her voice. When stressed, her accent grew stronger, making her unintelligible to the Americans.

"Don't look much like kitchen stuff," Bart said. He might have a job but he didn't get it through being able to read anything beyond primary level. He squinted at the tiny writing he knew to be Tala's. "Why have you got Tala's paperwork?"

Pauline replied, "They're notes about the dietary requirements of the patients, information I need to do my job. Gimme back them bloody papers and get on with your own bleeding job. Take another brownie and I'll clean up the mess you made. As if I don't have enough to do without having to clean up behind you lot, eh?"

Bart kept running his eyes over the words in front of him. Pauline suspected he couldn't even read half the words on the page. He threw the paperwork onto the table and snatched up two brownies, shoving a third one into his mouth.

Pauline kept her thoughts to herself, it wasn't worth antagonising the man, and she watched him leave the kitchen, a trail of crumbs in his wake. She swore under her breath and folded up the papers Benson and Tala had left in her safekeeping. That was too close for comfort. Searching around the kitchen, she settled upon the drawer where she kept her baking paraphernalia and slipped the papers under the rolls of foil and baking paper and turned her mind back to the problem of the missing ingredients. She didn't for the slightest moment consider that Bart Stubbs was responsible. He didn't have the skills to use the ingredients for cooking, being more a takeaway for dinner every night guy, plus he ate at the Rose Haven for the free food. Had been for years, skiving off work to grab a plate of free grub. He was a freeloader, not a thief. No, it was someone else.

She didn't have time to deal with it now, there was breakfast to serve and the lunch to prepare. After that she'd think on it, but bugger her if it didn't prey on her mind. What if Tracey accused her of stealing? She couldn't afford to lose her job, not now.

During breakfast, the dining room was filled with quiet apprehension. The empty chairs in the room did nothing to improve the overall vibe. Several residents hadn't made it to breakfast today.

The Rose Haven Retirement Resort was one of those rest homes which tried to pretend its residents didn't die, quietly ushering the bodies of the deceased out the back, away from the curious eyes. Pauline presumed that's what had happened. She bussed to work every day, so had no reason to go out the back. Apart from one old codger who'd died during lunch, she had nothing to do with the residents once they died.

Pauline was worried about one resident who hadn't made it down to breakfast - Muriel Lincoln, originally a Northerner like her. Muriel had been living in America since she'd come here as a teenage bride on the arm of an American soldier at the end of the war. Ancient and well past her use-by date, but still in fine fettle at breakfast the day before and Pauline looked forward to their daily chats. It was a small spark of home in a foreign land, despite neither of them having lived in England for too many years to count.

"Where's Muriel today?" she asked the nearest orderly.

"Did my job title change to Social Coordinator?" he replied, scratching at his arm. "Check out back, could be as stiff as a board waiting to be toasted with the rest of the wrinkly's out there stinking up the place."

Pauline would have slapped him but there was a strange sheen to his skin and something in his eye which stayed her hand. Not that she really would've hit him, she'd have lost her job if she had, but before the temptation consumed her, she stepped back. He wouldn't last long this one. Working with the elderly wasn't for the fainthearted and it had taken her a good few years to become comfortable herself. It was a hard slog, and you needed buckets of patience, compassion and empathy. This guy had none of that.

"You keep your voice down laddie, and don't talk that way about the residents," Pauline said.

"Whatever," the young man replied, before snaking around her and making his way to the other side of the dining room, ignoring John Gallows who'd knocked over his walking stick and was struggling to reach it.

Pauline watched the orderly making a rude gesture

with his fingers before leaving the dining room. She made her way over to the fallen stick and leaned it up against the table. "He's an idiot," she said to John, the owner of the silver-tipped walking stick. "Not picking he'll last long, doesn't have the balls to stick it out," she said, laughing at her own pun.

"He's not right that one," John replied, leveraging himself up with his cane. "Keep an eye on him, Pauline. He's got a problem, can tell from a mile off. He's as rotten as that bully Preston."

Pauline nodded. John's words gave her food for thought. Still it wasn't her battle, better keeping her nose out of things that didn't concern her. There were bigger things to worry about, like her old Mam and keeping a roof over her head. She'd keep an eye on things but she'd promised herself she wouldn't get involved, otherwise things could start getting messy.

Sulia retrieved the bottle hidden behind the curtain and a waterfall of desiccated moth carcasses fluttered to the floor, disturbed from their resting place.

Taking a sip, she stared out the window. Her cloudy eyes picking out the scurrying people living their lives, rushing off to appointments, pretending to be busy. Correction; imagining they were busy, caught up in the vicious treadmill of a capitalistic life. After school activities, gym memberships, chiropractor appointments, sessions with a counsellor. Being busy was a modern day plague. A vampiric drain on society. She'd been there herself. She'd lost her way, following the crowd, desperate to fit in, changing shape to fit the mould society brainwashed them to believe they needed to be in to win. To win what? Sulia realised life wasn't a race. They were all racing towards a finish line hidden under a blanket of lies. As she herself now lied to the world, and she wasn't sure how much longer she could carry on.

The bottle was almost empty, so she took the smallest of sips. In the beginning, she'd craved a never-ending supply of the stuff but now she'd outlived anyone she'd ever loved. There'd been so many funerals, and countless tears, that now she wanted it to end, but still she sipped from the magic bottle. She'd spent years finding her way to the Rose Haven, to Doctor Perry, and now she'd tracked him down, he was going to pay for what he'd done. Retribution would be hers.

Sulia fiddled with the contacts in her eyes. Now and then they bothered her, but she'd nearly finished with them. They made navigating the retirement home difficult, its bland décor blending into one, but she was sure the residents believed she was blind, which made her job that much easier. Twisting the lid on the bottle, she put it back behind the curtain before she took more than one sip. It wouldn't last forever, but she'd thought that about Doctor Perry too. Yet here he was, still alive after all these years as though time stood still for him, his face untouched by life.

She sat in her armchair waiting for the tonic to kick in. It always made her a little unsteady as her body adjusted to the toxins flowing through her bloodstream. She imagined they were toxins, but really had no idea what Perry's concoction contained other than she knew it was the work of the devil, or that Doctor Perry was the devil himself. Her skin crawled as tiny lines softened and evened out. Broken surface veins brightened and disappeared. Sulia struggled to keep her mouth shut as the roots of her old teeth burrowed deeper into her jaw, the pain unbearable but she knew for another month at least she'd be able to enjoy the foods she couldn't chew as she got older and her teeth loosened. Her muscles contracted, regaining the elasticity gravity denied them. She was always careful with how much she drank because if she had even one sip too much the changes in her would be too noticeable, and at the Rose Haven, she couldn't hide in her room for months, conducting her life through online ordering and a parade of ever-changing couriers.

Sulia waited as the changes slowly altered her body, she'd sleep afterwards, she always did, waking refreshed in a body two or three years younger than it should be. She wouldn't need to keep doing this now she'd found Doctor Perry. She was going to ensure he took a dose of his own medicine just like he'd dosed her mother, a woman too scared to go to a *real* doctor with her health complaints. Instead she'd gone to a little clinic in the deepest depths of inner Chicago, a place where no one asked too many questions, where most of the patients couldn't pay the full bill. She'd been with her mother that day, and Sulia had found a pile of children's books in the corner, more books than they'd had in their home. She sat silently reading when the receptionist showed her mother, the last patient of the day, through to the doctor's room, to Doctor Perry's consulting room. When the preoccupied receptionist left for the evening, she never noticed Sulia asleep in the corner, hidden behind a potted palm. Sulia couldn't have said how long she'd been there before screaming woke her from an uncomfortable sleep on the floor. She remembered she was waiting for her mother until realising it was her mother screaming. Sulia had crept to the doctor's door and turning the handle she'd peeked through the crack, too afraid to get any closer.

Sulia's legs twitched involuntarily, as the tonic made its way down her body and as she dredged up the memories which sustained her along with Doctor Perry's tonic. Through her childish eyes she'd watched a man in a white coat standing over her mother. She remembered how the deep brown leather of the bed absorbed her mother. But the bed wasn't absorbing her mother, her mother was shrinking into the bed, screaming as she morphed from being a grown woman to the height of a young teenager, to that of a child, then a toddler, until she was nothing more than a mewling baby. But it hadn't stopped there. Sulia recalled the doctor leaning over the tiny creature and administering one more drop of liquid. Sulia tried so hard to forget what happened next. The baby folded in on itself, imploding until only a gelatinous goop remained, writhing with the mess of intestinal worms which had caused her mother's discomfort. The reason for their visit.

What came next was a blur. She couldn't unlock the surgery door to escape, so had hidden behind the receptionist's desk until the doctor left. Her mother's cavernous handbag remained unnoticed, wedged under the doctor's desk. She couldn't have said why she'd taken the bottles lining a shelf in the doctor's office, but she'd stuffed them into her mother's bag, and had kept them with her all these years until she was old enough to work out the potency of the contents.

Too traumatised to do anything else, Sulia had slept curled up in a chair, scarpering as fast as a rabbit when the receptionist unlocked the door the next morning. The startled receptionist hadn't chased her, leaving Sulia to find her way home to an empty apartment and a lifetime of foster homes, burdened by her mother's handbag. She'd told no one what had happened to her mother, who would have believed her?

And like that moment so many years ago, Sulia slept. The sweet dreamless sleep of someone who'd spent her life with only one goal, a goal she was about to reach.

Ricky Donovan pushed the trolley through the long corridors of the Rose Haven, stopping periodically to dispense the teeny tiny medicine cups to the oldies. Normally there had to be two staff. There were *always* two staff on the dispensing cart. Can't trust the staff with the drugs, oh no, the staff absolutely categorically cannot be trusted to be alone with the drugs. Who knows what might happen? Stuff might go missing? Or the residents might be given the wrong medications and they might die, or worse, they might get sick and then people might find out they were given the wrong pills instead of just dying as old crinkly wastes of oxygen.

But tonight he, Ricky Donovan, was in charge of the medicine cart *all by himself.* Too many people had called in sick. And being Tracey's nephew, her very special favourite only nephew, he was trustworthy. Oh yes.

Pushing the cart off on its own down the hall, Ricky patted his trouser pockets affectionately. He was operating under a 'one for you and one for me' rule tonight and had amassed a huge number of pills. Party time at Ricky's house tonight. Some pills were enormous, and different colours. He was thinking of keeping the pretty ones, and trading the others for more stuff to fill his special pipe. Hadn't quite decided.

The medicine cart crashed into the wall, scattering the dozen remaining pill cups onto the floor. Paralysed momentarily, Ricky rushed forward and scooped them up off the floor.

> Eeny, meeny, miny, moe.
> Catch an old fart by the toe.
> One pill for Ricky and one pill to go.
> Eeny, meeny, miny, moe.

Singing to himself, he refilled the medicine cups until they looked about the same, and shoved another handful of pills into his bulging pockets.

> Eeny, meeny, miny, moe.
> Ricky is a chipmunk don't you know.
> All the pills for Ricky and no more pills
> for you.
> Eeny, meeny, miny, moe.

Satisfied with his work reallocating the tablets, he handed out the last of the medicine cups and left the trolley outside the room of his last delivery. Someone else would put it away. He, Ricky, was far too important, Besides, thinking about the pills in his pockets had given him an exceptionally important idea. A stupendously excellent idea involving the laboratory downstairs, the one where he'd seen the doctor magicking up… well, he didn't know what, but he could probably sell it, whatever it was, but that was a plan for another day. Tonight though, tonight he had all these pills, and he would keep them, or trade them, or keep them, he still wasn't sure, but now he was certain that his newest idea was the best one. He could use the doctor's laboratory — such a big word that, such an important place. A place where magic happened. Laboratories made pills, and if pills were made, they could be unmade. He could turn them into liquid and then he could put that in his special pipe, and he wouldn't have to worry about anything going wrong, because he was going to do it in a proper lab. He just needed his special pipe.

Ricky fair skipped down the corridor to grab his pipe from his car. Finishing his shift never crossed his mind. Nor did the consequences of what he'd just done. Someone else would deal with that.

When the detectives reconvened, the atmosphere in the briefing room was far removed from the heavy sense of nowhere from the last time they'd met. Half the officers looked like they'd won the lottery such was their eagerness to share their intel.

"Settle down, everyone. It's obvious you've made headway with our missing octogenarians. Whilst it'd be nice to hear you'd found our two wandering souls, I'm not getting the sense we're there yet? Am I right?" asked Clive.

A flurry of nods greeted his words. Pulling the lid off the marker pen he waited for one of his team to talk.

"I met Doctor Perry," Gary announced, and every eye in the room swivelled round to face him.

"You didn't want to give us a heads up straight away?" Clive asked.

"It was complicated. I had a few things going on," Gary mumbled. The team knew about his on/off relationship so he didn't need to go into any further details.

Clive shook his head at the front of the briefing room. He thought the doctor would be a dead end, but at this point in the investigation he was prepared to follow any lead, even the most ridiculous ones.

"Did your *brief encounter* with the doctor deliver any insights into our two missing persons?"

This time Gary shook his head.

"Moving on then, you can fill me in later. Right, anyone else got something more tangible to add?"

Emily Jesmond put her hand up, filling the team in about other reported crime which might be of interest. A mundane list most suburban cops knew well — disputes over tree branches, spousal abuse, weed smoking teens, excessive noise, car accidents. Nothing stood out until Emily mentioned an accident where a mother and her baby had died across the road from the Rose Haven Retirement Resort in an avalanche of bad luck.

"She was walking to school, along her usual route, but it was just bad timing all round. God knows why no one picked the stroller up. Poor baby."

"What about the child walking with her?" Clive asked.

"What child?" Emily replied, head cocked to one side.

"You said she was walking a child to school, what happened to the child?"

Flustered, Emily flicked back and forward through her notes, coming up with nothing. She shrugged.

"I don't know."

"You know what your next job is don't you?" Clive said, making a note on the board. The missing child wasn't a complication he needed, it was the worst development. He'd rather have a gunman on the loose than a missing child. Not for the first time did he think how much easier his life would have been if he'd just followed his father into the printing business instead of joining the police. Too late now.

He glanced towards Emily, burrowing into her jacket

and studying her notepad mortified she'd missed something so clear. If the woman run over by the car was on her way to school, then where was the school aged child?

It wasn't till everyone had left the briefing room that Clive realised Emily hadn't mentioned the Cavalletto link, so he still didn't know who'd picked the baby up from Doctor Perry's house. Of all the things he'd asked her to do, it was the simplest of tasks. Even a monkey could do it. And now she'd complicated his life a thousand times more than it needed to be by running traffic accident statistics into his investigation into two missing people. At this rate he'd need to see a doctor because he swore his arteries were hardening or he had the beginnings of an aneurism bubbling away, all because of the stress caused by idiots who didn't do their jobs.

EMILY COULDN'T HELP THINKING she was the naughty one, sitting in a stern high backed chair outside the principal's office. She hadn't made an appointment and the school principal was in a *very important* meeting according to his receptionist. Why were school receptionists cut from the same cloth? For the main part, childless, stern, bedecked in the most sensible of clothes and lacking in personality. Nothing had changed since she was at school. It was as if the universe had a production line allocating the most child unfriendly employees to every school the world over. She thanked her lucky stars she'd chosen a child-free life, missing the hypocrisy of her sweeping judgement.

"Principal Griffin is available now," the receptionist advised Emily, opening the faux mahogany door and ushering her through.

The principal was far from the typical principal mould and Emily paused, confused about whether she was meeting with the principal or with someone who'd climbed in through the office window of a school principal and was doing a poor impression of one.

"Good morning, Detective Jesmond, sorry for the wait but I was on a conference call regarding how the recent funding changes will affect us here. Sudden funding changes can be catastrophic for schools like ours, I'm sure you understand," said Trivelle Griffin, the principal of Crystal Lakes Elementary.

Emily was still coming to terms with the sight of a full head of dreadlocks and basketball boots, mixed in with khaki pants and an open neck shirt and had no words to answer him.

The principal watched her, his hands steepled on his desk as she flipped through her notepad, before clearing her throat, colour infusing her cheeks.

"You will have heard about the unfortunate accident down the road earlier this week and, well, and I understand she was a mother from this school and I'm here to check on the welfare of her child, who I presume is still away from school..." she tapered off.

Griffin seemed to weigh his words carefully before answering. "I'd heard about the accident. That intersection has concerned us for some time. You need to understand that we have a transient roll Detective Jesmond. Families come and families go, often with little or no notice. My team can't always follow up on truants. Do you have the name of the mother?"

"There's a small problem with that, she didn't have any ID, hence my question about children who have been absent from school. We haven't been able to contact any next of kin and a bystander said she was a mother from your school, so…"

Griffin's fingers flew across his keyboard, his dreads bobbing in time with his energetic typing. "Can you tell me her ethnicity?" he asked, before stabbing the enter button. A printer whirled into life behind his desk. He ignored the piece of paper the printer spat out, instead casting his eyes over Emily's pen poised above her notebook.

"Will you be requisitioning this information officially?" he asked.

"Eh?"

"I'm not new at this, Ms. Jesmond. I like my paperwork to be correct in every way and I have the information you need, but my main priority is the welfare of the children at this school, you need to understand that."

Emily nodded, confusion clouding her face.

"I have twenty three children absent all week and I'm sure you understand when I need to see a request in writing before I can give you those names?"

Emily swallowed her frustration. What an idiot, she was trying to help his kids.

"Fine," she said through clenched teeth. "I'll email something through, does that work for you?"

Griffin passed over the sheet of paper.

Emily's eyes absorbed the scant information, names marching down the page one after the other.

"Which one do you think is most likely to be the child of our deceased woman and her baby?"

"Her baby?" Griffin asked.

"Oh, yes, her baby suffocated on the plastic cover of his stroller. By the time they found him it was too late. One of the cars from the accident hid the stroller, it was just a small one. The worst sort of luck," Emily rambled, her brain calculating how long it would take her to work through this list. So much for putting his kids first, he couldn't even chase up the truants missing from his school.

"I can only think of one family on that list with a baby young enough to be in a stroller who would walk to school, everyone else drives," Griffin said, pulling the paper from Emily's hands. Tearing off the bottom section, he wrote two names followed by an address, and handed it back to Emily before standing up with a finality signalling their meeting was over.

"Thank you," said Emily, slipping the paper into her notebook.

"You'll let me know if the boys need our help? And Detective Jesmond, I look forward to receiving the appropriate paperwork from you. Good luck with your enquiries."

Still perplexed at the disconnect between the external image of the principal and his speech and insistence on protocols being followed, Emily couldn't help but suspect there was a con going on somewhere.

She left Griffin's office, and avoiding the archaic receptionist she checked the note Trivelle Griffin gave her. The address was within walking distance of the school if you walked past the Rose Haven Retirement Resort. But the paper didn't list just one child, it had the names of two boys, twins. She had an inkling where to find a set of twins, but first a visit to their home was in order.

THE FLORIDA SKY above Emily's head looked as if a toddler was let loose with pottles of blue and white paint and a broad brush. It was a sky which kept the humidity hovering around the seventy percent mark, bearable most of the time, except for times like this.

Emily Jesmond stood outside a small house on Mission Bell Drive. The carport was empty; the yard too. Even the house looked empty, but from the sickly sweet odour forcing its way through the windows, Emily knew there was someone inside, or rather, someone's body. The humidity didn't help with that.

With her face in the crook of her elbow, Emily opened the unlocked front door, and stepped through into a room entirely decorated with dark cane furniture. She couldn't immediately pinpoint the origin of the stench until her eyes adjusted to the gloom, and she spied an amorphous shape on the couch.

"Hello, Sir?" she said, although mainly she was talking to the flies who'd taken to the air as she approached their meal.

An ancient man lay on the couch, a blanket over his skinny legs, and an empty dinner tray beside him. Empty prescription bottles littered the coffee table. Emily suspected the old guy had either starved to death, or, having run out of medicine, his ticker had given out. Satisfied she couldn't do anything for him other than ring the coroner, Emily ignored her companion and wandered though the house.

Acclimatised to the smell, she took her arm away from her face leaving her hands free to rummage through drawers and open the few cupboards in the 1970s house.

At the end of the hall, she came upon the room she suspected belonged to the boys she was looking for. Sparse, and identical, right down to the soft toys propped next to their pillows. Goofy sat on both beds, with one missing its black button nose, sliced off with a knife at some point. Ignoring the toys, Emily poked about looking for photos. She hadn't seen a single photograph in the house and assumed they were in a box or in albums somewhere.

Opening a shoebox shoved on a bottom shelf, Emily found a bundle of photographs, which looked to be a mixture of generations, some from happier times. She shuffled through them. Half of the photos were torn in two, some shredded even more. *Bingo*. One clear snapshot of two identical little boys; blonde cherubs but lacking any sign of happiness. Looking around the tiny room which contained very little other than two beds and a set of shelves showing more shelf than beloved belongings, Emily was certain theirs wasn't a joyful life. She shoved the photograph into her hard-covered notebook and left the house, closing the door behind her.

Taking in lungfuls of air untainted with the decomposing flesh of the old man, Emily dialled Clive, smug with satisfaction at what she'd discovered. Her happiness didn't last long. Clive told her to get her arse over to the doctor's house and help Gary and Tony there. *Help*, he'd said, as if she were a child.

She didn't give a toss about helping Gary and Tony, or what Clive thought about her. She was in this job to make sure no one lived the life she'd had to live in order to get to where she was. And her priority would always be the children, no matter how much trouble that got her into.

48

Ricky Donovan's pupils filled his eyes as he inhaled the fumes bubbling inside the thin walled glass pipe. Drifting into a drug-induced utopia, he smiled at the food weighing down his grubby kitchen counter. He'd lucked in this time. It was amazing the strings one's family could pull when they wanted too.

Ricky inflated his cheeks, giggling at his resemblance to the chipmunks he used to see as a child. Laying his pipe carefully on the coffee table, he held his hands up like little tiny claws and mimed a crude impression of a chipmunk, "Hehehe, set for winter are we? We've got our winter supplies in haven't we? Thanks Aunty Tracey. It's good to have family support. Hehehe." Taking another deep breath, he puffed out his cheeks again. "Yummy nuts, nuts, nuts, nuts. And sugar. Oohh, Momma would be proud of me taking all the things, eating all the food. Clever little boy aren't I?"

A cockroach scampered across the coffee table, and Ricky's addled brain trawled through his memory reserves. Bugs! Chipmunks liked eating bugs too, not just nuts. He clamped his hand down over the prehistoric insect. It probed his hand looking for an escape route, and Ricky fancied he could feel its tiny little hands trying to force its way out. *Sucker*, he had it cornered. Lifting his hand an inch, he picked it up with his other hand, watching it squirming before dropping it into his open mouth and crunching. As he chewed the cockroach's crisp outer shell, he pondered what he should do next. What would a chipmunk do?

Scurrying around his lounge the way he imagined a chipmunk moved, he touched the trinkets he'd arrayed in an order of importance known only to him. A Lladro statue of a dog crouched at the feet of a young boy; an alabaster statue of the Egyptian deity Anubis; a brass stag — his antlers threatening to impale anyone who came too close. There were other smaller statues laid out like a trail of breadcrumbs leading to the door of his apartment. Ricky picked at the scabs on his arms, blood bubbling up like sulphuric mud. Selling these things would stop the bugs from burrowing into his skin when he slept. He knew that. Mind you, eating them could stop that too. He cackled. Going to work cramped his style, but he'd made a promise or they'd lock him up again. He couldn't handle that, there were so many bugs in prison, too many to eat, they crawled over him every night. He wasn't going back. The doorbell rang. The Black Man! he always came at the right time. Like a chipmunk, Ricky was preparing for winter and people came when he needed them, because he was special.

Before opening the door, he was lucid enough to hide his special pipe. He didn't do sharing, and he'd been no good at sharing as a child. It wasn't his Momma's fault — other children never gave things back. He'd always been surprised when other parents or teachers told him off for not sharing. It was self preservation, they were idiots for not figuring that out for themselves. Chipmunks didn't share their nuts. Neither did squirrels. Why then should he share his toys? They were his toys, and his alone. Satisfied he'd hidden his pipe, he checked his teeth in the mirror for any wayward cockroach legs and opened the door.

"Hello Ricky," said Nate Blackwell. "What have you got for me today?"

"It's the Black Man," Ricky cackled. "Come in!"

Blackwell sidled into Ricky's lounge. The almond tang of the crystal meth in the air gave Blackwell's step an extra lift. Buying off addicts was as easy as shooting fish in a barrel. As long as Ricky had half decent stuff, he'd be laughing all the way to the bank, again.

"What you got for me Ricky?"

"Lots of goodies, really valuable things. From my Gramma, she left it all to me. Sad, sad, sad days. But she was old. You know, a better place and all that. Lots of good stuff she had, I still don't know if I wanna part with it. It's hard, memories, family. Have you got family Black Man?"

Nate didn't believe Ricky's story. He'd been buying off him long enough that Ricky had lost various 'family' members twice over now. It's hard to keep the stories straight when you're in the clutches of the latest chemical offering. Ricky should stick to alcohol and gambling. "We've all got family, Ricky. It's a nice story, but keep those for your parole officer. I've got places to be, so what have you got?"

Ricky laughed again, puffing his cheeks out as he made his way around his elaborate display of wares on the floor. "It's all here, man. Laid it out for you. Gotta be worth a bundle. What do you reckon?"

Nate put on his game face, jotting notes on the stub of his check book. Whatever Nate offered, Ricky would accept. Happened the same way every time, and Nate kept it sweet by throwing Ricky a juicy little bone now and then.

"That's a nice statue, Ricky," he said, referring to the Lladro statue. "Are you sure you want to sell it? It's more high end than I normally handle. Not sure I'm the right person to buy it?"

Ricky twisted his head so fast, he risked twisting it right off. "Which one?" he asked, wild eyes scanning the assorted statuary.

"The boy with the dog. Market can't get enough of Lladro," replied Nate, throwing Ricky his bone.

Ricky had no idea who Lladro was, but he knew where more of them were. The Rose Haven was littered with them. "I've got more of them, but not here, they're at the... at my Gramma's house," Ricky stuttered as the twitching restarted. The bugs under his skin were telling him to get rid of Nate and to get back to his pipe. "How much then?" he asked, hopping about like a child on Christmas Day, eager to open his presents but also in desperate need of a toilet.

"Look, I can spring for two hundred for the lot," Nate hedged. He'd go higher if Ricky pushed him, but he recognised the behaviour in front of him, and knew he'd timed it right.

Ricky looked like a wide-eyed Disney cartoon version of himself. Two hundred dollars would see him through a whole week especially with his pay from the old folks home. He nodded seriously, or what he thought was seriously. To Nate Blackwell, it looked like Ricky's head would fall off, he was nodding so fast.

Nate wrote out a cash check and packaged up the treasures from the floor. He'd make his money back from this stuff at least four times over. A great day.

"Hey, Ricky, if you find any more of your Gran's

empathy. Myra however could not separate
from the scene.
ed her features and turned to face the twins.
u, but I don't think a coffee will fix today,"

ou sad?" asked one.
couldn't tell them apart and had no desire to
her heart hoped they were good kids, and
g so kind. Other than the tonic her husband
er a few times a month, she did everything
here was no one else to do any cooking or
dening or laundry. Her husband was barely
hen he was, it was to sleep and eat. His life
tine and predictability, a precise man who
hint of change. Which was why fostering
y was such an anomaly in his regimented
ilitated with every waking breath.
ny cat is dead," Myra explained, her
ncts overcoming her reservations. They
en, little boys who'd lost their mother and
brother. They had no one else.
linked at her, long lashes sweeping over
lue eyes. They couldn't have killed Tom,
ell, *wouldn't she?*
ant you to be sad," said one, wrapping his
legs. The second twin came in behind his
is arms to the tangle.
ou a coffee," said one. "And we'll bring it
nge," said the other. "Yes, sit down and
irst boy, a smile adorning his cherub-like

, leaving them to their good intentions. If
ess, she'd clean it up later. Their offer was
a lonely life.

Lladro, call me. And if you've got any silver you want to get rid of? With Christmas coming up, those things are easiest to sell. Just putting it out there." Nate smiled. He knew the stuff Ricky sold him was hot. He didn't know where Ricky sourced it from but it wasn't from his twice dead Gramma.

Ricky smiled, scratching at his hand, unknowingly smearing blood up his arm, a grotesque tattoo. He needed Nate to go now. Go, go. go, his pipe was calling him.

49

Patting the earth with the flat of the spade, Myra stood up and wiped the tears from her cheeks. With old Tom dead, her last link to life before marriage had gone too. Now nothing remained to bind her to the life before she became Myra Perry.

She hung the spade in its spot in the immaculate garden shed - everything had a place, and she kept nothing which wasn't useful. She didn't want to assume the twins had murdered old Tom, but it was the only explanation. Fiddling with the boxes of plant food and rust killer, Myra adjusted them so their labels lined up. If she could stay here and hide from reality, she would but life continued outside her little tin shed. Myra didn't have the strength to ask the boys if they'd killed Tom. What if they said yes? She didn't trust her reaction. They were only little boys. Maybe a fox or a coyote killed Tom?

As Myra straightened the last box, she spied a gap on the white peg board and ran her fingers over the space. There was no need to draw around her tools; she was the only one who used the shed and put things away. Tracing

her fingers over the ot
tools trying to rememb
hadn't used the garde
rushed to her ears, the
off a wave of nausea
old Tom, the clippe
Someone had used t
had happened to ot
should ask her neig
know she'd gone out
if they were respons

She closed the
two heads at the kit
couldn't have been
made her way slov
lead.

"Are you oka
concern.

Myra opened
the words choking
hands in the basir

"We can mal
said James.

"She likes cc
she won't get up,

Again Myra
her tongue. Eve
thinking about
turned her stor

Like an aut
and steam licke

"We'll do it

An outside
raised childre

abundance o
her suspicion
She stead
"Thank y
she said.
"Why are
Myra still
learn now, bu
they were bein
prepared for
in the house.
cleaning or ga
at home, and
was one of ro
bristled at the
baby after bab
life, a life she fa
"Because
mothering inst
were just childr
father and baby
The boys b
their innocent
she'd be able to
"We don't w
arms around her
brother, adding
"We'll make
to you in the lo
relax," said the
cheeks.
Myra nodded
they made any m
a rare moment in

THE BOYS WALKED into the lounge, huge smiles illuminating their angelic faces, and Myra smiled at the mess of jam spread across a slab of bread, which no doubt they'd helped themselves to, judging by the smear on one boy's cheek.

"We made you a coffee," said James.

"And an afternoon snack," said Jesse.

The coffee had splashed over the rim of the mug forming a muddy puddle on the wooden tray but leaving enough left in the mug to satisfy. The sight of the rustic jam sandwich made her stomach rumble, she hadn't realised how hungry she was.

"Thank you, boys," Myra replied with absolute honesty.

The boys giggled, their high pitched falsetto voices more at home in a church choir than her suburban home.

"Can we go outside to play now please, Myra?" asked James, his hand on his brother's shoulder.

"Yes but don't pick the flowers in the garden," she said. As they vanished from the room she followed with, "Because some of them are poisonous," but whether they heard, she couldn't be sure.

Myra closed her hands around the coffee mug. The aroma toyed with her senses and she took a sip. The boys had added too much cream in an attempt to cool the coffee, making it more lukewarm than hot, but at least they'd tried. The horror of what had happened to Tom would never leave her, but sinking into the cushions of the couch, she tried to let go of the afternoon's stress. So many nights she'd sat here on her own, a baby in her arms and a bottle in her hands, the soft scent of the baby filling the space left vacant by a husband never at home. But for now the space was hers. She took another sip and felt the caffeine kick in — the twins had made it stronger than she liked and the difference was noticeable, she felt her eyeballs popping open and her heartbeat increasing. She hadn't realised how much she'd needed a fix until now.

Myra tried closing her brown eyes but when she did, she imagined images of cats padding paw-less through her garden leaving smudges of blood on the grass, and fancied she could hear their exposed bones clicking on the tiles of the kitchen floor like a blind man with a cane *tap, tap, tapping* his way closer and closer. Myra swallowed the fear threatening to paralyse her. Shock, she was going into shock, and she gulped back the rest of the coffee, cold enough to knock it back in one long swallow. And then it hit her. It felt like she'd been pinned underneath a giant fan, the cyclonic air flattening her skin, forcing it into undulating waves over her tired cheekbones. Her eyebrows moved under their own volition, her jaw clenching. It felt as if hundreds of cats were stabbing at her with their crudely amputated bones as they clawed their way into her lap for blood-soaked cuddles. She tried screaming but couldn't find her tongue, her pulsating skin made that an impossible task.

The nightmarish vision of the cats vanished, leaving only the excruciating pain from their imagined amputations. Myra watched as her fingers shrank themselves, leaving stumpy shadows of her formerly long tapered digits. Her wedding rings slipped off onto the tray, sending up a tiny splash as they landed on the polished wood — the gold circles an empty promise of something never delivered.

Myra's head bobbed forward as she sank into the cushions. No, she wasn't sinking into the cushions, she was shrinking, the couch threatening to engulf her diminutive frame.

Through a deep reserve of inner strength, she reached up to touch her face, her tiny fingers pressing into her rippling skin. It was as if she'd plunged her fingers into the breathing gills of a shark — her cheeks, jaw, teeth, bones, muscles, and tendons pulsated under her touch. Her face had taken on a life of its own. Then, it was as if someone had filled her head with Fourth of July crackers, and then lit the fuse. The pain so excruciating that she found her voice and as her adult-sized cranium shrank and compressed her brain at an inconsistent speed with the other changes to her body, Myra's screams shook the house.

THE BOYS LAUGHED as they climbed higher and higher up the tree in the garden, a pair of garden clippers tucked into the waistband of Jesse's shorts. What fun they would have now! Two little boys doing what little boys did.

50

Doctor Perry stood in his office doorway and watched Molly stare at her phone. The girl was obsessed; she hadn't moved from her seat all day, held captive by the glowing square screen in her hand. Then the front door opened, distracting them both from their thoughts.

"Ah, Miss Swann, lovely to see you," Doctor Perry said, his face brightening.

Molly slipped her phone away and stood up with Clarita Swann's folder — one of Doctor Perry's late night clients.

"Sorry I'm late. They closed the I-95 to Gateway, the radio said it was a hit and run, so I had to come the long way."

"The sounds terrible, did they say what happened?" Molly asked.

"But at least you're here now," Doctor Perry interjected. "Thank you, Molly. That's all for tonight, I'll see you tomorrow. The folder?"

Molly sniffed and handed Clarita's file over before

gathering up her things, checking her phone one last time. No missed calls and no messages.

"Miss Swann, come through," Doctor Perry smiled at his newest patient as he locked the clinic door behind his receptionist. He followed his patient into his consulting room and engaged the lock on that door too — it paid to be careful. Unexpected interruptions weren't good for business.

"How are you feeling, Miss Swann?" he asked, as he sat behind his desk. The large desk gave him an aura of respectability, and power. From here, his patients believed everything he said.

"The lotion worked on my hands to begin with, but you're right, the stress of being alone in a new town is affecting me," Clarita replied, examining the eczema on her hands.

Doctor Perry kept the smile from his face, but her words were a balm to his troubled soul. So many things had gone wrong lately and yet here was Clarita Swann, a healthy young woman, with no friends or family in sight. She was what he needed, and what his clients, the Cavalletto's, wanted.

An idea formed in his mind; he guessed it had always been there, hence why he'd asked Molly to schedule Clarita's appointment for the last one of the day. He hadn't planned on finalising this patient so soon, but the opportunity was too great to pass up, and he had the latest variant of tonic which needed testing. Clarita was the perfect guinea pig.

Doctor Perry's cellphone vibrated — another call from the same number who'd rung half a dozen times over the past week, a police detective wanting to speak to him about two missing patients. He fingered his collar. Either the humidity was making him sweat, or it was the creeping unease pressing in on him at every juncture. Molly had switched off the air conditioning and it was unseasonably humid for this time of the year, but he knew it wasn't either of those things. It was time to pull the pin on the others and get out of town. The last thing he wanted to do was have a nice chat with the police. They always took things the wrong way.

He fingered Clarita Swann's file, the tiny red ink circle in the upper right-hand corner a reminder of his plans. He'd bring them forward, he'd done this a hundred times before, more probably, and knew nothing could go wrong.

"Come over to the bed, Miss Swann."

"Clarita is fine."

"Very well, Clarita. Hop up onto the bed if you will and I'll check your blood pressure and the rest of your vital signs."

With Clarita rearranging herself on the bed, Doctor Perry washed his hands and pulled on a pair of gloves. His bottles of tonic stood ready on the shelf over the sink. This was the newest batch, extra strength. He measured out five fluid ounces, then tipped in a little more. It was stronger than the last batch but he needed this done quickly. He checked the line on the cup, eight fluid ounces, more than enough for her weight.

Doctor Perry left the cup on the shelf, now wasn't the right time for her to drink it. "Are you ready?" he asked.

Clarita Swann smiled at him from the bed, excellent.

Doctor Perry used his stethoscope to listen to her chest, asking her to inhale, exhale, the usual doctor patter. Next he wrapped the modified blood pressure cuff around her arm, his own pulse racing. He'd rigged it in his lab, trialling it on a recently bedridden resident Tracey wanted gone. It had worked perfectly. Done in his lab, no one had bothered him as he'd tinkered with different placements of the hypodermic he'd concealed in the cuff until satisfied with the end product. Impossible to see, and a seamless delivery of the strong sedative he needed to use on patients not so prepared to swallow his tonic. He had no time to waste.

"I'll inflate the cuff now, so you will feel some pressure, which will ease off after a moment. Ready?" he asked.

"Yes," Clarita replied, with what would be the last word she'd ever speak.

The doctor pressed the power button on his blood pressure machine and the cuff inflated, the pressure around Clarita's arm slowly increasing. She squirmed a little as if trying to ease the discomfort.

"Please stay still, Miss Swann," Doctor Perry advised. She'd be immobile shortly, a shame but a necessity. He couldn't ignore the messages from his clients requesting fresh stock, and those requests hadn't come with any pleasantries. There'd been another message today, which he'd replied to by promising to deliver Clarita Swann tonight. After supplying them Clarita, the twins, and then Myra, the Cavalletto's would have more than enough to be getting on with, giving him ample time to disappear before they'd ask for more. And Mary Louise, he had forgotten about her, he still had her up his sleeve. And Molly, she'd go too. Over the years, his receptionists had been excellent stock, a ready supply. The money he'd earned so good, it was a shame to walk away, but the Cavalletto's were getting too pushy, and now with the police asking questions about two of his elderly clients… He knew where the two men were, and their files. He'd have to destroy those, but he worried that that might make it look more suspicious? He'd think on it later.

The blood pressure monitor beeped, and the cuff deflated automatically with a quiet hissing sound, leaving no other sounds in the room other than

Clarita's shallow breathing. A tiny prick of blood appeared as he removed the cuff from her arm, and Doctor Perry wiped the blood away with a fragment of gauze.

With his patient unconscious on the table, Doctor Perry unbuckled the straps from beneath the bed, and strapped his patient down. Elevating the bed, he opened Clarita's mouth, a mouth full of straight white teeth - an orthodontist had done excellent work here.

Bringing over the glass of tonic, he tipped it into Clarita's open mouth, massaging it down her throat, like you do with a cat and a worm tablet. The tonic's effect was instantaneous. Doctor Perry had barely poured the last drop in when the convulsions started and Clarita's body strained against the leather straps.

Doctor Perry rinsed the cup, his back to the machinations on the bed. Not listening to any screaming was a huge improvement. Why he hadn't thought of this earlier was beyond him, and he made a mental note to take the modified blood pressure cuff to Mary Louise's house, then he wouldn't have to bring her here which would save time.

A choking sound made him spin around - Clarita's eyes were open wide, her mouth frothing. Her bones undulated beneath her rippling skin. How was she awake? This was not the reaction he'd been expecting. He looked back at the cup he'd just washed out. Eight fluid ounces wasn't too much; five might have taken too long. The splash of liquid on the floor made him look back towards Clarita. The contents of her bladder, her bowel, gastric acid, vomit, her cerebrospinal fluid, dripped from the bed creating a virtually impassable lake around her.

Doctor Perry stood transfixed. He'd never had this reaction to any variation of his tonic, although he had lost several patients in the early years of experimentation, but none like this. Picking up the bottle of tonic, he sniffed it. The odour was no different. He daren't taste it, not with the potential outcome disintegrating on the bed in front of him; a disaster. Backing away, he stuffed the tonic bottles into his bag and snapped it shut. He'd have to clean up the mess, but it was still rippling and heaving, the limbs alternately shrinking and growing back.

Pop

A sound like a gunshot made the doctor jump. Clarita's lovely white teeth weren't even her own. A full set of dentures exploded from her mouth as her jaw shrank and expanded, landing several feet across the room, scattering the individual teeth in every direction upon impact.

Clarita now reminded Doctor Perry of the Old Croghan Man, an Iron Age body he'd read about years ago. With her skin split like a leather lounge suite left too long in the sun, and her tendons and arteries guitar string taut, her body pulled in on itself, distorting her into an unrecognisable tangle of muscles.

Fleeing crossed Doctor Perry's mind as he surveyed his consulting room, his bag in his hands. There was too much of Clarita left to stuff into the hazardous waste container and cleaning up would take the whole night. He could just run, now, and forget the others, and the Cavalletto's. He had enough money to hide from them, and enough tonic. He was looking forward to regaining his youth, but not with this batch. He needed to go to his lab to make another batch and then he'd run, which meant he had to clean up now.

The shuddering on the bed stopped and silence reigned until Doctor Perry pulled out the trash sacks, shook them open, and stuffed Clarita Swann's desiccated remains into the thick black plastic bags.

"It reminded me of the Grand Canyon," laughed the nurse.

"How?"

"It was as dry as hell, with those sparse prickly bushes your mother warned you not to touch."

The nurses laughed into their coffee mugs and sucked on their cancer sticks in the courtyard out the back of the Rose Haven. Bart Stubbs laughed with them, smoking his own cheap brand cigarette. He hated the residents with a passion. They stank and they nagged him, they always wanted more, and made the foulest of messes which they expected him to clean up. He hated the people here so much that listening to the other staff belittle the residents was a patch of sun in his otherwise miserable day.

"What's happening about you hitting that jogger?" the nurse asked.

"Heard she hasn't pressed charges, so I'm off the hook," Stubbs said sourly. Them mentioning the accident just ruined a perfectly good smoke break. He flicked his cigarette into the garden. "I'm due back now," he said, ignoring their stares. They would talk about him behind his back now, stupid bitches.

Walking back into the Rose Haven was like being hit with a rotten egg, and Stubbs coughed again. He hadn't seen the doc yet, cause the doc hadn't found time to fit him in. That slant-eyed nurse had lied to him, probably wanted him to die of the cough. He tried to call in sick today, same as yesterday, except Tracey told him over the phone he couldn't have any more sick days, and that it was his final warning. He'd had plenty of final warnings, but she'd sounded serious this time. So he'd reluctantly left a game of Counter Strike and come in for his shift.

So far Bart Stubbs had been to the courtyard twice for a smoke, had badgered Pauline in the kitchen for breakfast, and now fancied an early morning tea. He'd banged into the medicine cart someone had left in the middle of the hallway, so pushed that back to the nurses' station, ignoring the closed doors in the corridor. The residents had to keep them open during the day, to make it easier for the staff to check on them, but he was relieved he didn't have to see any of the old tossers in their pjs. If you were unlucky when you walked past, you'd catch them getting dressed, their saggy old butts hanging to the floor. Couldn't even see their dicks, they'd shrivelled up so much. No, Bart ignored the closed doors, intent on filling his stomach with the free food.

"Have you checked on the residents in the South wing?" Tala asked when he got to the nurses' station.

"Yup, just came from there, all good," Stubbs replied, sliding the trolley into its slot under the desk. "Just going to grab a coffee before breakfast duties."

Tala's eyebrows lifted, Bart Stubbs had never been known to help set up for any meal, other than his own.

Bart wandered towards the kitchen, feeling Tala's eyes

on his back. It was likely her who'd told Tracey not to let him have any more sick leave. Karma would get her, he was a true believer in that stuff.

Pauline was in a foul mood in the kitchen, and refused to give him the time of day let alone morning tea, so he helped himself to a handful of chocolate chip cookies left out for the residents and got well out of the way. He didn't want to be anywhere near the old-timers so wandered around until he found himself at the reception desk. No old farts here because it was out of bounds, being so near to the road. The only time the old biddies came through here, was when they arrived. Fancy decor, real potted plants and Cherie, the sweet little receptionist who sometimes shared her cigarettes and herself when they were on a night shift together. Today, the reception desk was busy and Stubbs sidled up against the wall to listen.

The two detectives stood at the desk asking Cherie if they could speak with Doctor Perry, and the other residents. This was not good. Not that he had anything to hide apart from the old Rolex on his wrist, but he'd helped himself to that a good year ago, after the old wrinkly had died on the toilet. Stubbs considered it payment for the shit he dealt with. Still, he tugged his sleeve down further, and shoved his hand in his pocket.

Cherie spied him lurking in the corner. "Bart will show you to Tracey's office, the manager, and you can ask her," she said.

Stubbs added Cherie to his karma list, the little slut, there'd be no more sharing his Camels with her after this.

He walked the two detectives to Tracey's office, knocking once, then opening the door. At least she'd see he was doing something and not skiving off the way she'd accused him over the phone this morning. His karma list was getting longer.

"The police want to speak with you," Stubbs said, enjoying the look of shock on Tracey's face as he mentioned the police. He wanted to be a fly on the wall listening to this conversation.

"Thank you, Bart," she said, standing to greet the guests. "Come in," she said to the men. "Close the door, Bart," she ordered.

He closed the door and stood alone in the corridor contemplating whether he should try listening at the door when he realised he wasn't alone. He glimpsed the weaselly nephew of Tracey's - Tricky Ricky Donovan, disappear down the stairwell to the doctor's lab-cum-temporary morgue. What was he doing going down there?

AT THE MENTION of the word *Police*, Ricky had scarpered. They wanted to take his pipe, or his pills or his trinkets, or everything. He'd hidden his trinkets here because the lab was full of old abandoned stuff, broken things, obsolete equipment, giving him a cornucopia of hiding places for the treasures he'd liberated from the residents. It was also a terrific place to hide from the police. No one came here, except him, the doctor, and dead people. And not at the same time — that would've given him more nightmares, nightmares like the bug one, and he hated that one and wanted no more bug nightmares, ugh. They put the dead people in the big chiller thing on one side, and no way, uh uh, was he going anywhere near that, ever.

He'd had such a fun time in the lab last night, playing with the pretty pills, crushing them into powder using the clever bowl thing he'd found — he'd seen people use those on TV so knew how to use it. Ricky was like the doctor, a professional laboratory worker, crushing pills and mixing them. The lab was half filled with a huge medical thing, all tubes and coils and things which were hot but were perfect for heating his pipe. He'd spent the whole night here using his finger to trace patterns in the powder he'd spilled on the ground. Ricky hadn't wanted to waste it so after he'd finished drawing patterns, he'd scooped it all up and had tipped it into the glass jars hanging all over the weird drug-making contraption. During the night, he'd watched it warm things up and then boil and then he'd followed the little tiny drops inching their way along the glass straws and dripping into another jar, where it would begin all over again. He'd been in meth labs before, and none of them looked as awesome as this. This was how you did it properly.

The stuff he'd pocketed from the residents made him sleepy and he'd used the toilet a hundred times but apart from that their pills let him sleep, free from the bugs. If he stayed, he might get to do the trolley run by himself again, and then it would be one for them and *three* for Ricky.

The full jars at the end had gone now, so he guessed the doctor had come by when he was upstairs, but no one said anything about it so they hadn't noticed, which was lucky. Ricky wasn't good at many things, but opening locked doors was a skill he'd mastered over the years. Most of the time here, he didn't need to open locked doors, he had a swipe card. They trusted him so much, they gave him his own special card, with his name and photo on and everything. It didn't work down here, or for the drug cupboard. Too many people were always near the drug cupboard so he hadn't been able to get in there, but if he did, it would be like Christmas presents and Easter eggs and Halloween candy all at once. But the lock on the lab door was so old, a child could have sprung it.

He'd wait here till the coast was clear and smoke his special pipe. The doc had his big lab thing running, so he didn't need to use his trusty lighter. And off he went to that la la land in the sky with enormous fairies and cookie dough bears and beakers full of meth.

Elijah limped through the beige corridors of the rest home trying to ignore the pain spreading its vicious tentacles throughout his body. Each day brought a new niggle, compounding the pain he'd endured in his fingers for years. Today's contribution was a flame of agony licking his spine. Like most football players of any note, he had old injuries which flared up but this wasn't one. This was a torment inflicted upon him by that most wicked of mistresses — time.

A gaggle of people whispering in the corridor gave Elijah a moment of respite. The Rose Haven Retirement Resort wasn't the place where residents gathered in corridors, the staff didn't approve. You ate in the dining room, relaxed in the lounge, and slept in your room. The residents paid for the privilege of living like toddlers deprived of external stimuli. And they all accepted it. Or they had. Even Elijah felt a change in the air, a paradigm shift in the atmosphere at the Rose Haven. There was something bubbling up. Nothing like an explosive regime overthrow by weary citizens rising against a cruel dictator, but something more subtle. It scared him.

"Where is she?"

"They said she'd gone to live with family."

"What family? She had none."

"Just saying what I heard."

"That's not what I heard. I saw them clearing out her room, she's gone to hospital—"

"Which hospital?"

"No, not the hospital, another rest home, better than here…"

"Where'd she get the money for that?"

"Was it the lottery?"

Elijah tried walking past the women congregating outside Muriel Lincoln's empty room but there wasn't room to slip by unnoticed. He mumbled a quiet *excuse me* but they pounced, hoping for fresh insights into Muriel's disappearance, which by now had gone in so many circles no one quite knew who knew what and how.

"You were with Doctor Perry last night, did he say anything?" Eileen Hislop asked.

"Benson would have said if Muriel was ill. Pity he's off duty this morning—"

"Isn't Benson the nicest man," Frances interrupted, quite forgetting her earlier concern.

"No one mentioned Muriel last night. Please excuse me," Elijah replied. He wanted to hurry past the women but even talking to the women pained his broken ribs.

"Hello, Elijah," boomed Sulia from the other side of the group.

He hadn't seen Sulia lurking in the shadows, despite being the largest person there. His heart sank, she'd want to talk with him too. He didn't have the energy for that and contemplated turning tail and going back to bed, despite knowing an orderly would find him and force him to go to breakfast. He could plead illness and get his breakfast delivered to him in bed. Isn't that the best part of being old? You got to play invalid and someone came and wiped your backside and held a sippy cup to your lips while you spent the rest of the time watching daytime television and sleeping? Elijah didn't even want breakfast, he just wanted to die. To be with Natalie.

"Will you walk me to breakfast?" Sulia asked.

It would have taken too much energy to decline, so Elijah nodded at the woman, then laughed at his own foolishness — the stupid woman was blind, she couldn't even see him nodding. "Sure, I'll walk you."

With her hand on his arm, they shuffled away from Muriel's room and along the corridor, an odd sight — the disgraced football coach, wasting away to a shadow, and a giant Indian woman, her colourful sari at odds with the beigeness of the surroundings, her ankles tinkling as her weight forced her to shuffle alongside Elijah.

"Wait!" Sulia exclaimed. "I need something from my room."

Elijah protested, but the woman had turned back, a slow laborious wheeling turn which left him following closely behind as she entered her room on the opposite side of the corridor.

Sulia's room was the mirror image of his own except she had even fewer belongings than he did. And where Elijah had framed photographs of his beloved wife, Sulia had nothing. The only nod to her past was a shoebox sized statue of an elephant. Upon closer inspection Elijah wasn't sure it *was* an elephant. It had an elephant-like trunk and ears but sat humanlike, cross legged, its feet beautifully rendered, as were its two pairs of arms with something held in each of its four hands.

"That's Lord Ganesha," Sulia replied as if she knew where he was looking. "The Remover of Obstacles," she laughed. "Close the door please," Sulia directed, her back to him as she gazed sightlessly out the window.

Elijah closed the door and Sulia reached in behind the curtain, pulling out a stoneware bottle, like an old ginger beer bottle from a century ago. Elijah couldn't have been more surprised.

"Alcohol?" Elijah asked.

He hadn't touched a drop since the accident. Not only was that one of his parole conditions but it was also part of his self imposed purgatory. Sulia's furtiveness meant only one thing and his mouth filled with the memory of bourbon. He wanted nothing more than to feel the heaviness of the alcohol on his tongue as he took that first sip, swirling it around in his mouth until it hit every tastebud... *no*. Natalie's beautiful face in the casket materialised like an old Polaroid photo coming into focus.

"I don't drink any more," he said, ignoring the saliva in his mouth which betrayed his lie. Elijah wanted a drink, but not now, not in this lifetime.

"It's not alcohol," Sulia replied. "Trust me, it will take away that pain, you try it," and pushed the bottle towards him. "Just a sip, you don't need more than that. Like how you'd try a hot tabasco sauce for the first time, a tiny sip," she coached.

Elijah took the bottle. It didn't smell of alcohol. He took a hesitant sip, his tastebuds protesting at the unknown milky substance coating his tongue instead of the bourbon they'd expected. Coughing, he handed the heavy bottle back to Sulia. The cloying scent of the woman's perfume mixed with the chalky aftertaste in his mouth didn't sit well in his stomach. He placed his hands protectively across his ribs as he felt a tickle in his throat, the precursor to a cough, the pain would be severe. But the sensation travelled down his throat and spread out through his chest, teasing its way through his limbs. He loosened his arms and straightened without noticing that the movement caused no pain.

"What is it?" he asked the woman who was staring at him with her cloudy white eyes.

"Magic," Sulia replied, stoppering the bottle and wedging it back behind the curtain. "We'll go to breakfast now, you take me before they look for us but we'll talk more later," she offered, squeezing past Elijah and shuffling to open the door herself.

Following behind, Elijah almost ran into Sulia as she bent awkwardly to scoop something up from the floor. Before it disappeared into her cardigan pocket Elijah caught sight of a pair of tiny white balls... pearls.

<hr />

BREAKFAST WAS A HUSHED AFFAIR; like a gathering of Cold War spies the residents huddled over their porridge and milky tea stifling their conversations every time an orderly came near. The empty chairs telling a curious tale, one which grew with every passing through the room. Elijah and Sulia slipped into their seats and waited for breakfast. Elijah spied the morning chef at the kitchen door, scanning the faces of the residents, as if she too were counting heads and coming up short every time.

Preston slammed plates of porridge onto the table sending small tidal waves of thin milk slopping over the sides of their bowls. He had a filthy smirk on his face, as if he knew a secret they didn't, one which involved them.

"Are you missing one of your friends today?" he

sneered, running a dirty cloth perfunctorily over the spilt milk.

Elijah ducked his head, refusing to make eye contact. He wanted no more trouble. Sulia however danced into the fray, toying with the younger man the way a cat does with a mouse.

"What have you done with them then, you filthy cretin?"

"Oi, you watch who you're calling a creation. Eat your porridge and be grateful, you old bat."

"You need your hearing checked. Where did you learn English, from the back of a cereal packet?"

Preston lost it, slamming his hand on the table, sending another wave of milk across the table and onto Sulia's voluminous lap.

Sulia leapt up faster than her size allowed and pushed her girth into the smaller man, towering over him. Preston cowered down, the confrontation too much, he weaselled his way from underneath her bulk, casting glances behind him as he scurried from the room. He left the other latecomers waiting in vain for their breakfast.

"It's best to leave that one alone," Elijah counselled, spooning another mouthful of porridge into his mouth. His eyes taking in the comings and goings, lingering on the empty seats. He didn't have any close friendships but a quick tally of the dining room confirmed that the people he was acquainted with were vanishing fast.

"You never said if you'd heard about what happened to Muriel?" Sulia said after sitting down again.

"I don't even know the woman."

"You had dinner together the other night. The night of the fight. Still think you should report him."

"Well I've got no idea what happened to her, so I won't stand around gossiping in corridors. She's old. Old people die. We all die. She's lucky she's gone," Elijah said. Talking about the other residents was the last thing he wanted to do. He wanted to eat his porridge and go back to his room. He had an Agatha Christie novel to read he'd found in the woefully understocked room the Rose Haven called a library. It was in his room, waiting for him.

"Maybe she's in her room? We should go check," Sulia suggested.

Elijah slammed down his spoon. "That's not my job. They have people to do that. I don't get involved in other —" He never finished what he was saying, staring instead at his hands and flexing his fingers. All ten digits moved with perfect synchronicity. Painless synchronicity.

"Told you it would work," Sulia said, smiling into her spoon.

53

Stubbs went to follow Ricky downstairs, but Tracey came out of her office with the two policemen in tow just as he took a step.

"Shouldn't you be helping at breakfast?" Tracey asked.

Stubbs muttered an apology and shot off towards the dining room. Shit, now she'd think he was listening at her door, when he'd only thought about listening in. Whatever their conversation was, she never showed the police through to talk to the residents, so he kept his big mouth shut lest she accuse him of spreading gossip.

Breakfast was easier than usual, a quarter of the residents were having a sleep in and never bothered coming. No matter, he'd eat the leftovers, it also meant there was less for him to clean.

Between him and Preston, they'd got the old farts served their porridge and toast in record time. He'd have plenty of time for another cigarette at this rate and put Tricky Ricky out of his mind. He had his suspicions about what the boy was doing down in Doctor Perry's lab, but that was Ricky's problem. As long as it didn't impact on his life, he didn't care. Ricky could shove all the pills up his nose and he wouldn't give a rat's arse.

Stubbs steered well clear of the big Indian woman who'd come in with the football dude, the one who'd killed his wife and kids in a drunken car crash. She scared the hell out of him, with bells on her ankles and that weirdo statue in her bedroom. He didn't even want to clean in there. Normally he liked having a good rummage through the resident's drawers, in case they kept cash hidden away, not that they had anything to spend it on. But he didn't like being in her room any longer than necessary. And the way she looked at you with her dead eyes, he'd wanted to spear them with a fork the first time she'd turned up at the Rose Haven.

He was on the other side of the room when he saw the creepy Indian biddy stand up and screech at Preston like a fish wife, and would've gone over to back him up, but Preston turned tail, the coward, and disappeared out of the room. He wouldn't have let that old freak get away with it, and Bart couldn't believe Preston had walked away. Still, he gave her table a wide berth when he left for a smoke. This day was turning out to be one of the hardest he'd worked and it was only the morning.

Stubbs had his packet of Camels in his hand and was in the middle of selecting the perfect smoke as he walked out of the dining room when a hand grabbed him from behind.

"You could have come over to help back there. You too scared to help after your little *accident?*" Preston sneered.

Bart's cigarette snapped in half when Preston spun him round, and he stood there stupidly, staring at his ruined cigarette. "You ruined my cigarette!"

"Forget the bloody cigarette, you need to come see what I found, unless you're too scared?"

The wide eyed excitement on Preston's face was enough to motivate Bart to follow him, his nicotine cravings stalled by the promise of something scurrilous Preston had discovered. He pulled up outside Sulia's room though, like a horse refusing a jump.

"That's the Indian's room," he said, hovering on the threshold.

Preston was already in the room, his hand on the curtain. "Come on Stubbs, she's eating her body weight in porridge, so get your arse in here and look at this."

Stubbs edged his way into the room, avoiding eye contact with the grotesque elephant statue thing, and Preston pulled the heavy curtain away from the edge of the window revealing a bottle hidden in the corner.

"Ooh, what's she got there? Against the rules isn't it, having alcohol in your room? Tracey will show her the door for this. Or did you put it there?" Stubbs asked, eyeing up Preston's reaction.

"It's amazing what you can find if you search hard enough, although this room is on your cleaning roster, so how do I know that you haven't hidden it there yourself? Thought I'd ask before we take the evidence to Tracey, you know, cover our own backsides before we get her kicked out on hers."

"It's not mine, don't touch the stuff. Anyway, that bottle looks to be as old as her," Stubbs replied.

"Come on, let's take it to Tracey now. You can say you found it when you were cleaning and you asked me for advice," Preston suggested.

Stubbs laughed, doubting Tracey would believe that. But, it was worth a shot and might just make her forget she'd caught him outside the office.

THE MEN LINED up outside Tracey's office and Preston rapped on the door.

"Now's not a good time," came the reply.

Stubbs shrugged, he didn't give a stuff too much either way, because the nicotine cravings had come back and his mouth was more parched than an old hag's panties.

Preston knocked again and turned the handle, walking through like he owned the place. Once again, Stubbs was standing alone outside the office, until Preston reached back and yanked him in, slamming the door behind them both.

"You tell her," Preston said, holding the bottle out like a stick of dynamite.

Stubbs explained, before realising Tracey wasn't alone in the room, Doctor Perry filled the other chair and he had aged.

"Where did you get that bottle?" Doctor Perry asked.

"I said now wasn't a good time," Tracey said on top of Perry.

"It was in that Indian woman's room," Preston said, pushing the bottle in Perry's outstretched hands, stepping back from the doctor who looked ready to lynch him.

"You can't have found it in her room," Tracey said. "We search everyone's belongings when they first arrive, you know the rules. Alcohol is on the prohibited list and we confiscate any we find."

"Where did you find it?" Doctor Perry asked again, staring at the stoneware bottle in his hands.

"Told you, behind the curtain in Sulia Patel's room, the one stirring up the trouble," Stubbs said, his bottom lip sticking out, suddenly afraid of missing out on the praise for a job well done.

"Is Bart telling the truth, Preston?" Tracey asked, her frozen face looked incredulous despite not moving an inch.

Preston nodded, his eyes on the doctor, who'd pulled the stopper free and was sniffing the contents.

"It can't be," Doctor Perry muttered to himself before sticking a finger in the bottle and sucking the milky substance from the tip of his index finger. With his eyes closed, he licked his lips, and then his body rippled, as if there were a series of tiny earthquakes happening right underneath him.

"Thank you Bart, Preston, we'll take it from here," Tracey said, rushing to her feet and shepherding the men from the room. "I don't want you talking about what you've found, to anyone, understand? Doctor Perry and I will have a word with Miss Patel," and she closed the door, locking it.

Outside Tracey's office the men looked at each other. Neither had any words to describe what they'd just seen, but it wasn't natural.

"I need a cigarette," Stubbs said.

"I think I'll join you," Preston replied.

54

Ricky still had a handful of the big pills left. He'd been saving them to trade later, but now he had to hide from the police down here with no one to play with, and his special pipe was empty, so he might need to use them instead. He scratched at his arms; the bugs were back, and he needed something to kill them with so spent a fruitless ten minutes looking for a fly swat or a knife or a gun, anything to kill the nasty little beasties. They mostly came at night so he didn't understand why they were being so bothersome now, it was only the morning.

He found a staple remover on the doctor's desk and sat quietly chasing the bugs up and down both arms with the sharp teeth of the staple remover, oblivious to the pain and blood. Ricky didn't have as much luck killing the ones on his right arm; he had difficulty using his left arm to chase them; they were so quick, but he killed enough of them so now he could focus on crushing the big pills into powder and give them a snort to see what happened.

The Namenda pills he'd swiped from the drug cart, the ones to treat Alzheimers, looked like huge flesh coloured candies, with the number '5' on one side, and the initials 'FL' on the other. He didn't know if the 'FL' was a good omen or a bad one, but if he said them together — the 'FL' and the '5' it sounded like he was saying *firefly*, which Ricky thought was clever. He'd hidden them inside a fancy silver coffee jug, which he was pretty sure the Black Man would pay him good money for the next time he saw him.

Ricky put the handful of pills into the special crushing bowl and ground away at the pills with the ceramic pestle until the pills became powdery flesh, well it looked to him as if someone's skin had flaked off. Ricky cackled to himself. There was lots in the bowl and he didn't want to snort the lot. Damn, damn, damn, he shouldn't have crushed them all, he should have kept some to trade. What a dumb thing to do. He didn't even know if the powdery flesh would be any good. If he snorted up someone's flesh, did that make him a cannibal? He pondered the idea while he searched the doctor's desk for something to snort the powder. There was nothing glamorous on the desk, not like in the movies, where someone always had a Washington. The best he came up with was a Post-it note, which he folded carefully to make sure the sticky side wasn't facing inwards. He wasn't dumb enough to fold it the wrong way.

Sticking the yellow paper up his nostril, Ricky snorted straight out of the bowl, the pink powder firing around the mucus and into the blood vessels in his nose, and straight into his bloodstream, then it skipped past the blood-brain-barrier and into what remained of his brain. And then the bugs came. Ricky sat terrified at the doctor's desk as he saw hundreds of tiny black beetles, and brown bugs, and red ants, crawl from every corner of the room and scurry towards him, running over each other in their haste to get him. Ricky watched ants being trampled to death by the larger bugs who wanted to get to him first. He couldn't move, or breathe, and then they almost touched him so he pulled his legs up to his chest so they wouldn't climb up them. Rocking back and forth, he wanted to close his eyes, but didn't know if they were jumping bugs and he wanted to see them jump so he couldn't close his eyes, even to blink. Ricky tried counting them, but every time he counted the big ones, they moved and he had to start again, and it was so hard counting when his eyes were so dry, but he couldn't blink because the bugs might be waiting for him to blink before they jumped on him, or for him to fall asleep, and then they'd burrow into his skin through the little holes he'd made. Ricky checked his arms, they hadn't made it there yet, so he was okay.

"Shoo," he yelled, braver now they weren't coming any closer. "Shoo, shoo!" He threw the heavy pestle at them and his aim was true because they scattered, and reassembled further away. There were other things on the desk he could throw, the stapler, the hole punch, the pens and pencils, and he was a fantastic thrower, and the bugs moved further and further away. The bugs were scared of Ricky Donovan. He'd showed them, which felt good, he was the master, and all the bugs and beetles would obey him. Should he have another snort of the pinky powdery flesh in his professional laboratory bowl? Probably not, but he should add it to the doctor's glass beakers, like last time. He was a superb laboratory assistant. Tracey would probably give him a pay rise, and then he'd have enough money to fill his special pipe more often. Yes, that was a fantastical idea.

Ricky tipped half the remains of the pink powder into the beaker in the middle of the chemical laboratory and the other half into the end beaker. The colour changed a little, so he grabbed a glass stirring rod, and gave both beakers a good stir, and the milky liquid went back to being white, just the way the doctor liked it.

"Get back," he warned the bugs, who were getting closers, and they tip toed backwards. Good, this was the right way to treat them, Ricky wished he'd done this when they'd first crawled under his skin, nasty filthy bugs. But now he was tired, so tired. He'd slept on the old couch last night, the one at the back facing the wall, so he'd had to climb over it, no one could have seen him, but the couch smelled of urine, so didn't fancy napping there now. There wasn't anywhere else, except... The chiller wasn't on, he knew because Tracey told him it used too much power, so if he slept in there, with the door shut, the bugs couldn't get him.

With his reasoning sound, Ricky pulled open the closest drawer, the empty one, and climbed in. Ricky didn't realise he was sharing the space with anyone else, when he called out a merry "Goodnight," to the bugs on the floor only he could see.

55

Pauline was desperate for a cigarette, almost as desperate as she was to give up, but it kept sucking her back. She'd cut right back, she'd made a promise. Her old Mam had done some complicated maths sums and worked out if she stopped smoking for four months, and saved all the money she normally spent on cigarettes, she'd be able to fly home. So she promised herself, after she'd finished this packet, she'd quit, go cold turkey. She'd done it before, loads of times, it was working in this place that did it, the stress of her budget being cut, and the poor people who lived here. She felt so bad for them and wanted to take half of them home with her.

Taking her usual seat in the courtyard, Pauline pulled out her cigarettes, but the wind was well up today, racing through the courtyard, so she shuffled her chair round the corner, out of the wind and out of sight.

With the unlit cigarette halfway up to her lips, her moment of peace and quiet interrupted by the sound of that lazy oaf, Stubbs and the bully Preston. What were they doing out here together? Preston didn't smoke.

The wind carried their words right into her Northern ears and chilled her heart.

"I'll never forget what I saw for the rest of my life," Stubbs said.

"Was it a seizure?" Preston asked.

"I've worked here for a long time, and I've seen nothing like it. It wasn't any seizure I've ever seen."

"Drugs?"

"Could be, he's got his big lab downstairs, don't know what he does there, for all we know, he could be trying his own stuff," Stubbs said.

The men both took a long drag of their cigarettes and foul scent of nicotine and tar and a thousand other chemicals made Pauline gag.

"What was in that bottle, can't have been drugs—"

"Or alcohol," Preston interrupted.

"It wasn't natural, what his body did, moving that way."

"No, it wasn't."

The door into the courtyard creaked, it always did, the maintenance schedule was loose at the best of times. And Pauline almost looked round the corner to check they'd gone, when another voice joined the conversation. The last voice she expected to hear.

"I trust you're following my last instruction to you both?" said Tracey Chappell.

Pauline nearly fell off her garden chair. She couldn't have been more surprised if the President himself had walked into the Rose Haven's courtyard.

"Just having a quick smoke before heading back to work," Preston said.

Stubbs had flicked his into the bushes the moment he realised it was Tracey coming through the door.

"Stubbs, you need to start the morning medicine

rounds. Tala's rung to say she has a family emergency and won't be coming in. Preston, I need you to do a small job for me, if you can find our friend, Miss Patel, and check her blood pressure. Doctor Perry will join you when he's collected his medical bag. It's possibly why she's been playing up, drinking whatever was in that bottle. Doctor Perry suspects it contains a psilocybin, similar to magic mushrooms, which is why you saw the doctor have such a strong reaction to it."

The men said nothing to refute her claims, although to Pauline, it sounded like Tracey was talking out of her arse, making it up as she went. And why on earth would she ask an orderly to check a resident's blood pressure? That wasn't right. It would be like asking her to do the catering for the next NASA mission, just because she knew how to cook, didn't mean she knew how to feed astronauts in space. The woman was barking mad.

"Here's the blood pressure cuff. It's automatic. Slip it on over her arm, and press the start button, simple. And remember, not a word to anyone," Tracey said, handing the equipment to Preston before disappearing back inside.

"Psyclo-what?" Stubbs asked, lighting up another cigarette and drawing the smoke deep into his lungs.

"Magic mushrooms, you must have tried those?"

"Never in my life. Cigarettes are the only poison I put into my body; that and Pauline's food."

The men laughed and Pauline felt her own blood pressure rising as she tried to refrain from giving them both a knuckle sandwich. Calling them wankers was too kind a word to waste on them. The situation called for something stronger, but she was more worried about what might be in store for Sulia Patel to risk letting them know she'd overheard their conversation. Damn it all to hell, now she had to get involved.

She waited them out, and after Stubbs had finished his second cigarette, the men disappeared back inside, Preston with Doctor Perry's blood pressure machine. Pauline didn't have the foggiest idea what to do next and dithered a bit before putting her shoulders back and reentering the Rose Haven. She had every right to be walking these corridors, no one knew she knew anything, and she didn't, but Tala and Benson's inconceivable accusations were growing some legs.

Pauline rarely ventured anywhere other than the kitchen, dining room, the courtyard, so didn't know where to find the Indian woman's room. She wandered the halls peering in doorways, too nervous to give anyone more than a little wave instead of her usual boisterous greeting. She stumbled past Sulia's room by accident and had to double back to see Preston manhandling the blood pressure cuff onto the large woman's arm. Sulia was protesting, but Preston relished his role as the enforcer, making up poppycock about how the residents had their blood pressure checked every month, and it was her turn.

She waited outside the door, hidden from Preston's view, listening to Sulia complain before Preston told her to shut the hell up, and that he would press the button now. The unmistakable sound of the inflating cuff was followed by a loud beep and then the hissing of the deflating cuff, and then by a massive thump. Pauline peeked round the doorway, stifling her shock, as she saw Sulia's unconscious body half on and half off the bed, with Preston swearing like a bloody trooper manhandling her bulk onto the bed.

Pauline turned tail, hurrying away, ignoring the calls from the residents she passed.

What to do? Who to go see? It wasn't the weekend, so Benson wasn't here, and Tala had called in sick, should she call the coppers? What were they going to say? That the woman had passed out from nerves? Maybe medical tests made her nervous? Oh hell and damnation and bloody Nora. Who else was trustworthy in this place? No one. All, except Tala and Benson, were tossers, with no bloody compassion. Who was Sulia friendly with? She'd been here such a short time, Cone, she'd seen her hanging out with Elijah Cone. She hadn't believed half the stuff they'd printed in the papers about him. Poor guy had lost his wife, and some kids from his team, but he wasn't over the limit, and still they found him guilty. He had been drinking, and the hospital said he wasn't over the limit, that's what she remembered reading. He'd made someone jealous enough to have him prosecuted for what was an unfortunate accident. Sadly most people believed what they read in the papers.

So she walked the rest of the corridors, looking for Elijah's room, and sank onto his bed when she found it, the one room without a bloody TV blaring.

Elijah was sitting at his window reading but closed his book when she rushed in. An Agatha Christie novel, *Appointment With Death*.

"It's Sulia, they've done something to her," Pauline got out. Christ she sounded like a madwoman.

"And why are you telling me?" Elijah asked.

"Don't be a bloody plonker, you're her friend. She needs your help," Pauline said.

"I don't know if I'd call her my friend, we've sat together twice for meals. You should tell someone in management."

"Don't play that game with me. I've been round the block just as many times as you have, and I'm telling you, the woman needs your help. Now git your arse out of that chair and gimme a hand sorting it out before it's too late." Pauline heaved herself off the bed and stood in front of

Elijah with her hands on her hips and a battle-axe look on her face.

Elijah put his book to one side, and stood up, with none of the grimacing and incremental pauses he usually did. She didn't comment because it wasn't her place to pass judgement on someone else's health, or self medication, she was happy she'd got the urgency through to his thick skull.

"So talk me through it," Elijah said as Pauline hurried him along the corridor.

"There's no time, but it's got something to do with Doctor Perry, and Tracey Chappell, she's the manager here, and then Preston checked her blood pressure, even though he's only an orderly and not a nurse, so that's bloody dodgy and then she collapsed or fainted. Anyway, she was unconscious on the damn bed, and then I came here to get you."

They got to Sulia's room to find she wasn't there, and nor was her bed, only the space where it had sat.

"He's taken her somewhere, I know it. It's exactly like what Benson said, and I didn't believe them, not really," Pauline fretted.

Elijah walked to the window and pulled open the curtains.

"What are you doing man? There's no time to be fussing over curtains. Come on, they're probably cutting her open now and stealing her heart and lungs and stuff."

Elijah ignored her, and she didn't know if her blood pressure could take much more of this. Men were all the bloody same, only listened to what they wanted to hear. What was he doing behind the curtains? Pauline watched as Elijah pulled the curtains right away from the wall, and reached into the corners of both sides of the window, coming up empty handed.

"Did you see anyone with an old bottle, or talk about something in a bottle?" Elijah asked.

Pauline racked her brain, the whole thing had rattled her. "One of them said something about something being in a bottle, Stubbs or Preston, can't remember which one," she said.

"They've found her bottle then, the one she had hidden behind the curtain. It was there before breakfast. Where would they take her?"

"Um, to the doctor's office? Or to Tracey's office?"

Elijah shook his head. It was the first time in a decade he'd been able to do that without being in pain. "No, it'll be somewhere more private."

"They mentioned Doctor Perry's lab, a big lab downstairs somewhere. I didn't even bloody know we had a downstairs, shows how often they let me out of me kitchen," Pauline said, her attempt at humour falling flat as Elijah hurried forward.

He paused next to the motel's old fire escape diagram, running his finger along the sections of the motel, before stabbing at a symbol next to the motel's office.

"There, is that Tracey's office?"

Pauline adjusted her glasses, peering at the tiny writing.

"Yip. Is that a staircase next to her office then? That little block of lines?"

"It is, when you've stayed at as many hotels, motels, budget inns and airport accommodation as I have, reading the fire escape plan before you go to bed at night is a routine you get into if you want to live through the night."

Pauline nodded at Elijah's homily. She could count the number of motels she stayed in on one hand. Wasn't any spare cash around for that carryon in her life, although she went to Spain once, with her Mam. She'd got bloody sunburnt, and they hated the food, so not the best experience.

"Do we go to the lab now? Sneaking into a lab sounds very James Bondish, eh?" Pauline said.

"I'll have a look, see what's happening. Be best if you rang the police, you're an employee here, they'll believe you. No one ever believes me," Elijah said.

"I believe you, eh I do, I never believed what they wrote about you in them papers," Pauline said, her hand on Elijah's arm.

Elijah stared at her, "Thank you."

"Right, I'll ring the coppers, and you only have a look mind, no heroics. If they're cutting her up for body parts, they'll have knives, so you watch yourself, you mind, eh?" and she hurried back to her kitchen. She'd ring from there, and then at least she'd have her kitchen knives if she needed to protect herself.

56

Called into the Rose Haven by Tracey, and told the police were looking for him and that they wanted to question the residents about two of his patients, had sent Doctor Perry's world spinning out of control. Tracey was livid that his activities outside the Rose Haven might jeopardise their financial *arrangement* and he'd been incredulous at that. Tracey lived a life of luxury because of what he delivered. It wasn't his fault if she frittered her cash away like there was no tomorrow, while he squirrelled his away, always thinking of the future. Despite all the best-laid plans that rainy day was here.

He'd delayed the Cavalletto Cartel boys with a creative message about him picking up something infectious from a patient. It would take the pressure off for a few days, not that he would be here to care. He had a flash of concern for Myra if they turned up at the house and he wasn't there, but shrugged it off. It wasn't his problem, and he was sure they'd deal with her in their usual manner, the twins too.

Losing identical twins was a shame, he'd been looking

forward to experimenting on them with some different formulas he'd developed. He'd have to find another set after he moved, it couldn't be that hard.

But then, to face a bottle of tonic missing for sixty odd years, he didn't know whether to laugh or cry. After the disaster with Clarita Swann, he didn't trust the last batch of tonic, and had emptied it down the sink, starting a new batch which should be ready by now. Doctor Perry hadn't analysed what could have gone wrong. But now he had this bottle of his original tonic, the one he'd used back before he reduced the potency to avoid any more accidental deaths, which had been getting out of hand. One sip was enough to take three years off his age. Tracey was so wrapped up in worrying about herself, she hadn't even noticed. Doctor Perry wasn't tempted to offer her any; let her spend her money on Botox and collagen and the rest of the false beauty she pumped into her body to keep herself young. He had the real thing.

He'd spent the whole night at his clinic cleaning up the remnants of Miss Swann, who was now in the dumpster out back, although her teeth were in his pocket. He had accumulated a nice collection of teeth and he would have to remember to grab the tin from the garage before he left. It would be a comfort to have those little memories near him, to show him how far he'd come.

Doctor Perry told Tracey he needed to gather some things to deal with the patient who had his tonic. He couldn't recall ever interacting with her, but they must have met in Chicago, because that was the only time he'd ever mislaid any bottles of tonic. He'd never figured out how it had happened, and the first person he took his frustration out on was the receptionist — stupid girl, she mustn't have locked up properly, or a boy distracted her.

There was only one reason he'd gone back to his office, self preservation.

Doctor Perry pulled file after file off the shelves, shoving any file with a red circle in the top right-hand corner, into a sports bag. The bag bulged at the seams, threatening to split with every additional file stuffed inside. He couldn't remember having this many patients and stopped to wipe the sweat from his face. The air conditioning was off, along with the lights. Molly would be here soon and he needed to go before she arrived. He'd lock his office behind him and call in sick. That'd give him another day or two before anyone asked questions here.

Doctor Perry paused, he'd been at the clinic all night, yet Myra hadn't rung to find out what time he'd be home. Should he worry? No, Myra wasn't worth the worry, she had the twins to look after, and was probably too tired to care about his whereabouts. As she so often told him, she was always tired these days, and looked it too.

With all the marked files off the shelves, he heaved the bag over his shoulder, locked up behind himself and dumped the lot into the trunk of his car. There was no reason to hang around any longer. If the police had already been to the Rose Haven, they were coming here next or home. The Rose Haven was the safest place for him and his files right now.

Sulia moaned as the room came into a fuzzy focus. It was like looking through a white veil because she still had her contacts in, making it hard to tell where she was, but she wasn't in her room and confusion clouded her mind. She tried lifting her arms to remove the contacts but concrete blocks held them down. No, not blocks, straps, straps which cut into her wrists and her ankles too. A white coated orderly appeared on the periphery of her vision.

"Hey," Sulia croaked, but the figure ignored her. Clearing her throat, she tried again, louder this time. "Hey!"

"Are you comfortable?"

"What?" asked Sulia.

"I asked if you were comfortable?"

Sulia couldn't think of a response when she didn't know why she was restrained and had no memory of coming here.

"I'll be off now, but I'm leaving you in the safe hands of Doctor Perry," Preston said, and laughed all the way upstairs

WHEN PRESTON WENT UPSTAIRS to wait for the doctor, the lab door didn't engage behind him, leaving it ajar for whoever came next, and that was Elijah, who paused at the open door, nudging it with his toe, until it swung open exposing a room jam-packed with everything. It bore little resemblance to a doctor's surgery, with a wall of pullout freezers on one side, the other side dominated by a complex laboratory set up with test tubes and gas burners bubbling away in a complicated network of pipes and coils,. The body of a woman he now knew to be his friend was strapped to a hospital bed jammed into the corner among old filing cabinets and broken office chairs.

"Sulia?" Elijah called out, stepping into the room.

"Elijah? Is that you?"

Elijah wedged a stapler he'd randomly found on the floor into the door jamb to stop them from being locked in, before stepping over to the bed.

"It's me, now hold still while I try to undo these straps," he said.

Elijah eyed the leather straps tight around Sulia's wrists and ankles. He flexed his fingers expecting the pain to return any minute, he'd do the best he could but his faith wasn't strong.

"How'd I end up down here?"

"Can you keep the noise down," Elijah whispered. He'd got the first strap loose and was working on the second one when he felt a familiar prickle in his fingers. No, not now, he needed to get Sulia out of these straps, then the pain could come.

"Can you let me out?"

"Sulia, shh, please, the door is open,"

"I didn't say nothing," Sulia said.

There was a dull *thud* coming from the wall of pullout freezers. Elijah assumed the staff used them for the recently deceased residents, so if the noise was coming out of there, they have even bigger troubles.

"If the bugs have gone can someone get me out? There's no handle in here."

Elijah looked at Sulia, who'd turned her heard towards the noise.

"Go let him out, then come back and finish this. I'll keep working on it," she said.

Elijah pulled open the freezer drawer he thought the noise was coming from. It wasn't an empty drawer, but the person inside wasn't capable of speech or of drumming their heels against the tray.

Stripped of her pearls and her angora twinset, Muriel's skin was a filthy grey colour and her hair lay limp around her face, the wispy strands scarcely covering her skull. Elijah swallowed the bile which had crept up his throat. So this was where Muriel had disappeared to. As Elijah moved to open the next drawer, he properly saw what was left of Muriel's face, and fear twisted in his gut.

Muriel lay sightless, her eyes gone, although the empty sockets seemed to search out Elijah's eyes.

"Have the bugs gone now? I'm only coming out if the bugs have gone, although I am their boss," came a voice from the next drawer.

Elijah pushed Muriel back into her drawer and wrenched open the drawer speaking to him. A familiar face peaked out, his blood encrusted uniform even more dishevelled than the man in it.

"Thanks man. Didn't check if I could get out. I've been in there for hours," Ricky said. "Have you seen any bugs? Have they gone?"

Elijah had spent his life learning how to get the best out of a team, how to inspire individuals, and this was no different, he needed a different motivator.

"What's your name, son?"

"Ricky."

"Ricky, I can tell you that the bugs have gone, for now, but when Doctor Perry comes back, he's bringing them back with him, and their friends. There will be so many bugs, that unless we take out the doctor, those bugs are going to crawl under our skin and eat us from the inside. Do you think you can help? It's Doctor Perry who brings the bugs into the Rose Haven, you ever see them anywhere else?"

Transfixed by Elijah's words, Ricky's eyes were saucers. Elijah didn't know if his words had made any difference to the kid, but it was worth a shot.

And then Ricky nodded. "I'll hide behind the door, you grab him, and then I'll have a go at him before all the bugs get here."

"Perfect kid, now you get behind the door, and wait, and don't say a word until I raise my hand like this," and Elijah showed the boy what he meant.

"A secret signal?"

"Just like a secret signal. But be silent, you got that?"

"Silent, like the bugs. I'm the king of the bugs. Silent, yup, got it," and Ricky walked unsteadily over to the door and waited, picking at his arms.

Footsteps echoed down the stairwell, and Doctor Perry appeared, his doctor's bag in one hand, his car keys in the other. He hesitated before striding over to the desk and placing his things down.

"Mister Cone, I wasn't expecting to see you here," Doctor Perry said. "But you're here, so we may as well chat. Your friend has been causing mayhem at the Rose

Haven and it's not good for the morale of the residents. You understand don't you? She stole something from me, a long time ago now. People shouldn't steal, it always comes back to haunt them."

Ricky looked ready to explode on the other side of the room, and Elijah tried placating him with subtle hand signals.

"The procedure won't take long, it'll be over as fast as you took the lives of your passengers the night you drove drunk into a tree. You remember that night don't you, Mister Cone?"

Elijah ignored the barb. He'd heard much worse.

Doctor Perry pottered about the chemical array in the centre of the room, fiddling with the burets, and adjusting the heat of the flames under the beakers.

"What's all that for?" Elijah asked.

"This? This is something I've been refining. Let's call it a *mood enhancer* shall we? It's had its difficulties but I've got it right now. It didn't have the correct levels of the key ingredients but I've rectified that. Having access to the Rose Haven residents has been a boon to my research because you keep yourselves in tip top condition, not a single meth head among you. It has been wonderful, you've got no idea." Doctor Perry rambled.

"What are you going to do to Sulia?" Elijah asked.

"Sulia? I will try her on my new tonic to see the reaction, I've been experimenting with the potency, There've been a few failures so I need to get it right before I move on, might not have another old folks home to, ah, *aid* me in my endeavours. I think I've got it right now but I will warn you, some patients experience a higher than normal level of pain."

At that, Elijah gave the signal, and Ricky launched himself at the doctor with a primal scream, his fists pummelling the doctor, with punch after punch after punch.

Doctor Perry fell down, flailing at the unexpected assault, his arms by his face fending off the drug-crazed madman attacking him. Elijah grabbed Doctor Perry's arm, his concern for Sulia masking the pain threatening to bloom in his own hands.

For the age he was, Doctor Perry gave a good fight, and at one point Elijah spied a handful of what looked like Ricky's teeth on the linoleum. The meth would have made them fall out eventually, the doctor only hastened the event.

And then Sulia materialised above the three men, her eyes now dark brown without the white contacts disguising their true colour. And in her hand she held one of Doctor Perry's narrow necked flasks and a funnel. Sulia lowered her heavy bulk onto Doctor Perry's prone body, rendering him immobile.

"Hold his arms for me, Ricky," she said.

Like a puppy on speed, Ricky wrenched both the doctor's arms above his head, pinning them down, and waited for his next instruction.

"Remember me, Doctor Perry? Do I remind you of my Momma in Chicago? You tell me the truth now," Sulia demanded.

Doctor Perry's eyes weren't on the woman squashing the breath out of him, they were on the flask in her hand, the one from the end of the chemical process, containing the tonic he hadn't tested. Through the transparent glass sides of the flask the tonic had a pinkish tinge.

"Ricky is the best lab assistant ever, Doctor Perry. See that there? I helped make that, like yesterday's batch, I added in some good stuff, the stuff the residents take. If you mix it all up, it's better for everyone. Stops the bugs, no one needs the bugs in their lives," Ricky played with Doctor Perry's arms like a marionette doll.

"Keep him still, Ricky, he will drink your super medicine now, and that will stop all the bugs, I promise," said Sulia.

Doctor Perry clamped his lips together, his head twisting from side to side.

"Elijah, I'm gonna need you to hold his lying head still for me. He's got a terrible thirst for revenge, and I've got just what he needs."

Elijah used his forearms to hold the doctor's head in place, the four of them making the strangest tableau on the floor.

Sulia pushed the funnel deep into Doctor Perry's mouth, shoving it past the lips the doctor refused to open, and battering it through his teeth, until he lay there gagging.

"Hold his nose, Elijah," Sulia said.

Elijah shuffled backwards to make sure he could hold the doctor's head and clamp his nose at the same time. And although he had no expectations of what the liquid would do, the memory of Muriel's eyeless corpse gave him the strength he needed to hold the thrashing man as Sulia poured the entire contents of the flask into the funnel and down Doctor Perry's throat.

Doctor Perry's body convulsed, once, twice, and was still. Elijah looked at Sulia.

"Just wait, it's coming. You can let him go now, he'll be no more trouble," she said.

"No more bugs?" Ricky asked.

"No more bugs, Ricky, but head on home now for a proper sleep, away from the mess. Elijah and I will clean it up, don't want you getting into any trouble," Sulia suggested.

Ricky nodded and released the doctor's arms. Ricky rescued his special pipe from the silver coffeepot, and then with the pipe in one hand and the plated coffeepot in the other, scarpered up the stairs. The woman was okay for an oldie.

"Stand back, Elijah."

They both struggled to their feet, backing away from the body on the floor. They'd made it as far as the desk when Doctor Perry yelled out, his yelling turning into a gurgling choking sound as his tongue engorged and flopped backwards in his mouth which was changing shape the same way dough moves when it's being kneaded.

Doctor Perry's legs shrank with incredible speed, the sound of his femurs snapping under the pressure masked by his screams before his body went rigid and his teeth clamped down on the huge tongue in his mouth and bit it off cleanly.

After that, Elijah looked away. The sounds were enough to let him know what was happening, he didn't need to see. He watched Sulia's face though and in front of his eyes, the stress of her past sloughed off her, relaxing every fibre of her body. She was still old, but contentment covered her like a cloak, softening her.

The room fell silent and Sulia walked over to Doctor Perry, and she wrapped the newborn baby using the stole from around her neck, scooping him up in her arms.

"This is what he'd been doing," Sulia said, offering the infant to Elijah.

Elijah wanted nothing to do with the creature in Sulia's arms, it was unnatural and sickening. He shook his head.

"I'll take him upstairs and figure out what to do. I wonder if he'll remember any of this, I hope not, don't want to think I've spent my entire life tracking him down for what he did to my Momma, just to let him grow up and do it all over again." Sulia walked up the stairs, cooing to the baby boy.

Elijah sat in shock in the lab, in denial about what he'd seen. He'd have to go upstairs to Pauline, to tell her everything was okay, unless you were Muriel Lincoln, or Johnny Paulson, or whoever else the doctor had used for parts or in his experiments. He wouldn't open any more of the freezer drawers, he'd leave that to the police.

Pushing off from the desk, the familiar pain back in his hands, and there in the middle of the chemical array was an identical flask to the one Sulia had tipped down Doctor Perry's throat. Just a sip couldn't hurt him. Elijah picked up the flask by its narrow neck, he had nothing to lose so took a small sip and waited, he almost took a second sip, the flask was at his lips when he felt the tonic kick in. And it was wonderful.

AND IN A MODEST BRICK HOUSE, in a quiet working class street a few doors down from Mary Louise's empty house, the curtains twitched a little. With Doctor Perry gone, there was no one left to worry about Mary Louise... no one with her best interests at heart.

Gary Pemberton and Tony Street pulled up outside the Perrys' house. Today had been another wild goose chase, with the good doctor missing. His office looked abandoned, and he hadn't made it into the Rose Haven yet, so the house in Heming Way was their final port of call.

Walking up to the front door, Gary rang the bell and waited, sending Tony round the back, just in case.

He rang the bell a second time, nothing and had his finger poised for a third ring when the door opened. Instead of Myra Perry, or the Doctor, or the twins, Tony stood there, shrugging, with a baby in his arms.

"What the hell, Tony?"

"No idea, ask the boys, found them in the kitchen with a baby bottle warming in a pot on the stove. They haven't seen Myra since last night, or Doctor Perry since yesterday morning."

A shiver ran down Gary's spine. Myra hadn't seemed like the type of woman who would readily abandon the children she cared for. Based on his experience, a mother going missing like that was bad news, for the mother.

"You ring Social Services and ask for advice, I'll have a quick search," Gary said.

Tony disappeared inside with the baby. Tony had his own kids, so he'd know how to handle them. Gary didn't.

He checked upstairs and nothing looked out of place, the rooms downstairs were clean and tidy. There were dishes on the countertop but with the boys fending for themselves overnight that was to be expected. The bottle was still warming on the stove but Tony seemed to have everything under control there. The twins watched him from the breakfast bar with their peculiarly matched sets of eyes.

Which left the garage, and it was with a heavy heart that Gary opened the door from the hall to the garage and flicked on the lights and stepped down onto the concrete. He'd taken only two steps when there was a crunching underfoot. Bending to have a closer look, he instantly knew what was on the floor and they weren't a collection of white pebbles, they were teeth - human teeth. The biggest question now was where were the Perrys'?

———

THE POLICEMEN HAD SEALED the front door to the house with a strip of bright yellow police tape. One edge hadn't stuck properly, and it flapped about as if waving goodbye to them as they climbed into the back of Gary's undercover police car.

Schoolbags on their laps, they stared out the window as the policeman drove them to the KID Palm Beach County Campus, an orphanage, with Myra in a baby capsule strapped between them.

They'd told the policemen that the baby's name was Arabella, the name of their favourite teacher, and the policemen had believed them. Jesse and James weren't entirely sure what would happen at the orphanage, but they'd come prepared with the last bottle of magic milk from the refrigerator, and their pocket knife. Whatever happened, they'd have fun, they always did.

REVIEW

Dear Reader,

If you enjoyed *Doctor Perry*, I would love it if you could please post a review on your favourite digital platform?

POST A REVIEW ONLINE

POST A GOODREADS REVIEW

Thank you

Kirsten McKenzie x

CAST OF CHARACTERS

ROSE HAVEN RESIDENTS
Elijah Cone - resident
Sulia Patel - resident
Muriel Lincoln - resident
Ryman Spittle - resident
Nancy Brood - resident
Jennifer Withers - resident
Polish Rob - resident
Frances Merriweather - resident
Eileen Hislop - resident
Ginger Bruce - resident
John Burrows - resident

ROSE HAVEN STAFF
Tracey Chappell - manager
Benson - weekend orderly
Ricky Donovan - orderly
Bart Stubbs/Smokey - orderly
Preston Sergeant - orderly
Pedro Garcia - orderly

Tala - head nurse
Jules - Yoga instructor
Pauline Kerrigan - chef
Cherie - receptionist

DOCTOR PERRY'S CLINIC

Lily - receptionist
Molly - receptionist
Don Jury - patient
Sarah Miller - patient
Clarita Swann - patient

OTHER

Mary Louise Jackson - jogger
Myra Perry - Doctor Perry's wife
Trivelle Grifin - principal of elementary school
Tom Williams - antique dealer
Nate Blackwell - second hand trader
Jesse and **James** - twins

POLICE

Clive Jeffries - lead detective
Gary Pemberton - police detective
Tony Street - police detective
Emily Jesmond - police officer
Burton - police officer
Michelle - police officer
KID Palm Beach County Campus*

*This is a real orphanage in Florida. Please consider making a donation, to help with the the treatment of abused and neglected children. www.kidinc.org

ACKNOWLEDGMENTS

Once again, a huge vote of thanks to my editor Emma Oakey. And thanks also to Kate Sluka for her early developmental suggestions. And to Carolyn McKenzie for her proofreading.

For medical advice, thanks go to Dr. Kimberley Thomson, and paramedic Joshua Sanders. Between them, they provided some exceptionally disgusting advice and if I translated it wrong onto the page, it's my fault not theirs.

Nothing would be on these pages if it wasn't for the support of my wonderful family - Fletcher, Sasha, and Jetta. Thank you.

If you enjoyed reading Doctor Perry, or if he made you feel squeamish, could you please leave a review on your favourite digital platform. Reviews are essential to authors.

Thank you

Kirsten xxx

ABOUT THE AUTHOR

For years Kirsten McKenzie worked in the family antique store, where she went from being allowed to sell postcards in the corner, to selling Royal Worcester vases and seventeenth century silverware. She has also worked as a Customs Officer in both New Zealand and England, fighting international crime.

Her historical time travel trilogy, *The Old Curiosity Shop* series, has been described as *Time Travellers Wife meets Far Pavilions*, and *Antiques Roadshow gone viral*. The audio books for the series are available through Audible.

Kirsten has also written the bestselling gothic thriller *Painted*, and the medical thriller, *Doctor Perry*. Her latest novel, *The Forger and the Thief*, is a historical thriller set in Florence, Italy.

A full time author, she lives in New Zealand with her husband, her daughters, and two rescue cats.

You can sign up for her sporadic newsletter at:
www.kirstenmckenzie.com/newsletter/